GOOD
THINGS

Kate MacDougall is the author of *London's No. 1 Dog-Walking Agency*. She writes freelance for *Country Life*, the *Telegraph*, *Homes and Antiques*, *Horse and Hound* and *Period Living* among others. She lives in Oxfordshire with three children, three dogs and one very patient husband. *Good Things* is her debut novel.

 @MacdougallKate

 @katemacdougall1

First published in the UK in 2024
This edition published in the UK in 2025 by
ZAFFRE
An imprint of Bonnier Books UK
5th Floor, HYLO, 105 Bunhill Row,
London, EC1Y 8LZ

This is a work of fiction. Names, places, events and
incidents are either the products of the author's
imagination or used fictitiously. Any resemblance to
actual persons, living or dead, or actual
events is purely coincidental.

A CIP catalogue record for this book is
available from the British Library.

ISBN: 978-1-78870-638-4

Also available as an ebook and an audiobook

1 3 5 7 9 10 8 6 4 2

Typeset by IDSUK (Data Connection) Ltd
Printed and bound in Great Britain by Clays Ltd, Elcograf S.p.A.

The authorised representative in the EEA is Bonnier Books
UK (Ireland) Limited.
Registered office address: Floor 3, Block 3, Miesian Plaza,
Dublin 2, D02 Y754, Ireland
compliance@bonnierbooks.ie
www.bonnierbooks.co.uk

GOOD THINGS

Kate MacDougall

ZAFFRE

For Belle, Milo and Jesse

PART ONE
Winter/Spring

Chapter 1

Of all the eventualities that Liz had considered when pre-paring to host the Little Martin village council meeting for the first time, her father's dog arriving by pet courier from Spain was certainly not one of them. George had inherited Albert when their grandmother died, and wher-ever Queen Vic (as she was known by Liz and her younger sister, Maggie) was in the afterlife, she would have surely found the whole situation deeply satisfying. Albert had not only been one of her very favourite corgis, but Queen Vic had always believed that humans were simply not capable of managing their lives without the help of a dog here and there to help show them the way. She would have sensed a certain synchronicity in it all, the way his-tory likes to repeat itself, and how glorious it was that dogs could just drop in like that and shake up a situation in the most spectacular way.

Nobody was exactly sure how Queen Vic's tenure as chair of the parish council had ended all those years ago, but it was almost certain that one of her corgis was involved. She told everyone she had just got bored of it all, but this seemed unlikely as Queen Vic never gave anything up without a fight and had taught her granddaughters to do exactly the same. So there sat the committee, perched on Liz's brand-new John Lewis sofa, when the topic turned (as it so often did) to the provision of dog-poo bins in the village. Carolyn Sewell, current chair and owner of a spaniel with unpleasant digestive issues, was in favour of three additional bins and Liz was just in the middle of a very measured rebuttal on behalf of the non-dog owning residents when there was a knock on the front door. It was Albert, looking all casual and fat and wearing a red bandana.

Liz's previous exclusion from the meetings' monthly rota had been described by the council clerk as 'an administrative error', but it seemed far more likely to Liz that it was due to the fact she lived on the new-build estate, Fair Meadows, at the edge of the village. There had been a long-winded and very messy crusade against its development, causing (in the eyes of some) Rosemary Peterson to fully commit herself to sherry, the Roper family to move back to Ireland, Mary Jane Laing to divorce her husband and half of the parish council to resign. There was also the hefty bill for the 'Unfair Meadows' leaflet campaign, the responsibility of which was still being disputed. As far as the remaining councillors were concerned, Fair Meadows was the ninth circle of hell, the place where traitors and deserters are sent to be tormented for eternity by Satan himself.

As with many things in life, Liz quietly hoped she might be a little bit better than most other people. She had always assumed she was exempt from such petty snobbery and scorn as she lived with her husband and small children in an Executive Family Dwelling (or the lipstick on the pig, as her sister Maggie liked to say), one of four high spec, four-bed houses at the front of the estate, all of which were clad in real Cotswold stone and twice the size of the basic red brick ones behind. Moreover, she was an Addison by birth. She grew up in the Manor House and that was no small thing in a village like Little Martin, so for the parish council to lump her together with the miserable masses in those tiny brick boxes behind her was both confusing and troubling.

But Liz had often struggled to see the bigger picture in life, to grasp how she might be seen by others, even now at the age of forty. It was actually one of the things that Maggie envied and admired about her sister the most. Liz would always lean towards thinking the best of herself, whereas Maggie invariably leant to the worst.

Once everyone had been to the house and seen how charming and tasteful and warm it was, how contemporary yet classic, how energy efficient, how easy to run, how much better than some of their draughty, money-pit period properties, they would know what a clever choice she had made. They wouldn't voice it, of course. Nothing would actually be *said*. It never was. But Liz knew that she would be able to see it in their faces. She would see it in the way they moved, the way they glanced at each other, the way they touched her integrated appliances and the days of having to coax Carolyn and Mrs Wilson and the rest of them 'all the way out' to Fair Meadows would be over. They would come willingly. They would come enthusiastically, because aside from anything else, Liz was the most immaculate and organised hostess in the whole of The Martins and the evening had been planned with a level of meticulousness rarely seen outside of the military. Nothing could possibly go wrong.

'It's all there. All the forms and the passport,' the man at the door said as he handed Liz a thick folder of paperwork. Albert looked up at her, his dark, cloudy eyes tired and befuddled. 'Ferry was delayed. Some problem at Calais, God knows what, there's always something going on over there and now there's this bloody wind. Anyway, we're a bit late I'm afraid.'

'*Albert*?' Liz gasped.

'Err, yes, Albert, that's right,' the man said, checking his clipboard. 'Nice dog really.'

'Oh, thank you,' replied Liz in as polite and as casual a tone as if she had just been accepting a parcel and not her late grandmother's beloved corgi. The exceptionally well-mannered and formal Liz was the role she chose to play for most of her life and she found it always served her well, even in the most unexpected of situations.

'Although he was sick on the way over,' the man continued, wiping his sleeve under his nose. 'On the crossing. Puked bloody everywhere. All over the car upholstery.'

'Oh?'

'It happens quite a lot. Dogs get seasick. Dogs get carsick. We will have to take it off the deposit though, miss. It's all in the terms and conditions.'

'Right, I think there might be some sort of mistake here,' she continued as Albert plonked his bottom on the floor.

'No, no' the man said. 'No mistake. It's in section five, miss. Any additional cleaning of the vehicle will be charged to the client. And that's the receiving client, miss, not the one at the other end.'

'I meant the *dog*,' Liz hissed. 'Why is the dog here? I am sort of in the middle of something.'

'He's here from Spain, miss. This is the relocation from Santa Pola.'

'But he lives there, in Spain, with my father. Why is he *here*? Where is the man that should be with him? Tall, English, very irresponsible?'

'I don't have back stories I'm afraid, miss. We're just the couriers. But it might be on the paperwork if you want to have a read through.'

'I would *love* to have a read through, I really would, but I am right in the middle of a very important meeting and I am going to have to ask you to come back later.'

'Later?'

She nodded. 'Yes. Or tomorrow perhaps? Tomorrow is very free at the moment actually, so anytime would suit.'

'I can't come back tomorrow, miss. I have a chihuahua in the back who needs to get to Bristol.'

'A *chihuahua*?'

'Yes. Long-haired one. He's come from the Dordogne.'

Liz took a deep breath in. The silence from the living room as ears strained to hear the conversation at the door had begun to turn to whispers, and Liz knew that this would not do at all.

'Right,' she replied with a short, sharp sigh. 'You had better give him to me then.'

The man grinned and handed Liz the lead and Albert sauntered slowly over the threshold, the weariness of his journey on top of the eleven years he was carrying clearly visible in his tired, heavy bones.

'I had him up in the front with me for a stretch,' the man said. 'He's good company, aren't you Albert?'

But Albert was already half asleep on the floor of the hallway, and Liz found that she could push him by his bottom quite easily over the smooth, shiny flooring and into the downstairs loo without much effort at all. She returned to her guests with a spotless smile and resumed her speech about how there were just *too* many dogs in Little Martin while also wondering how she would explain to her guests that the downstairs bathroom was now out of use.

In the centre of the village, another unexpected visitor was arriving.

George Addison was not the type of man to slip quietly into the back of a room. He arrived in the same manner that he did most things in life – with a roar or a quip or a gibe, a bottle of something nice and chilled under his arm, Stephanie or Vicky or Mel on the other, and enough charm and panache to cheer even the most miserable of mortals. For it was George's sincere belief that any gathering, large or small, domestic or municipal, would be so emphatically improved by his appearance that everyone present really should know about it so that they could finally relax and get on with life.

It was then something of a surprise that for a man so keen on making an entrance, so determined to be noticed, that his return to Little Martin after a considerable absence was such a mute affair. There he was on that chilly spring evening, climbing the steps of the Manor House with nothing more than an overnight bag and a very nice bottle of

Rioja to show for his Spanish sojourn. George had always travelled light, so as he knocked on the large wooden door of his former home, it was not clear how long he would be staying. Perhaps he didn't really know himself, for life had always unfolded in the most unusual of ways for George Addison, and the people who knew him best knew not to expect a normal course of events.

'Hello, darling,' he said when Maggie opened the door, his skin tanned and creased, his smile as familiar as her own. He was wearing his favourite suit, the one he always wore for special occasions, the old dark sage tweed that marked him out as a man who had, at least at one time in this life, both money and taste.

'*Dad*? What are you doing here?'

'I have some very sad news I'm afraid,' George said, gravely, as he placed his bag on the top step.

'What? What's happened?' Maggie said, feeling a sudden lurch in her stomach.

'Rhonda has betrayed me.'

'*What*?'

'Rhonda was not who she said she was. Not by country mile.'

'Who's *Rhonda*?'

'She took my heart right out, Margaret, and then she threw it into the very darkest part of the bin.'

'Oh. Dad,' Maggie said, feeling her heart begin to sink.

'The same bin we bought together at the market in Murcia on our one-year anniversary.'

'What happened to Janet?' Maggie asked, remembering a small, red-haired lady with cats who George had written about on a postcard.

'I have had the most terrible, wretched, *ghastly* time. I am a wreck, Maggie. A husk. I am a shell of a human being with all the good bits sucked out. There is nothing left of me anymore. *Nothing!* Rhonda has taken it all. She has taken everything.'

Maggie sighed and then stood back against the open door so that the warm light from the hallway slunk outside and began to creep into the deep contours of his face. He must be seventy-five now, Maggie thought, but still as handsome as ever; the noble, angular nose, the cheekbones now excavated by age, the royal blue eyes set off against his warm Spanish tan. However much trouble George Addison got himself into, however many times he disappointed or cheated or left you in the lurch, he never looked anything less than dashing, dapper and distinguished, a man in perpetual search of an adventure, a man with many stories and no shortage of an audience to hear them. And here he was again, with yet another tale to tell, a tale that would change the lives of the Addison family forever, or what was left of them anyway.

'You had better come in, then,' Maggie said, as she picked up the overnight bag.

They hadn't seen or spoken to each other for over two years.

Chapter 2

June

Two and a Half Years Earlier

Victoria Addison, Queen Vic, had died of a common or garden heart attack on a Tuesday in late June, just a week shy of her ninety-fourth-birthday. She had managed to see her Royal Jubilee roses in full bloom before she expired, although a fair few of them were squashed as she fell forward onto the accelerator of her mobility scooter, driving it at some speed into the flower beds. The housekeeper, Debbie, was alerted to her demise by Albert, her last corgi, son of Louise, grandson of Ham, great grandson of Darling, from a line of corgis stretching right back to a dog who'd had the very good fortune of belonging to the Queen.

The Queen often came to mind to people who met Victoria Addison. Being regal in both manner and appearance was possibly the least interesting thing about Queen Vic, although always the first thing people noticed about her. The hair, set tight in short curls, the calf-length wool skirts and sensible brown shoes, the hats and white gloves on special occasions, the dogs she so doted on . . . none of that mattered to her granddaughters. Her voice, firm and steady, her hands, always warm and soft, her wisdom, her kindness, the laugh, no more than a chuckle but more infectious than any other, these were the things that mattered to Liz and Maggie. These were the things they lost that day.

Albert, rarely an outdoor barker, had been intermittently tugging on the corner of Victoria's kilt while calling for help and getting filthy in the process as the front wheel of the scooter splattered mud and manure right up his fur. Debbie fished her off the scooter and laid her on the grass near the croquet stump before running off to call 999 as Albert lay down quietly next to her and put his muddy paw on her chest. For a while it was just the two of them there in the garden, their faces warmed by the sweet yellow sunshine, the birds still singing as if nothing of any significance had just happened.

The ambulance came, a formality more than anything since there was never any doubt about her being dead. 'She died the way she did everything,' George would say at her cremation. 'Properly,' which had made the vicar chuckle. Everyone in the street had ventured out to see what the flashing lights were about, and although it was no great shock to hear that she had finally passed away, Victoria, rather like the Queen herself, was one of those people who you thought might just go on forever. Everyone was there to see the hearse leave the Manor House for the crematorium, heads bowed respectfully, but not because they particularly liked her. It was the end of an era, a marking of time, and the passing of one of their own – born, bred, stayed till they're dead – was an event in a village like Little Martin.

'She's dead,' Liz said down the phone to Maggie the day after it happened.

'When?' Maggie replied, although she already knew. She always had one eye on home, even when she was hundreds of miles away, her connections to the village, to her home, running through her like veins. She'd had a text, a school friend who worked at the funeral home, and Maggie had spent a full night grieving while she waited for her sister to call.

'Yesterday. Late afternoon. They don't need you to come back. Not now anyway.'

'OK.'

'It's going to be just as we thought. No fuss. The crem. Only George.'

'Right.'

'But she wanted us all there for the will. We're reading that a couple of days after.'

'But there isn't anything left, is there? George has spent it all.'

'There's a few bits and bobs,' Liz said. 'And the house, of course.'

'I can be back whenever you need me.'

Liz sniffed sharply, a noise that Maggie knew translated to irritability. They had been mostly irritated with each other since Liz got married and had children and Maggie decided to travel and they both thought the other had abandoned them.

'How is Paris?' Liz asked.

'It's fine,' Maggie replied.

'Have you finished the cooking course?'

'Yes, Liz. I told you that already.'

'Well, are you working?'

'I'm trying,' she said as she looked across at the sleeping Frenchman next to her in the bed. 'I'm not sure I'm very good.'

'Of course you are good. You just need to get on with it.'

'Fine.'

Maggie thought she heard Liz make a snorting sound before her daughter climbed onto her lap and told her mother she wanted a chocolate roll.

'No, Sophie,' Liz scolded. 'It's lunch soon. Maybe later but you have to eat an apple first.'

'You sound grumpy,' Maggie said, goading.

'Yes, I am *grumpy*,' Liz snapped back. 'I have two children, in case you hadn't noticed.'

'Of course I've noticed. You talk about it all the fucking time.'

'Aren't you sad? Aren't you even going to ask *how*?'

'*How*?'

'How she died?'

'Heart attack? Stroke? I presume she wasn't shot? Or mauled?'

'Heart attack. On the scooter, in the garden. Albert found her.'

'So, that's it then. The house will have a new owner soon,' Maggie said, matter-of-factly, although the enormity of such a statement would take a long time to sink in. It had been in the family for generations, and none of them knew who they would be without it.

'He wasn't there, by the way,' Liz continued. 'George wasn't there. We had to track him down.'

Maggie sighed. 'Where was he?'

'He was with a woman called Beverly in Shipston. Recently widowed. He was valuing her furniture apparently.'

George had in fact been in Beverly's paddling pool with a glass of Pimm's in one hand, Beverly in the other, and a small oak dresser, a Soumac rug and a pair of 18th century silver candlesticks in the back of his van. He had got out, towelled himself down and sobbed briefly but purposefully on the lawn before driving to the hospital morgue. There his mother lay, more majestic than she had ever looked before, and George wondered why he couldn't feel any emotion whatsoever. He had been waiting for this moment for as long as he could remember, and now it was here, he wasn't sure what he would do with it.

Chapter 3

Spring

Albert sat beneath the kitchen table looking expectantly at the cereal and toast that was making its way back and forth between table and mouth as Tom and Sophie ate their breakfast, his front leg occasionally sliding off to the side on the engineered wood flooring. How adaptable dogs are, Liz thought to herself as she watched him while she sipped her tea. How effortlessly they accustom themselves to their new environment, even in his advanced years and after a particularly bilious channel crossing. She'd had more than enough canine interaction in her forty years though, and the thought of having to actually own one was more than she could bear. She could admire their resilience and composure for this one, definitely temporary, definitely very short-lived moment. Then he would be gone.

Since starting her third maternity leave, Liz had felt that the various strands of her life were becoming far too entangled and unruly and she hadn't found an easy way to smooth or separate them out. She often imagined herself as the maypole from the children's primary school, sturdy and level and strong, yet surrounded by screeching, skipping children who wound ribbons around her, tighter and tighter, until she could no longer breathe and had to start punching them all just to get a minutes' peace.

Any additional complication, whether it came from a faulty washing machine, a child's earache, school dressing-up days or a corgi unexpectedly arriving from Spain, had become completely intolerable. The third child, an entirely unplanned and troublesome addition to an already busy household, had almost tipped Liz into the arena of the disorganised. Once or twice she had felt herself being full almost to the brim, the washing piled just a little too high, the school uniforms not quite straight enough, the kitchen surfaces given only a cursory wipe, but she had thankfully managed to pull herself back from the brink. The thought of life actually tipping over that edge, of letting any of her standards slip, was too terrifying to contemplate.

'I thought Albert died,' Tom said thoughtfully between large mouthfuls of Cheerios.

'No, darling, he didn't die. Look, there he is, perfectly well. He was just having a nice, long holiday.'

'You said he died two years ago when Granny Vic died.'

'Did I?'

'You said he went to the big kennel in the sky because he was sad and lonely and that's what happens to dogs sometimes, but I know that's not true because God didn't make a kennel in the sky.'

'Didn't he?'

'He made the heavens and the earth and then lots of other things like rivers and fish and snakes—'

'—and hamsters,' Sophie added, cheerfully. She had been campaigning for a hamster for a number of weeks and did not seem to be giving up, despite Liz's explicit objection to any sort of animal in the house, especially one from the rodent family.

'And hamsters and sharks and cake and cars and people and bicycles and all of those things,' Tom continued. 'But he didn't make a kennel. It wasn't on the list of things that Mrs Jones said he made anyway.'

'Well maybe God did some extra bits on the side when nobody was looking,' Liz said briskly as she began to clear the breakfast things from the table. 'Or maybe whoever wrote the Bible couldn't fit it all on the page or ran out of ink or something. They didn't have gel pens and felt tips back then, you know.'

'Did God make toast?' Sophie asked as she finished off her last crust.

'Mummy made the toast,' Liz replied, rather firmly.

'I think I might like toast more than I like hamsters.'

'Well that's *very* good news because toast doesn't poo everywhere or need cleaning out once a week.'

'Can we get a dog?' Tom asked. He had also been campaigning.

'No.'

'Why not?'

'Because there are three of you already.'

'I'll keep asking until you say yes.'

'Jolly good.'

'*And* I'll have to check with Mrs Jones about the kennel,' Tom said, eyeing his mother suspiciously. 'She'll be able to tell me what *really* happened.'

'Righty-ho,' Liz said, feeling a small but familiar poke of sadness. 'Let's all get our teeth done then and get ready for school. We don't want to be late.'

When had Tom stopped believing everything Liz said? When had she stopped being his favourite person? Everything she did was wrong or silly or untrue and she felt like she was losing tiny morsels of him with each disagreement, of which there were many. The mistrustful phase had coincided with Lily's arrival, and according to all the parenting books was completely normal, but she couldn't help finding it unsettling. She couldn't help finding everything unsettling, or sad, or dull or just very, very annoying. Everyone's lives were carrying on all around her while she was back in the dreaded, swampy land of The Baby. She was sour and she was spiky and that's just the way it was for now.

Liz's husband Doug, as straight and as measured as a Helix ruler, was back behind his accountancy desk a week after Lily was born, which had suited Liz in many ways as she found his weekend, trackie-bums persona deeply irritating. She had fallen in love with him in a suit, in sterile meeting rooms talking about deficits and balance sheets, or behind his desk, his computer glasses just off the bridge of his nose as he submerged himself in a spreadsheet. They had met in their first jobs out of university, an accountancy firm in Coventry that was oppressively grey and ugly and smelt like oxtail soup, but they'd had cubicles next to each other and the little spark had grown and grown until it was a flame.

'Got much planned today?' Doug said cheerfully as he came into the kitchen, dressed and ready for work, shirt tucked in, trousers all pressed and the domestic arena soon to be utterly forgotten about for another day. He was never more attractive to her than when he got dressed in the mornings, his sense of purpose for the day ahead pulled into his suit trousers and buttoned firmly into his ironed blue shirt, the careful tucking in, the silver cufflinks, the shoe trees placed neatly back on the shelf. All of their children were conceived at this time of day, in those moments when Liz's desire for him pushed against her desire for him to leave, creating a small, golden window.

'No,' she grumbled, trying her hardest not to feel hideously, murderously resentful. 'Apart from that.' And she pointed to a baby bouncer where Lily was contentedly lying, her feet gently kicking. Lily was, in so many ways, the most perfect baby; always content, always smiling, slept well, fed well, hardly ever cried and yet Liz could not help seeing her as another obstacle. Another bump in the road on the way back to her old life. In quieter moments, Liz worried that Lily might be so good-natured because Liz might not love her enough, hadn't given her as much attention as the other two, hadn't always felt the same joy on seeing her face in the mornings. Lily was trying to charm her mother into wanting her. Wasn't that what she and Maggie had done?

'Why don't you try baby group?'

'Why don't *you* try baby group?'

'I could take her at the weekend perhaps?' Doug said as he started to line up a series of vitamins from various pots laid out in a line on the windowsill above the sink.

'They don't do it at the weekends, Doug,' Liz sighed. 'That's when you are all meant to be having 'super fun family time'. They do it in the week so that mums have someone to talk to and don't go insane with boredom and start clogging up GP waiting rooms. Except that it *is* boring. It's possibly the most boring thing you can do in your whole entire life.'

'I'm not sure it's meant for men anyway, is it?' Doug chuckled nervously as he began to gulp down his supplements.

'Of course, it is,' Liz snapped. 'It's just that it's the women who still get lumped with the babies while the fathers all bugger off back to work. There wouldn't *even be* baby groups if men all did it. You'd all be standing around mumbling bollocks at each other or hiding in the loo and it would all just be too excruciating and would have to be cancelled.'

'Do any dads go?'

'Only one or two. Occasionally. Nobody talks to them.'

'I thought you quite liked the whole baby-club thing. You used to do it with Tom and Sophie, didn't you?' Doug said.

'That was then,' Liz replied, and she sat back down at the kitchen table, suddenly feeling very flat and tired. Those first few years of motherhood, their little family unit of three and then four seemed so simple somehow, so symmetrical and neat and easy. She knew how to be that person, she knew how to be the person she was before children, before Doug, before any of it, but that all felt like such a very long time ago.

'Well, you've got Albert for company today,' Doug said as he gave the dog a little awkward pat on the head.

'Great.'

'Lucky Albert! Any word from your dad?'

There had been no word, but Liz had already decided that as soon as everyone was out of the house, she would take Albert for a walk across the village to the Manor House and see what her sister knew. She would then leave Albert there and when she got back home and had put Lily down for her nap, she would dig out the 'pet turbo' attachment that came with her Dyson and she would hoover with it for as long as she liked.

Chapter 4

Maggie had only ever lived in one home in England, and that was the Manor House in Little Martin. It was just in that middle bit of the Cotswolds where the stone turns from a pale, schoolboy chino to a warm, flat ale, where everything is a little bit less clipped and a little bit more muddy than its smarter, paler neighbours, and the villages known as The Martins sit among the pleasing hills of the Whichford Valley.

Little Martin was actually bigger than Great Martin, but smaller than Martin St John, Lower Martin and Upper Martin and further south than Lower Martin, which seemed to annoy everyone except for the people who lived there. Maggie and Liz had always firmly believed that their village was the best of the Martin clan. Small yes, but underestimated. They used to picture their Martin in human form as canny and insightful, diminutive but snappily dressed, creative and original, well-read and morally superior but humble too, gracious, charming and magnanimous. A good neighbour, a good friend, someone you would look to for advice and for wisdom but also the one you would go to for a very good time.

Great Martin and Upper Martin were naturally the pompous ones. Lower Martin had been shunned for some sordid indiscretion and Martin St John was far too churchy and hypocritical, so Little Martin really was the only acceptable Martin to live in. He had everything you wanted for village living: schools, a pub and a church, thatched roofs and tiny cottages, quiet neighbours and nosy neighbours and everything in between, and the Manor House right in the middle, its size and its splendour sometimes seeming horribly out of place, almost like it had been there since the dawn of time.

Set back a little way from the street, the Manor House was imposing and handsome, classically Georgian in design with a slate roof, sash windows and steps leading up to a huge wooden front door that held the sign, 'NO TIMEWASTERS' above it. The façade was covered on one side with an ancient wisteria and on the other with thick ivy, and there was a point around mid-May when the soft purple flowers were in full bloom and the ivy was a deep, glossy green that you would have thought it was the prettiest house in the whole of England.

Maggie's favourite time of year had always been late autumn. The ivy turned cherry red and the wisteria was an afternoon-sunshine yellow and it seemed as if the two plants might finally reach out and touch each other above the doorway after their new summer growth, that they were somehow striving to be together in all their ripened, mellow glory. But then the leaves would fall, and the frost would come, and you would see that all the roots and branches were really just all tangled up with themselves and couldn't possibly have had the energy to reach for anything other than their own botanical enrichment.

Although rather emptier than it once had been when piles of antiques filled every room, the Manor's style was still eclectic, colourful and curious, dotted throughout with furniture, paintings, sculptures and other assorted trinkets deemed too cheap or too weird to put to auction. For the first-time visitor, there was a seemingly endless tangle of rooms and it wasn't uncommon to find a guest in a cupboard when they had only meant to get themselves a drink. Some of the rooms had formal names such as the 'orangery', the 'study' or the 'parlour', but Maggie and Liz found that it was far more manageable and infinitely more sensible to name the rooms after their colour.

On the ground floor there was the Blue sitting room, two green rooms (Dark Green and Light Green, although sometimes just referred to as Dark and Light) and the very pretty Pink Room which hardly ever got used, as well as the large kitchen, pantry and cloakroom. Upstairs there were two floors of bedrooms in Apricot (Queen Vic's), Violet (Liz's), Lemon (Maggie's), Burgundy, Olive, Grey and Cream, as well as a number of bathrooms and linen cupboards and a very long corridor that they threw balls down for the corgis. At the very top of the house there was an enormous attic, packed full of boxes of the stock that had failed to sell, and at the very bottom there was the basement. It was out of bounds to the girls when they were children, firstly because its stairs were quite narrow and steep, and then because it became George's domain and there was no knowing what he would be doing down there.

Connecting the house together were staircases and passageways that led up and down the building, so it was a very brave child that joined in with the girls in a game of hide-and-seek. The sisters' favourite room and the one they used the most, the one Maggie thought of when she wanted to be back home, was a snug-like space just off the entrance hallway. It was technically beige, fawn at a push, but it looked and felt like the perfect cup of tea, and so they just called it Tea.

Tea was what Maggie thought about when she thought of home. However, many times she moved abroad, however many ways she attempted to reinvent herself, she was always drawn back to the Manor, always felt its pull and tug as if she had left some vital part of herself within its walls. 'This time will be different,' she would tell herself as she packed her bag and headed off somewhere new. 'This time I will not come back,' and she could be quite happily entertained by men or cooking for a month or two, but nowhere felt quite the same as the Manor House. Nowhere else had ever felt like home, regardless of the fact that the house was everything about her and also nothing at all.

This is how the Manor stood that spring, undressed and still wintering, its only adornment the 'For Sale' sign planted outside, its only resident Maggie Addison, rattling around the house like the last pill in the pot. Despite the large number of rooms, Maggie lived quite contentedly between the kitchen, the lemon bedroom, Tea and occasionally the garden and that seemed like a sensible and modest way to exist as the house was to be sold and Maggie was only really there to deal with all the estate agents and help keep things ticking over. She was just one person after all. Liz liked to call her 'the caretaker,' if she was in a particularly combative mood. 'Here comes the caretaker,' she would say as if it was something they both found funny, but Maggie knew it was because Liz hated asking people to do things for her, particularly favours as enormous as taking the Manor on, and would usually cover up her gratitude with some sort of veiled insult.

Whenever Maggie looked back on the time before George came back, the time when she had the house all to herself, she would recall the stillness and simplicity of those days, especially when she needed reminding that life didn't always have to be complicated or dramatic, you didn't need to keep moving or changing, and that easy, everyday living was actually more than all right. She had never felt particularly lonely in life. She liked her own company more than most and she always said that the house kept her company, its rooms as familiar and as comforting to her as any person. It had helped her feel pleasantly tethered and rooted, a balloon tied safely to a chair. Although she didn't realise it at the time, these were the days that the Maggie of the past thirty-five years was being dismantled, piece by piece.

This was when George returned. There he was, ensconced in the guest bathroom the following morning, moaning and muttering his way through his early ablutions and Maggie was struck with just how long she had been so isolated and how very happy she was to have some company.

'All right in there, Dad?' she called through the bathroom door. He had been in there some time. 'Do you want any breakfast?'

'What? Yes, yes. I'll be out in a minute.'

Now she had a guest. And not just any guest. George was back, and Maggie wasn't sure if the rolling feeling in her stomach was one of excitement or just plain old everyday worry. He could easily summon both in her, often at the same time, a confusing cross-wire of emotions that fought for dominance in the bottom of her stomach.

She waited awkwardly by the door, listening to the taps being turned on and off, the indistinct mumblings then, quite surprisingly, turning into song. Humming at first, then singing. Definitely singing. God, was he really *singing*?

The key then turned in the lock and he was suddenly standing in front of her in a long silk maroon dressing gown, his towel draped around his neck and a washbag under his arm as if he was making his way out of a country hotel spa.

'Good morning, darling,' he said, all bright-eyed and bushy-tailed, the anguish of the night before nowhere to be seen. He looked rather jolly.

'How did you sleep?'

'Fitfully,' he replied.

'I, um, just wondered if you want anything to eat?' she asked. George had always been her favourite person to cook for, right back to when she was six and she first learnt how to cook. 'Aren't you a clever girl,' he would say as she put down a plate of sloppy eggs or soggy cake. Pleasing George had been her lifetime's work.

'Ah, yes. Breakfast,' he mused, as though he had just been approached for his order at The Ritz and was having trouble deciding. 'I'm not sure I can really face anything right now. Heartbreak does rather scupper the appetite, don't you find?'

'No problem,' Maggie said, smiling. 'Maybe later.'

'But perhaps I will have a small, little something.'

'Oh, good.'

'Maybe just some egg and bacon, mushrooms, if you have them?'

'Sure,' Maggie said, and that warm and wholesome feeling of being able to do something nice for a person you love just a tiny bit more than they love you began to fill her from the bottom up, like a beautiful warm bath.

Liz had only ever wanted to get away from the Manor House. She had always found the jumble and clutter and ridiculousness of it all upsetting and would create small, ordered corners of her things so that she could retain some sense of sanity and control. She had left as soon as she could, first to university, then on to do an MSc, a year abroad in the States with an accountancy firm who specialised in insolvency and then into full-time work in London, Birmingham and Coventry. When she finally returned to the Cotswolds with Doug by her side, she bought a house so utterly different from the one she grew up in that it could only be seen as a statement of intent. This was who Liz was now. This was the house she had dreamt about during all those years spent tripping over Persian carpets in the hallway or eating her breakfast next to a stuffed fox or badger at the kitchen table. She was now part of the new side of the village: progressive, tidy, forward thinking. Normal.

'Morning Elizabeth,' a voice called across the village green. 'Morning! Morning!'

'Morning, Mrs Wilson,' Liz called back before she had even turned to see who it was. Mrs Wilson's voice was as distinctive as her appearance, both hearty and voluminous, a stout and ruddy Toby jug of a woman who dressed in sensible navy trousers and a wax jacket and interfered as much as she possibly could.

'Jolly good meeting last night,' Mrs Wilson panted, as she finally caught up with Liz. 'Seemed to all go well, didn't it?'

'Yes, very well. Very well.'

'A few too many interruptions for my liking, but I have always been a bit of a stickler for a tight agenda.'

'Hmmm,' said Liz, vaguely.

'It *is* nice to see the modern part of the village once in a while. Reminds us all of how lucky we are to have the old part, I suppose. There is so much history in these beautiful buildings. So much to cherish and preserve. It is *so* critical that we remain vigilant and not let anything else slip under the radar, don't you agree, Elizabeth?'

Liz sighed deeply but managed to cover it with a weak smile.

'A bit of an expedition though, isn't it, out to you? We shall all have to bring picnics with us next time.'

'There was plenty of food on the table, Mrs Wilson, and drinks. I provided plenty of food and drink to cover any and all dietary requirements.'

'But I suppose it gets the steps in, doesn't it? My Fitbit was very pleased with me. It even sent me a sort of firework display!'

'How nice.'

'Not everyone was happy to be there, of course. There were quite a few grumbles, quite a few, but you can't please everyone can you?'

'No,' replied Liz, thinking that if anyone had started grumbling it was most likely to have been Mrs Wilson.

'Are you girls off anywhere nice?' Mrs Wilson asked, cocking her head to the side so she could see Lily's face squidged into the baby carrier.

'No, just to see my sister.'

'Ah. Any interest in the house, dear?'

'We have had an offer, actually.'

'An offer?' she said, eyes widening.

'Yes, but it's early days.'

'I wonder who that could be. Anyone local?'

'I'm not a hundred per cent sure, Mrs Wilson. It's early days.'

'I shall have a little ask around and see what I can find out,' she said, tapping the side of her nose.

'You really don't need to do that.'

'No, no, it's my pleasure, Elizabeth, my pleasure.'

Mrs Wilson chuckled to herself, and Liz found her eyes drawn to her neck, the fold of extra skin that sat on the collar of her salmon pink shirt and how it jiggled up and down when she laughed. She had an unbelievable urge to squeeze it very, very hard.

'That's not Albert you're walking, is it?' Mrs Wilson asked once she had composed herself.

'What, *this* dog?' Liz said, looking down at where Albert was loitering. She had almost forgotten he was there. 'No, no. Just a friend's dog. I'm just walking him, somewhere.'

'Looks *just* like Albert, doesn't it? It's uncanny. Poor old Albert. He must hate it over there in Spain or wherever it is he's landed up. All that sand and heat. All those dirty stray dogs.'

'I'm sure he's fine, Mrs Wilson.'

'Well, nice to see you, Elizabeth. You look a little tired. Don't forget the Martin Players auditions, will you? There's the fundraising meeting right after.'

Mrs Wilson turned and walked back in the direction she had come from, and feeling intensely irritated, Liz tugged Albert sharply to his feet and continued across the green towards the centre of Little Martin. The Manor sat there at its heart, the older back streets, terraces and cottages surrounding it forming the village's arteries, veins and bones, the curves and kinks in the roads and the rolling hills behind creating the outline of Little Martin. Liz did not enjoy coming here anymore. She would feel uneasy until she returned home again, back to the order and calm of her house, its straight lines and shiny surfaces and everything in its place.

If she had been a dog person, she might have suspected that something was awry when Albert became suddenly quite animated as they turned onto Green Lane. As they approached the stone steps of her old family home, he lurched forward with unexpected fervour and almost pulled Liz off balance as he bounded up towards the front door, tail wagging furiously.

'Albert!' she cried, as she was yanked along behind him. 'Albert, Albert, *slow down*!'

He reached the top step and started to sniff frantically around the bottom of the door, and as Liz caught up with him, a window on the first floor was pulled open and a nicely brushed, slightly balding head poked out.

Chapter 5

The very last thing that Liz had said to George before he left in a huff for Spain was, 'Get off the floor, you terrible, useless shit of a man,' which was rather a lot for Liz.

She was typically quite restrained, the outburst being evidence of just how cross she had been to see her father, rolling around on the carpet clutching his throat while telling the solicitor's rather attractive assistant that he might need medical assistance on account of shock. Maggie and Liz had looked on from the hard-back chairs in Dark Green and sighed. The reading of Queen Vic's will had been far more dramatic than anyone could have possibly imagined, even with Maggie just back from Paris, George dressed in full mourning garb and Albert in his black bow tie. She had left the house to Elizabeth and Margaret, and nothing would ever be the same again.

'He's been up since about five o'clock, Liz,' Maggie said, turning to her sister. 'He was like a kid on Christmas morning.'

'Shame,' Liz had replied.

It was unfortunate for all concerned that the Addison family solicitor, a serious and sensible man in his late sixties, was having his hip replaced the week that Queen Vic died. That meant that the reading of her will was passed to his assistant, a perky woman in her late forties called Henrietta Huggett: a name so wonderful, Maggie thought, that she doubted the woman had ever had to try very hard in life. She had only been recently hired, and while she had very little in the way of legal training, she was a friend of his wife's, so that was fine. It worked like that in the Cotswolds. Knowing people was sometimes more important than knowing things.

Henrietta had then got down on the floor next to George to loosen his top button and lightly pat his cheeks and from there it was only a matter of a few readjusted limbs before they were fully embracing, George sobbing into her auburn hair that something somewhere had gone terribly wrong. Perhaps she had felt sorry for George, a man whose inheritance had just leapfrogged over him and landed right in the lap of his two daughters. The Manor House, the only thing he had ever wanted, was not to be his after all.

Albert had somehow got involved then by mounting the side of Henrietta's elbow, in a protective way no doubt, and it was around then that Liz lost her patience and having shouted at George, ordered him out of the house. Her house, the house that she now owned with her sister. So, it was no surprise that the reunion between George and Albert in the Manor House hallway was rather more exuberant than the one between father and eldest daughter. George was overwhelmed to see Albert, who made noises that sounded like a small child in pain and turned himself around and around in circles. George rubbed his back and cooed at him in Spanish while his two daughters looked on, speechless.

'Why did you post your dog to my house?' Liz asked, after the greetings had all died down.

'I couldn't really say, darling. I must have got in a muddle.'

'You didn't mention Albert was coming, Dad?' Maggie said, giving Liz a quick kiss on the cheek.

'You look very well, Liz, very well,' George said. 'Very well. Very well indeed. How lovely to see you.'

'You didn't mention *Dad* was here, Maggie!' Liz said to her sister.

'He only arrived last night, Liz. I've hardly had a chance!'

'And the dog just arrived, out of the blue!' Liz continued, throwing her arms up in the air. 'On my doorstep. While I had *people* over.'

'Perhaps I have dementia, girls? Is that a possibility?'

'You've been here since *last night*, Dad, and you didn't mention Albert at all,' Maggie said.

'Didn't I? Well, there you go. The brain is definitely on the slide. Not long now, darlings, and I'll be dribbling into my cornflakes.'

'Jesus, Dad,' Maggie said.

'I'll be in those giant nappies before you know it, wandering around the streets of Banbury.'

'There's nothing wrong with you,' Maggie insisted.

'Albert gets seasick, did you know that?' Liz blurted. 'There's a vomit bill to pay.'

'Right. Well, we can sort that out, can't we?' George said, looking distinctly awkward.

'*Vomit bill*?' Maggie said, eyebrows raised.

'Dogs get seasick, did you know that? And then they puke all over the vans they are being transported in from Europe and then *someone* has to pay the cleaning bill.'

'Right, right,' George said as he rubbed his forehead slowly.

'Why didn't you get the tunnel, Dad?' Maggie asked.

'Can you take dogs on the tunnel?' he replied. 'Seems extraordinary, doesn't it? A dog, in a tunnel.'

'What is going on, Dad?' Liz interjected, 'Why didn't you tell us you were coming? Why didn't you tell us Albert was coming?'

'Well, it's a long story, Elizabeth. Long and complicated. But I'm here now and I would love to tell you all about it.'

'The bonkers thing is that *you* haven't even been to my house,' Liz exclaimed. 'Albert has, but you haven't!'

'Haven't I?' George chuckled. 'Well, I suppose it *is* a new build, isn't it darling?'

'It's not a *new build*. It's an Executive Family Dwelling!' Liz retorted. 'And you haven't even met my daughter.'

'No, no, I haven't, have I? Is she, a, um, good baby?' he asked tentatively while pointing feebly to the lump on Liz's chest.

'She's your *granddaughter*, George,' Liz replied as she unbuttoned the baby carrier. 'Of course, she's *good*.'

'Well don't disturb her now, darling,' George said, taking a step back. 'I'm sure she's happy where she is.'

But Liz had already undone the straps and Lily was removed, legs and arms all tucked in like a little beetle.

'Hold this,' Liz said firmly, and thrust Lily into George's arms. 'I need the loo.'

George held Lily at arm's length for a few moments before resting her gingerly in the crook of his arm and half-heartedly jigging her about. Lily was sleepy but waking in what seemed to be an amicable mood, gummy and smiling with limbs now flailing around, her fists balled up tight. He turned to Maggie, a look of sheer panic passing over his face.

'Bit, um, confusing at this age, aren't they?' he said, his nostrils flaring slightly as if he might be smelling something unpleasant. He was hard to look at, all awkward and pained. Still, after everything, Maggie realised she desperately wanted him to look strong and fatherly, even in some small way.

'She's sweet,' said Maggie, reaching over to have her finger grabbed.

'I was never very good with babies,' he said thoughtfully, as if he'd come into his parental stride at some later developmental stage. Maggie smiled but didn't reply. 'They're confusing, aren't they? What do they *want*?'

'Not very much really. Just food. And love.'

'Ah ha, rather like me and Albert, then,' he said, smiling at Lily, and for a short while he seemed rather transfixed by her. Albert looked up, concerned, clearly wondering whether he should be feeling jealous. 'I do remember you and your sister as babies. Holding you like this.'

'Do you?'

'There wasn't much to it, was there? Parenting . . . just jig you about a bit, give you something to eat.'

'I'm fairly sure there's more to it than that.'

'Although they are a bit of a blur, those years,' he said, wistfully.

'I don't think you were around for them that much, Dad.'

'Perhaps not,' he said, as Liz swept back into the hallway, scooped up Lily and shooed them all towards the kitchen table so that everyone could sit down and hear what George had to say for himself. To Liz's utter dismay, the remnants of breakfast were still all over it.

'I thought Rhonda might have been the one,' George began, carefully placing his hands on the table in front of him and taking deep, measured breaths. 'But it was not meant to be, girls. She is not the woman I thought she was. Not by a country mile.'

'Was she a man?' Liz said archly.

'There were other men involved.'

'How many?' Liz asked.

'I don't know how many. Does it matter, Elizabeth?' he said, rather curtly, before then lowering his voice. 'Spaniards came to the house.'

'*Spaniards?* Couldn't they have just been friends?' Maggie asked.

'Rhonda changed. She was different. She was distant, distracted. She said she no longer wanted to play Cribbage with me or explore the local towns. She said she wanted us to buy a Skoda Yeti together. They had an excellent deal on at the Multimarca, and we were going to drive to see her sister in Zagreb and then maybe even drive on to Venice and then who knows where else. But she suddenly said she didn't want a Yeti and she started talking about how she might actually just go to Malta where some friend of hers was living, instead.'

'And what happened to that other lady, Janice?' Maggie said.

'The thing is, girls, that I have been left in a very, very difficult position. Financially speaking. The deposit for the Yeti was quite substantial and I am now in a bit of a quandary.'

'You're broke,' Liz said, flatly.

'Perhaps a little . . . *chipped*,' George said.

'Why don't you just ask Rhonda for it?' Liz asked.

'We haven't left on the best of terms. She threw some kitchen utensils at me.'

'Which ones?' Maggie asked, ever the chef.

'Is that it?' Liz said, clearly incredulous. 'A wooden spoon and you run away?

'There was a whisk, Elizabeth! And a masher. Rhonda has a very violent temper. And there was a lot more to it than that, girls. She wasn't right in the head. She went all peculiar. Doolally.'

'But if she owes you the money, Dad?' Maggie said.

'I don't care about the Yeti, girls!' he protested. 'The Yeti is done. It's gone. I don't want to dwell on the Yeti.'

'What about your pension?' Liz asked.

'It's a very modest amount, Elizabeth,' he said. 'Although it will help to keep me from malnutrition.'

'I thought you were going to get back to selling antiques?' Maggie said. 'Spanish antiques, sold by an Englishman? That was going to be your thing.'

'Well, it turns out the market is actually quite challenging.'

'Oh, really?' Liz asked.

'Yes, Liz, it is. And Rhonda didn't particularly like me to travel for work so I couldn't do as much as I would have liked.'

Liz snorted loudly and pushed her chair back, knocking into Albert as she went, who yelped rather pitifully and shuffled off into a different room. She began pacing up and down the kitchen, swivelling so precisely on the balls of her feet that Maggie wondered if it was something you only learn once you reach a certain level of adulthood.

'What do you want?' Liz asked eventually, her eyes narrowing at George.

'I don't need much, girls. Nothing at all really. Just somewhere to live, and only until I can make other arrangements of course.'

'Are you serious?' Liz asked.

'We can spend some proper time together. The three of us. I'd like that.'

'What about what *we* would like?'

George looked startled for a moment; the face of a schoolchild put on the spot about something he has not prepared for.

'This is not an easy thing for me to have to ask, girls,' he said, his tone skirting dangerously around the edges of belligerence. 'If I am not wanted here, then you must say and I will not bother you anymore. I can knock on a few doors perhaps? See if someone will take me in until I can get back on my feet.'

'Don't be silly, Dad,' Maggie said, softly. 'You can't do that.'

'What about two years ago? Liz said, increasingly irate. 'What about the enormous hissy fit you had when granny didn't leave you the house and you decided to flounce off in a sulk? What about what *we* needed then? I moved house. I had another bloody baby. Maggie's just been sat around here on her own doing goodness knows what.'

'*What?*' Maggie said.

'Where have you been for all of that, George? Where were you after mum left? Where have you been ALL OF OUR LIVES?'

George put his head in his hands, slowly rubbing his forehead, before looking up again. His face seemed slack and loose as if it had somehow lost all its bones.

'I have made mistakes, Elizabeth,' he said slowly. 'I know that. And I am very, very sorry. But I am here now, and I must try to look forward.'

Maggie looked up at Liz. She always looked to Liz.

'We will need to talk about it,' she said eventually. 'Maggie and I will need to talk.'

Chapter 6

From the very first inklings that her father might end up spectacularly ruining his life, Liz had planned her future out in meticulous detail.

'Your mother and I are getting a divorce,' he had said, all those years ago, as he lit a cigarette. Maggie was six and Liz eleven when their mother, Pat, had finally decided that enough was enough after overhearing George tell Sylvia Thrupp on the telephone that he wanted to 'set about her like a terrier in a barn.'

'Ugh, thank God!' exclaimed Liz, who had worked it all out a long time before and wondered why they hadn't just got on with it. It felt as though their mother had always been looking to escape, and there was almost a sense of relief about her finally having done it.

'Does that mean you don't love each other anymore?' Maggie asked, slowly.

'It's not quite that straightforward, darling. Love just isn't enough sometimes.'

'Or it's going in the wrong place,' Liz said pointedly, glaring at George.

'Yes, well I am afraid that your mother doesn't approve of some of the friends that Daddy has been seeing recently.'

'He's been having sex,' Liz said to Maggie. 'It's called *extra-marital* sex and it's the type of sex you are not allowed to do if you are married.'

'The important thing is, darlings, that nothing with *us* will really change. Not really. I will move downstairs to the basement and you can see me when I'm not busy, so long as you knock very loudly first, and then I won't have to be in the way of you girls and all your baking and shopping and whatnot.'

Maggie had cried and Liz had got a Viennetta out of the freezer and then not eaten any of it, as she knew wasting food annoyed George intensely. He moved down to the basement, which had two large bedrooms, a kitchen and a bathroom and was actually quite nice and not at all the chastisement that everyone had hoped it would be. This was interspersed with frequent 'buying' trips abroad where he would set out to acquire dressers or tables or bureaus but would become distracted by Jaqueline or Heather or Sue and not return for months on end. When in residence, he would see them formally on Saturday afternoons where he would say things like, 'I can do no right in this world,' or 'your mother despises me,' while puffing on back-to-back Silk Cuts and failing to ask them a single question about their lives.

'She hates me like the plague, girls. Does she say anything about me? What does she say? Does she talk about me?'

'Not really,' Maggie would reply, before trying to change the subject. She had learnt by then to give him short and conclusive answers or he had a tendency to try and squeeze out a tear or two. The truth was that nobody talked about him, not even Queen Vic, whose disappointment in her only child had peaked years before, and it wasn't long before Pat moved to Brighton and Liz had her own exit strategy planned.

On her twelfth birthday she announced that she was going to be an accountant, a very good one, and that she would not allow herself a moment of indulgence until she had at least £20,000 in the bank.

'What about buying a tiger?' said Maggie. She liked to quiz Liz on what the money was for and how exactly she was going to spend it.

'I don't like tigers, Maggie. I only like lions. Lions are far more intelligent.'

'Are they?'

'Yes of course they are.'

'OK, a lion, then?'

'A lion would eat Darling and Ham, Maggie, and then Queen Vic would be very cross with us.'

Darling and Ham were their grandmother's beloved corgis at the time. She always had corgis, a series of mothers and daughters who tended to be overweight, spoilt and extremely loyal. Their portraits hung in the downstairs loo; photographs mainly, but there was one painted in watercolours and that was of Albert. They marked time by the passing of corgis, each dog's life marking an era in theirs. 'Was that during Diana or Caroline?' one of them would ask when trying to recall something from the past. Ham was really Anne, after the Princess, but it sounded too much like Ham to the girls and they enjoyed the reaction they got when they yelled 'HAM' into the garden. Anne was also no name for a dog, even a corgi.

'Will you buy a pony?' Maggie asked. They were big fans of horses at the time and having a pony seemed like an essential purchase if you wanted any sort of happy life.

'No. No ponies.'

'What's it for then?'

'I am going to invest it in Premium Bonds and, if I am very careful, it should yield a profit of at least £1000 in five years.'

They were very different, right from the word go, but it was around this time that Maggie really began to feel it. Of course, people pointed it out all the time, right in front of them too, as if being a child meant that they wouldn't care about these things or even remember them. Adults seemed to like easy labels. They liked to plonk the children into neat categories, saying things like, 'Elizabeth is *so* poised,' or 'Isn't Margaret a character,' while they sit there in front of them, minding their own business, and the child wonders if it should react in some way, be grateful or cross or even contradictory because this person standing in their kitchen has only met them a handful of times and how the hell would they know? The adults move on, to another room, to the rest of their lives, but the girls are now 'moody Margaret' or 'clever Elizabeth' and those things seep in after a while.

The problem with these girls was that they were *Elizabeth* and *Margaret*. *The* Elizabeth and Margaret, and from the moment they became their namesakes, there was a sense of expectation about who they were to become and how they were to behave. At least in the minds of some people.

45

Maggie often wondered whether her sister's single-mindedness and tenacity was what made her quite so laid back, as though they needed to balance each other out somehow, a cosmic equilibrium between the first and second born that was way beyond her control or understanding. While Maggie was essentially a practical and realistic girl (there really was no other way to be when you grew up as an Addison), she sometimes leant into the belief that in order for Liz to thrive, for her to yield Premium Bonds and get accountancy qualifications, she needed to dally and to stall. It made her complete inability to cope with the multitude of decisions that life threw at her more tolerable somehow, as if it was all part of the sacrifice she must make to preserve a sense of harmony at the Manor House, the harmony of Little Martin, the harmony of the whole entire universe. Elizabeth, clever, hard-working and compliant Elizabeth, shone brighter with Maggie standing in her shadow.

Maggie fell into her choices like she was falling in a dream, disconnected and in slow motion and then waking with a jolt to find she had picked physics GCSE or tennis club or a relationship with Callum Collins. At some point in her latter teenage years, she just stopped trying altogether and let the current take her where it wanted to go. Life felt easier when you weren't fighting against it, and besides, that wasn't her job. That was what Liz was for.

It was only just midday when Maggie and Liz got to the pub, but after the meeting with George, they ordered two double gin and tonics, two packets of salt and vinegar crisps and asked for a bottle of milk to be warmed.

Standing there, side by side at the bar, you wouldn't have known them as sisters unless you had been told, and then you might start to notice the slight curve of the nose, the eyes that pulled down slightly at the edges, the somewhat aloof expression that they could both arrive at almost simultaneously if they were talking about cars or football or something else that they had no interest in. They were beautiful in that traditional English way; noble, pale faces and bright blue eyes, high fine cheekbones and porcelain complexions, as if the years spent in a Manor House had smoothed and sculpted them the way the sea does with glass.

Maggie was still dark haired like George, and Liz still blonde like Pat, although there was now regular upkeep with bi-monthly highlights. They dressed in direct correlation to how they used to be clothed as children – Maggie as far removed from it as possible and Liz in the adult, watered-down version: stiff collars, neutral colours and pleats, everything with a purpose, everything just so. In recent years, she had also returned to the hairstyle of her infancy, a neat bob which she saw as practical and time efficient, but Maggie saw as middle age resignation. Her hair was long and wavy and very much without style, and while she knew that one day she would do something more interesting with it, she'd never quite got around to it.

'I haven't just been *sitting around*, Liz, by the way,' Maggie said pointedly as they settled down in the corner of the pub. 'I do work you know!'

'I know, I know,' Liz said, taking Lily out from the baby carrier.

'Just because I don't have fifty kids it doesn't mean I'm not busy.'

'Fine. I'm sorry, OK?'

Maggie took a large gulp of gin. She could feel it slide down to her stomach where it lit a small and very pleasant fire. 'What are we going to do, then?'

'I don't know,' Liz replied. 'I need to think about it.'

'I don't mind having him at the house. It's not like there isn't room. And it's got to be better than having him wander around the village, hasn't it?'

'But we're meant to be selling the house, Maggie. You are meant to be moving out.'

'We've only just had the offer though. Doesn't it all take a few weeks to go through?'

'He'll settle in and spread out and then it will be impossible to get rid of him. He'll be one of those squatters you hear about. You know what he's like.'

'But where else is he going to go?'

'He's *not* staying with me.'

'Right. It will only be for a short time anyway. He'll have to sort himself out by the time the new owners want to move in.'

'So will you,' Liz said, pointedly.

'I know. I know.'

'Any progress?'

'I'm looking round places this week. With Joe.'

'Joe Church?'

'Yes.'

'Good,' Liz said. 'That's good.'

She shook the milk up and down and tipped Lily back onto her arm to feed her. Maggie watched while the words sank in. She had noticed how calm and serene Liz became when she was feeding Lily, ethereal almost, as if she was partly somewhere else, somewhere otherworldly, a place where only mothers were allowed. It was perhaps the only time when Liz fully submitted to the stationary demands of parenthood. The sitting still of it. The quietness that was sometimes required. She was so beautiful, Maggie thought, when she just sat long enough for you to have a proper look at her.

'What are you thinking about?' Maggie asked her eventually.

'I'd almost forgotten about him, hadn't you?' she said thoughtfully.

'Yes,' Maggie lied.

'I'd got used to the idea of being a sort of orphan. I thought it made me a bit more interesting, in a way.'

'To who?'

'I don't know really.'

Maggie took a large gulp of her drink.

'I mean, I thought about him occasionally,' Liz continued. 'He popped up every now and then, but I didn't know if we'd actually *see* him again. And I was fine with that.'

'Me too.'

'I just don't think he should get to waltz in here like nothing has happened and have us look after him. He needs to actually *do* something.'

'Like what?'

'I don't know. Help. Muck in! Be a parent for once in his life.'

'A *parent*?' Maggie said, the word seeming so utterly strange and unfamiliar in her mouth, at least in regard to George.

'Yes, a parent! It's bloody hard work, in case I hadn't already mentioned that. Or he could get a job. Volunteer. Pick up litter. Pick up the kids!'

'Your kids?'

'Yes, my kids! Who else's kids would he be picking up?'

'I'm sure he'd pick them up if you asked him to.'

'When has he ever done anything with my kids?' Liz snapped.

'I don't know, Liz! Why are you getting cross with me?'

'I'm not. I'm sorry,' she said, and sheepishly looked around to see if anyone had noticed her raising her voice. A pair of ramblers had come into the pub and were shaking out their coats by the bar. It had started to rain outside.

'Is this about childcare?' Maggie asked. 'I can help if you need someone—'

'No, of course not, it's not about childcare,' Liz replied, looking down at Lily who had fallen asleep in her arms, a stream of milk snaking down from her mouth to her chin. 'Not just about that anyway.'

'Maybe we just shouldn't expect too much,' Maggie said. 'He's not particularly practical, is he?"

'Of course, he's practical!' Liz said. 'Everyone is practical. Everyone has hands! He just pretends not to be, so he doesn't have to do anything. He's got used to people doing everything for him, Maggie, and I don't think we should let him this time. This is our chance to have a functioning parent in our lives.'

Maggie laughed. 'It's a bit late for that, Liz, isn't it?'

'Everyone says that the older kids get, the more they need their parents.'

'But they mean teenagers, don't they? Not adults!'

'I want to see if he can do it, Maggie,' Liz said, leaning in. 'I want to see if he can do things for other people. For us.'

'OK,' Maggie said, and she thought back to the breakfast she had made for him just an hour before, how readily she had agreed to do it and how pleasing it had been to cook for him again. She realised that she would probably be quite happy just doing that and not expecting anything at all in return. She had learnt not to.

'We can't let him be repeatedly shit. Or sit around moaning all day or saying he's going to die of gangrene or gout or some other disease of the month. He'll bugger off again before we know it, without having lifted a finger to help any of us, and he'll probably create God knows how many disasters along the way. We can feed him and we can house him until he's back on his feet or he's met some other woman. But we have to keep him busy. He's going to have to be useful if he wants to stay.'

Maggie nodded and downed the rest of her gin.

'I'll make a list,' Liz said, and the prospect of having a genuine reason to use a notebook and pen for the first time in weeks filled her with an instant shot of pure, undiluted joy. 'A list of helpful, constructive things he can do with his time. Family things. Good things.'

'Good things,' Maggie repeated.

'Maybe he just needs a bit of guidance and instruction?' Liz said, while she began to stuff Lily's legs back into the carrier. 'Maybe someone just needs to remind him how to be a decent, normal human being. *How* to be a father. I mean, he never really had one, did he?'

Maggie considered this for a moment. Queen Vic's husband had died very young, not long after George was born, and she hadn't liked to talk about him. But there was never any doubt about her devotion to George. She was, by all accounts, the most loving and steadfast of mothers, and if her calm, firm and kind parenting was anything like the care given to Maggie and Liz, then it was more than enough.

'Queen Vic was often working, wasn't she, and then she had to help bring us up. Maybe nobody told him?'

'But nobody tells anyone how to be a father, do they?' Maggie asked, thoughtfully as she nursed her gin.

'There is a lot of new thinking about how to parent these days,' Liz continued. 'Doug and I have read a lot of books.'

Maggie stopped herself just in time from rolling her eyes. 'Normal, everyday parenting is OK too, isn't it?' she said. 'Any parenting, really.'

'You have to do things right in life, Maggie. There has to be an order to it. You have to follow the rules or else it's just mayhem.'

Maggie nodded. Despite all their differences, despite everything that had happened to them, she still believed that there *must* be something more to Liz than the control and the neatness and the towing the line. She still

52

thought, even now, that one day Liz would beckon her over and whisper how it was all part of an act, a much bigger plan, and that they were in it together all along. They would do it together because it just wasn't possible for Maggie to do living all on her own.

'So, we have a plan,' Liz said, standing up, her sense of purpose radiating off her. 'Sisters formulate a plan! Have a think about the list, OK? Let me know what you want to put on it. I'll call you later.'

She turned and left the pub, and Maggie was unsurprised to see that she had barely touched her drink. She pulled the glass across the table towards her, sensing in her marrow that something about the two of them was going to change, and then she got out her phone and googled, 'What do fathers do?'

Chapter 7

It was with enormous satisfaction that George opened the front door of the Manor House a few days later after hearing the tinkling of the bell. Albert had barked only once, unsure if he was on duty or not, and Maggie had shouted downstairs that she would be ready in a minute.

'Yes?' he said, with what he hoped was some degree of proprietorial gravitas.

'Hi. Mr Addison? I'm the estate agent, Joe. Joe Church. But Joe is fine. I'm here to see Maggie.'

'Ah, yes! Come along in, Joe,' George said, shaking his hand enthusiastically and then ushering him into the hallway. 'You come highly recommended.'

'Do I? Gosh!'

'I should imagine so. Doesn't everyone come highly recommended these days?'

'I suppose they do, yes,' Joe chuckled.

'But you, Joe, look like a man who knows a thing or two.'

'Well, that's very kind,' Joe replied, smiling stiffly as Albert began to sniff his trousers. 'I am actually quite new to the job. I worked in property development before. In London. Commercial mainly.'

'Apologies for Albert. He's a terrible one for the trouser leg I'm afraid.'

'He can probably smell the cats,' Joe said.

'Cats, eh? I wouldn't have pegged you as a cat man, Joe.'

'They're my mum's really. I just live alongside them.'

'Ah, spoken like a true cat man,' George said, giving Joe a friendly tap on the arm. 'How is your mother, by the way? Is she healthy? Keep herself fit?'

'Yes, she's fine, thank you. Do you . . . know her well?'

'No, not at all,' George said. 'But we are all of an age, aren't we?'

'Oh, yes, I suppose so.'

'I'm afraid you have caught me in the middle of a particularly gruesome heartbreak, Joe. That and the beginnings of a possible degenerative brain disease. It's quite a potent cocktail.'

'Oh, goodness, I'm very sorry—' stuttered Joe, as a voice from another room yelled, 'HE'S FINE!'

'My daughter is 'putting me up' in her enormous house,' George said. 'I used to live here, you know? It used to be mine.'

'I think I came here once or twice, many years ago,' Joe said, taking in his surroundings. 'For kids' parties.'

'It's not *my* house, Dad,' Maggie said as she came into the hallway in dungarees and knitted cardigan. 'And it never used to be yours. It's being sold anyway, isn't it, Joe?

'So, you two know each other already then?' George asked.

Joe said, 'yes' at the same time as Maggie said, 'not really.' Joe chuckled awkwardly.

'I used to do, um, archery club with Liz, back in the day, and Maggie and I were in the same year at school,' Joe clarified.

'Different classes,' Maggie added. 'Different friends.'

'We did PE together though.'

'Did we?'

'Mrs Porter? She didn't like me. PE wasn't my best subject back then.'

'Oh, I'd forgotten that' Maggie said as she tried to remember the face of the PE teacher, or even the schoolboy face of Joe, who it seemed she had very little recollection of at all.

'So, you've had a good offer, have you? George asked. 'On the house?"

'It's a good starting point,' Joe said, smiling at Maggie.

'What I tend to find with these things,' George said, stepping forward towards Joe and placing an arm around his shoulder. 'Is that the buyer doesn't really know what he wants. He may think he does, but actually he wants to be gently persuaded into it a sale. You turn the ship very slowly you see, very, very slowly, so that the passengers on board don't realise it's happening until they are already facing in a completely different direction.'

'Dad used to sell antiques,' Maggie said to Joe. 'The family business. Now folded.'

'Yes, yes, I think I remember,' Joe said. 'And I remember you on *Antiques Roadshow*.'

'Good lord, do you really? How marvellous!' George looked delighted, hands perched on hips, an enormous smile across his face.

'He was only on a couple of episodes,' Maggie said to Joe.

'Did you see the one with the footstool?' George asked. 'Very unusual thing, designed for a man with one leg. Did you happen to see that one?'

'I'm not really sure, actually. I might have done.'

'Or the one with the desk that came from France? The owner was wearing a purple dress I think, terrifying looking woman, but she'd brought the desk all the way from the Alps, if you can believe it.'

'We'd better get going, Dad,' Maggie said gently. She recognised the look on George's face, the one which seemed to take him far away, and she started moving towards the front door.

'What? Yes, of course, you must go. What time will you be back?' he asked, with just the smallest hint of concern.

'I don't know, Dad. Does it matter?'

'No, no. Just want to know you are safe, darling.'

Maggie was about to say she had been safe without him for most of her life but decided against it and instead smiled, giving him a kiss on the cheek instead before turning to leave.

Joe was far more handsome than Maggie had remembered, now that she could see him properly in the crisp, cold light. He was tall and broad, athletic, Maggie thought, at least for someone who hadn't liked PE. He looked a little awkward in his navy suit, shifting slightly in it as he walked, and he carried himself like someone still unsure of their place in the world. He had a warm, kind face, dark curly hair that was very slightly greying at the sides, brown eyes behind tortoiseshell glasses and a smile that leant slightly to the right.

As they set off down the street together, he walked quickly and purposefully in long reaching strides, but then stopped every few steps to slow down so that he could walk alongside Maggie.

'You're too quick for me,' she said, panting slightly.

'Sorry, sorry,' he said. 'I've got used to running about the place.'

'Professionals in suits always walk quickly.'

'Do they?'

'Of course. They're very important.'

'It's probably because they are so unhappy with what they are wearing,' Joe said, adjusting the suit jacket around his collar. 'I am not really a fan of all this.'

'No, I'm not sure I would be either.'

'What do you wear then?'

'For work?'

'Or for fun?'

'For fun I wear my pyjamas.'

'For work then.'

'Nothing very smart. I'm a chef so I don't really have a job as such, not in the traditional sense anyway.'

'A chef is a proper job, isn't it? It's a great job.'

'Yeah, I suppose so.'

'Who do you cook for, if you don't mind me asking?'

'Well, I catered the Little Martin wine club's AGM the other day so, you know, I'm in the big league now!'

'I'm very impressed.'

'I did do quite a lot of work abroad and I do bits and bobs here and there. My sister always says that I *lack focus*.'

He smiled at her. 'Do you wear the white jacket and the big white hat?'

'Not really. Only if a customer asks. And then I definitely charge them more.'

'Maybe I should start doing that with the suit?' he said with a grin.

'I'm not paying you more for wearing that thing!' she laughed.

'What, you don't like it? It's a Marks and Spencer classic.'

'You look very smart. And very grown up. You must be one of those adults I've been hearing about.'

Joe laughed. 'I hope not. Not yet anyway.'

'You were always quite sensible though, weren't you? At school? You were one of the good ones. The ones that all the teachers liked.'

'I thought you didn't remember me?' Joe said with a smile.

'I didn't. Which is how I know you must have been good.'

'I got by.'

'You *got by*?' she scoffed. 'What does that mean?'

'I got through it, I guess. School wasn't that much fun, was it?'

'Maybe you were doing it wrong?'

Joe shrugged. 'I got good A levels. Went to university. Is that doing it wrong?'

Maggie thought for a minute about pushing it further but instead just shook her head. 'No, not at all. Sounds like you did it exactly right.'

They walked on, down Fox Close and on to Kings Road where The Brown Owl came into view. It was a thatched building and very pretty from a distance, the sort of place a tourist might have taken a photo of, but when you got up close it was in some disrepair. The cream paint around the windows was chipping off and the thatch was heavy with moss.

'I've seen you in The Owl once or twice,' Joe said, pointing towards the pub.

'Why didn't you come and say hello?' Maggie asked.

'I don't know really. You were with some of those blokes we went to school with, Callum and Mike and all that lot. They never really liked me.'

'That was years ago,' she said. 'They're harmless really. You'd probably quite like them now.'

'Maybe I would,' Joe said, pushing his glasses to the top of his nose. 'It's all a bit weird being back here, isn't it? Seeing everyone again . . . you have to remind yourself that you're not in school anymore, all the rules about who you can and can't talk to.'

'So, you are *back*, back? Back for good?'

'I am back back, and I am living the actual dream,' he said, gesturing down to the suit and the glossy home brochures in his hand. Maggie laughed. 'How about you? You've been here a little bit now, haven't you? Do you have a plan?'

'A plan? God, I don't know really. I keep wondering if I should be somewhere else but can't seem to figure out where. I hear there is life elsewhere.'

'There is, there is. I have actually seen it.'

'*Wow*! Really? You're amazing!' she teased.

'Some of it is not that bad either. Some of it's crap too, I mean really, really crap, but some of it's OK. I can tell you about the good bits if you like?'

'That's a very kind offer, thank you, Joe.'

'Anytime,' he said with a grin.

'I have actually seen some of it too, you know. Foreign bits too. Maybe we should compare notes?'

'I'd like that.'

'Although everywhere is really the same, isn't it, once you get past the front door.'

'But then here we are,' said Joe as he lifted his arm up to show the scenery in front of him, the village, the houses, the fields and hills. 'Back where we started.'

'Here we are. Looking at houses.'

'They do exist elsewhere too, you know. You don't *have* to buy a house here. Or one at all.'

'Are you talking yourself out of a job, Joe?' she teased.

'No, no. I guess I was just wondering if you really have to sell? It's such an amazing house.'

'I think we do. I think we do, yes. My grandmother left the house to me and my sister and we have to split it somehow. She needs help with childcare costs and family stuff, plus there's some debts to pay off from the family business.'

'Ah.'

'I'm sure you remember my sister? She's blonde and married and is generally very good at things.'

'She was smart, wasn't she? Head Girl of school, quite competitive, always winning stuff? She thrashed me at archery.'

'Yep, that's her.'

'What about you? Are you good at *things*?'

'I'm not sure,' she replied. 'I might be a late starter.'

'There's no rush, is there? I mean, not really.'

'I don't know. I sort of feel like people want you to get on with life. They don't like a dawdler.'

'Or a backtracker. They *hate* a backtracker.'

'Urgh, backtrackers are the *worst*!'

He laughed, his head tipping right up to the sky and Maggie felt a smile appear on her face that she had not planned.

'Well, come on then,' she said, giving him a little nudge. 'I thought you were going to show me, what was it you said, some "exceptional properties".'

'Did I say that? Jesus.'

'You've got the estate agent chat down already. I am very impressed.'

'Please don't tell anyone, but I haven't got a clue what I'm doing.'

Maggie smiled. 'That's fine, neither do I,' she said.

'Perfect. We can just muddle along together, then. What do you reckon?'

Joe showed her four properties, three of which were horrible, and one which seemed as if it might be all right, more than all right really, if only she could just picture what her life might look like living in it. Small but perfectly formed, it was a Cotswold stone, end of terrace house on the corner of Rosebank, and it was bright and cheery and felt exactly like the sort of place a person could be very happy in.

'This one is the right one, yes?' Maggie asked, as if it might have all been a multiple-choice test. She still didn't trust herself to make important decisions.

'It does have a lovely feel to it,' Joe said. 'Good location, airy rooms, period features. It will probably go quite quickly, so . . .'

'And if it's a mistake, I can just sell it again, right?'

'Err, you could do, yes. Or you could rent it out . . . although it might be a good idea to have a think about it if you're not really sure. It is quite a big thing to buy.'

'Sorry, Joe. I'm just trying to picture it all.'

'I think you'd like it here. It ticks lots of boxes. But it is just a house, Maggie. It's not . . . *you*.'

She smiled at him, grateful for the perspective. 'You're good at this, aren't you?' she said, as she opened and closed the kitchen drawers and knocked on the walls like someone who knew what they were looking for. She had found herself impressed by Joe's professionalism and his ability to say the right things, despite the ridiculousness of it all. There was something about his willingness to take it all seriously, to be positive, even cheerful about it, that Maggie found completely enchanting.

'Will your dad be living with you too?' Joe asked.

'Oh, no. God no! He's just visiting.'

'I don't remember him being quite so—'

'—unusual?' Maggie offered.

'I was going to say funny, actually. And charming. He must be good company.'

'He is, I suppose. When he's around anyway. He's certainly an attention seeker,' Maggie said.

'Ah, well, all the best ones are. Mine was such an attention seeker he died.'

'Oh, shit. I'm sorry, Joe,' Maggie said, taken aback. 'I didn't know that. I'm so sorry.'

Maggie suddenly remembered Joe's dad very clearly. She remembered them both, how they were together, how similar they looked: both tall and cheerful and slightly goofy, as though they never quite got used to their adult bodies. He drove a clapped-out navy BMW and often wore a Panama hat and Maggie remembered the way he greeted Joe when he picked him at school, how happy he was to see him, how enthusiastic and joyful he was about everything. She always noticed those sorts of dads.

'No, it's fine, it's fine. It was a year or two ago now. He was ill for a long time, so . . .' He drifted off.

'I'm really sorry to hear that, Joe,' she said, placing her hand on his arm and then feeling a little awkward that she had. 'I remember your dad. He seemed really lovely.'

'Thank you. We miss him a lot.'

'So, is that why you are back here?'

'Um, sort of. Mum's lonely and has crap knees and a bit of a dodgy heart, but I also lost my job in London and my girlfriend dumped me – well, actually, she was having an affair with someone I used to work with, which was nice. The obvious next step, clearly, was to move here and become an estate agent!'

He chuckled to himself, and Maggie noticed he had the smallest of dimples on his left cheek, a tiny dark divot like a keyhole.

'I mean, it does seem like a perfectly normal life path to me,' she said. 'And there's nothing wrong with being an estate agent.'

'Oh, I know, I know. Some of my best friends are estate agents.'

'*Really*?'

'No. Not at all,' he said with a grin.

'Sorry about the girlfriend though,' she said.

'Don't be. She's fine. She's great actually. She went off with a banker so, you know, she's doing really well.'

'A *banker*? Oh no.'

'And she didn't like potatoes, so it was never going to work.'

Maggie laughed. 'Wow, that is a double whammy. Who doesn't like potatoes?'

'Stephanie Robertson doesn't like potatoes,' Joe said.

'Stephanie Robertson,' Maggie repeated. 'That is a shame,' and they smiled at each other for what felt like a whole minute but was probably only seconds, and Maggie felt her cheeks get warm. She stepped away then, shy, and looked around the house one last time, telling Joe all her favourite ways to make potatoes, the dauphinoise, the mash and homemade chips and all the chef's secret tips for cooking roasties. He laughed and he smiled at her and she couldn't think of a single reason to not like him. She liked him. She actually liked him very much.

'I like the house,' she said. 'I do. You're right, Joe. I like it. Shall I just buy it?'

'Well, you could make an offer. That would be a good start. We can't really do much until you accept an offer on yours.'

'Oh, right. Of course. I'll talk to Liz.'

'There's no rush. Have a think about it.'

'We've been thinking about it for over two years. We probably just need to get on with it now.'

They left the house and began to head back towards the Manor, taking the longer route around the edge of the village so that they could walk alongside the school playing fields and past the bench where Maggie used to sit and smoke cigarettes and waste time before going home again. They talked about school and growing up in the village and the inevitability of being drawn back to where you came from, the tide that washes you out and then back in again. They talked about the days when they all drank in the same pub, groups of them in the beer garden all crowded onto picnic benches, elbows and arms and the galloping hormones all tangled up and the wondering if there was anyone there you might want to kiss; wondering if you stood out, to anyone, at all.

'What's it like living with your mum again?' Maggie asked as they finally headed back towards the centre of the village.

'It's all right. We get along most of the time. She's old and a bit grumpy and she misses my dad, but she watches murder mysteries and she does the crossword and drinks quite a lot of sherry, so I think there's probably quite a lot to look forward to in our later years.'

'That's a relief!' Maggie said. 'The middle bit isn't that much fun. Not so far, anyway.'

'It's not is it?' he replied. 'It's all a bit of a swizz this adult thing, isn't it?'

'*Swizz*?'

'Swizz. God!' He winced and put his hands over his face.

'No, no, swizz is such a good word!' she said, grabbing his hand and giving it a quick squeeze. 'I LOVE swizz. I haven't said it since I was about ten!'

'I don't think I have either. Shit, it's being back here again, isn't it? I'm in my old bedroom with all my old stuff. I'm backtracking again.'

'Well, I think it's great,' Maggie said. 'Who wants to be an adult anyway? All the adults I know are boring and miserable and weird. Let's just stay here on our little middle thirties island and hope nobody comes looking for us.'

He reached out then and took her hand in his. It felt warm and soft and unexpectedly light, as if he was somehow taking all of its weight.

'Do you want to go for a drink, Maggie?' he said. His eyes were so wide and bright and such a deep velvet brown that Maggie thought that they might completely envelop her.

'With me?'

'Yes. With you. With me. If you want to. But it's absolutely fine if you don't want to, I was just thinking I might have one and then you might like to come with me but if you have things to do and I am sure you have lots of things to do then that's absolutely fine.' His cheeks had gone slightly pink and he was fidgeting with his feet. He had suddenly forgotten how to be around her.

'Sure,' she said, not letting herself think any further or deeper about it than the sudden, acute need for alcohol and male company being fulfilled. They went to The Owl and drank rather a lot in a very short space of time and it felt utterly wonderful, like being allowed outside for the first time in weeks, like being seen by someone for the first time, the thrill of being really seen and really liked. How brilliantly seductive reminiscence was, Maggie thought. Remembering the person you used to be was like a part of you had come alive again and the world was full of endless exciting, ridiculous possibilities. She wondered if she would have liked Joe quite so much if they hadn't already known each other for so long, if they didn't have a shared history, a history that reminded them of a time in their lives before death and decisions and worrying if they had left living life too late. She thought about her mind then and how it always looked for the darkness and she hoped, more than anything, that this time she would not find it.

'I'm quite drunk, actually,' Joe said as they stumbled outside on to the pavement at closing time, their hands clasped tightly together to steady themselves. It had turned completely dark since they had been in the pub, so dark and so clear that they could see every single star in the sky, and even though Maggie had been in that singular moment many times before, the moment just before it all becomes something else, the anticipation of what was going to happen next was as intoxicating and as wonderful as ever.

He shuffled up close to her and put his arms around her waist, his smile small and sleepy, as if everything had been turned right down and the spotlight beam rested only on them.

'Is this all part of the service?' she said, and instantly wished she'd said something cleverer. Something funnier, something more aloof. She wanted to impress him.

'This is actually the premium service, where the estate agent who shows you around the properties then takes you to the pub and gets you very, very drunk and then asks if he can kiss you, and because, you see, you have already signed up for the premium service in advance and you sort of have to say yes to the kiss because you were brought up not to waste a single thing by your very sensible and very lovely relatives, and they would be so very disappointed in you if you turned down the *most premium* part of the premium service.'

'What's wrong with you?' she mumbled as they leaned towards each other.

'What do you mean?' he said, taking his glasses off and resting his forehead onto hers.

'What's the thing, what's the thing that's not right?'

'Nothing,' he said. 'Everything.'

She couldn't remember much of that first kiss after-wards, but she remembered that it wasn't disappointing when so many others had been. He was sweet and gen-tle, and there had been something surprising about it, this new mouth she was kissing, the new body she was pressed against. Had he put his hand on her face when he leant in? He seemed like the sort of man who might. She remembered she was laughing, and she remembered that she hadn't wanted to go home. She had meant to cook George supper. She had meant to update Liz on the houses she had seen and come up with something for the list, but all of that had been so easy to forget.

Chapter 8

Maggie often thought that she had the most coherent thoughts about life, about herself, about everything, when she was dreadfully hungover. There was a clarity to her reasoning, the aches in her body and the queasiness of her stomach allowing her to see the many errors of her ways without sentimentality or forgiveness. Regret is so much more resonant and longer lasting when it is accompanied by sweating and nausea.

She would replay scenes from the night before with rigorous commentary, the voice in her head like a teacher who despaired of her pupil, the pupil who couldn't seem to stop making the same mistakes over and over again. The voice liked to point out the moments where Maggie could have been clearer, kinder, less stubborn, more picky, less picky, less everything that she was. It liked to encourage her to give good people another chance, that everyone was flawed, just like she was, and that the flaws were the parts that you grew to love and cherish about a person because Maggie was always, always looking for a reason to leave.

There was always *something*. Something small, something silly; bad toes or bad taste or just too much hair, and she'd walk away so easily because that meant she could never get too tangled up. And it wasn't just that she'd pick unsuitable men; men with wives or goatees or glaringly obvious commitment issues. She also let the kind, decent ones go. Men who wanted to be with her, just her, men who wanted to make her happiness the most important thing in their lives. Men who brought her toast and tulips and hardback books, men who wiped away her tears with their fingers and told her she looked young for her age. Men who wanted to introduce her to their friends, their mothers, or who suggested weekends at the beach and wrote her poems about how her face reminded them of the sun pushing through the clouds after heavy rain.

But the poem would be typed instead of handwritten or all in capitals, and there would be a line about cat's paws or rose petals and the man who wrote it would wear bad jeans or call his mother too often and that would be it. Queen Vic had always said that the true test of a person is how they treated dogs, specifically hers, but Maggie thought it was how early a man opened his mouth after their fork left their plate, or which loaf of bread they would pick in the supermarket, or how long they spent in the shower, or any number of inconsequential things because it didn't really matter what the *thing* was, it mattered that they had the capacity to break her heart.

She was, as Liz called her, *persnickety*, a word that seemed to encapsulate Maggie's particular brand of fussiness, but that also had a childlike quality to it, as though it might just all be a game that she would one day grow out of. That morning, as the hangover revealed itself to be a steady headache with a background of dry mouth and nausea, she remembered that she hadn't wanted to go home but she went home anyway. Replaying the scenes from the night before, she was struck with just how quickly the worry had come in, how it came out of nowhere and without any warning like a sharp stab of pain. Despite everything kind and funny and wonderful about Joe, she had still felt the need to run, and the part of her that needed to do that was bigger and louder than the part of her that didn't.

'I should go,' Maggie had said as the kissing finally stopped. 'I am going to go.'

'No, no, don't go,' Joe said. 'Don't go, Maggie.'

They had been standing outside The Owl for a while, their hands intertwined, their bodies pressed close, but as the first feelings of attachment began to appear, she had the urge to push them away, to shove them so hard that they would tumble over and not come back. He asked if he could drop by and see her another time, the next day perhaps, the next week, but she had already gone cold.

'It's not a great idea,' she said as she untangled her hands and took a step back.

'Why?' he had asked. She remembered that he looked hurt, confused. He asked if he had done anything wrong. Whatever it was he was sorry, he didn't mean it, he was tipsy, he'd overstepped a line, he liked her, so much, hadn't they had a good time? But she couldn't give him an answer. It was just better to do it now rather than later, wasn't it?

Noises from the house were slowly coming into focus. George, clearing his throat and speaking to Albert, talk radio on in the kitchen and a debate about immigration, and for a moment she thought she was back in childhood again when the house was busy and noisy and had life again.

'Morning, darling,' George said as she eventually shuffled into the kitchen. 'Your sister is on her way over.'

'*God*, why?'

'She has a task for me, from a list. George is being *instructed*!'

'Already?' Maggie said, and then quickly realised she was not at all surprised. Maggie had noticed a particularly ferocious strain of efficiency in her sister over the last few weeks. Liz had said it was because she was now so busy with three children that she had become a machine at managing her life, but Maggie suspected it was far more likely that she didn't have enough to do.

'Oh, you know about this, do you?' George asked.

'Err, not the specifics I'm afraid,' Maggie said as she flipped the switch on the kettle and then slowly lowered her elbows onto the kitchen counter. Her head pulsed angrily as she rested it in her hands.

'So, am I to expect requests from you too, darling?'

'*Requests?* No. I don't know,' she stuttered. Perhaps she should make something up for the list so Liz didn't get cross with her. Perhaps she should just blame Liz for the whole thing. 'It's not really like that, Dad. It's a good thing.'

'Elizabeth said that's exactly what it was like. I was to follow instructions from you if I wanted to stay here.'

'I think we just thought that it would be good for you to be busy,' Maggie said with a shrug as she turned back to face him. 'So, you don't have to, you know, dwell on things too much.'

'Ah. I see,' George said, nodding. 'This is for my benefit.'

Maggie managed a weak smile. The kitchen, which Maggie had spent so many days and weeks in alone, seemed different somehow. It seemed bigger and brighter, as though some of the lamps had only just been turned on, and in the light was George, looking reassuringly dapper and so perfectly at home as he read the newspaper that Maggie felt as if she was the one who had just returned.

'What are you wearing?' she said as she began to digest the retro burgundy roll-neck jumper, moss coloured cords and red socks that he had on. There was something vaguely festive about him, a misplaced elf who hadn't quite made it back into the Christmas box.

'From the attic,' he said. 'Eighties, I think. I have a whole wardrobe up there. There's some quite nice bits.' Maggie had forgotten that he had stored some of his things in the Manor's enormous attic. He always said that one of his only good investments in life had been the shirts, trousers, jackets and jumpers he had bought in better days from The Cotswold Gentleman, a shop whose sole purpose seemed to be dressing George. The look was timeless country casual at top volume, outdoor pursuits and pheasant motifs, old-money tweed stitched with a hint of mid-life adultery. It suited him.

'Sorry if I woke you last night,' Maggie said, as the kettle finally boiled. 'Albert was barking when I came in.'

'Excellent guard dog, Albert. Did you know he scared off some wild boar in Spain? Enormous bloody things. *Tusky.*'

'I didn't know, no. I haven't seen you in two years, remember?'

'Did it not make the news back here?' he said with mock surprise. 'I am astonished, Margaret. It was big news on the continent; big, big news.'

'Don't call me Margaret, please,' she said with a smile. 'And Albert is *not* a good guard dog. He licked the postman yesterday.'

'Ah, well he does have a bit of a thing for postmen, don't you Albert?' Albert looked up and sniffed the air. 'It's the shorts, I think. Coffee, darling? You look like you could do with some.'

He lowered his newspaper and there was the coffee pot, half full and definitely still warm, a jug of milk, some fruit in the fruit bowl and toast in the toast rack, the old cornflower-blue butter dish with proper butter in it, a jar of jam and a jar of marmalade, all laid out. She couldn't remember the last time the table had looked so full, so welcoming, so exactly how it should be.

'Yes. Please,' she said, slowly taking a seat. 'This is . . . nice.'

'I popped to the shop. Thought I would get a few bits before we all starve to death.'

'That's kind, thank you,' she said, pouring herself some coffee. 'But there is food in the house, Dad. In the pantry.'

'There's a whole load of nonsense in there, darling. Couldn't work out what much of it was to be honest. Sometimes you just need a piece of toast.'

'Well, thank you,' she said, taking a sip of the coffee. 'It's very kind of you.'

'Not at all.'

'Are you going to be OK for money?'

'Not really, darling, no,' George said as he took a piece of toast and began to butter it firmly with his knife. 'I have been pillaged.'

'Pocket money, I mean. Just day-to-day stuff?'

She knew that he wouldn't have any. He never had any actual *money*, even when the business was doing well, but he was excellent at getting credit. The day-to-day of bills and bank accounts and making sure you were not overdrawn had never seemed to concern him, because he had always somehow found his way back to money, even when it wasn't his. It had seem so grown up to Maggie as a child, so sophisticated and successful, as though cash was for other people.

'I have my pension, darling,' he said. 'Did you know that I am an actual *pensioner*?'

'I think I worked that out, yes.'

'You're all right then are you, darling?' he said, giving her a good look up and down. 'You're OK, are you?'

'Me? In what way?'

'I just thought I should check in. See how you are. That's what fathers do, isn't it?' He smiled warmly at her, clearly pleased with himself.

'I suppose it is, yes,' Maggie said, realising they were both speaking in a hypothetical sense. 'When you feel like it.'

'Any news?' he asked, ignoring the last comment.

'News? Err, not really, no.' Not in the Liz sense, anyway. No new babies or houses or significant grievances. 'I'm just, you know, muddling along.'

'How's work?'

'It's picking up a bit. I have a few jobs coming up, so—'

'—Excellent. Any more travel?'

'No, I'm going to stay put for a bit I think, at least until the house is all sorted out anyway.'

'Good, good,' he nodded at her in between bites of toast. 'I always said you would make an excellent chef.'

'Did you? I thought you wanted me to be a dealer like you?'

'Nonsense. Selling antiques is a mug's game. People need food, not trinkets.'

'I suppose so . . .' she drifted off, realising how small her life all sounded.

'Anything else to report?'

'Like what?'

'I don't know, just general *news*?'

'*Men* you mean?'

'Well, not necessarily,' he floundered.

'You don't have to tiptoe around me just because I am single, Dad. It's not an illness.'

'No, no, of course not.'

'It didn't work out with the French guy if that's what you're wondering. He was married.'

'Oh?'

'And a dick.'

'Right.'

'But I'm fine. I'm more than fine.'

'Yes, of course you are, darling. Of course.' He sat back in his chair and smiled at her. 'We're not too different, you and I, wouldn't you say? Hopeless in love, happiest here, in this house, in this village, in our own little worlds.'

'I've never really thought about it,' Maggie said, when in fact she had in fact thought about it endlessly. It was what she thought about most of the time, analysing every facet of her personality over and over again and where it might have come from, looking for the clues that would help her to understand who she was. She worried that she would never work it out, that she would always be a vague mystery, someone without a purpose or a definition, or even worse, just someone's sister, someone who used to live in a big house, someone who used to have a family. She worried that she would always choose the worst man in the room, or that she would hurt people again and again, but even worse than that, she worried that she wouldn't care, that she would become so far removed from the person that she hoped she could be, that there would be no way back.

'Did you know that Rhonda is a very good cook?'

'Rhonda? No, I've never met her, Dad.'

'Ah,' he said, nodding slowly. 'Of course.'

'You're going to be fine, Dad,' Maggie said, pouring herself some more coffee. She was going to be fine. Everything would be fine. 'This is just a hiccup.'

'You can die of hiccups,' he said, despondently. 'Did you know that?'

'You're not going to die from hiccups.'

'And I have a pain in my leg that's probably cancerous.'

'Maybe it's just a pain in your leg?'

'It's probably a blood clot. It will travel up to my lungs and kill me before lunchtime. It's an unfussy death

I hear, so you'll have me back out of the house by this evening, with any luck.'

'Oh good,' Maggie said as she took a piece of toast and began to nibble it at the edges.

'Unless the undertakers are busy, of course. It is death season, after all. Spring is their busiest time of the year which could postpone the body removal until tomorrow.'

'Well, there's no rush, is there?' she said with a smile, and then to change the subject, 'Anything in the news?'

He flicked through the pages of the newspaper again. '"Local woman eats large brie for cat charity",' he read in his RP newsreader voice. It was the same voice he used to pass parenting orders on from Queen Vic: 'Your grandmother wants you to get into your pyjamas,' or 'Your grandmother says something about brushing your teeth.' The girls often imitated it, creating their own headlines if a situation needed describing in a nice, succinct way. There hadn't really been much direct parenting from George. He thought somebody else was doing it.

'There's a chicken terrorising people in Barford St Michael,' he continued. 'And a lot of people getting irate about parking.'

'Average day then,' Maggie said.

'Some nice houses for sale here though.'

'Oh?' Maggie said, glancing over.

'Joe will be on to that though. Lovely man, that Joe. I rather liked him.'

'Yes, yes he is,' she said as a sudden wave of nausea rolled through her and crashed down into her stomach. Lovely Joe. Lovely, wonderful Joe.

'It's important to get onside with estate agents, don't you find?'

'I don't know any estate agents,' she said. 'Apart from this one.'

'And you think he's the right man, do you?'

She looked up at him. 'For what?'

'Selling the house, darling.'

'Right. Well, he's about the only man, Dad. Unless you want to get someone, over from Chipping Norton?'

'Good God no,' George spat, scrunching up his face. 'They're all idiots over there. Better to keep it local, don't you think?'

'You know we have to sell the house, dad,' she said. That was the crux of it. They had to sell the house, but however many times she said it out loud, it never quite rang true, even two years on.

'Just as long as you're happy, darling,' he said, taking her hand. 'You and Elizabeth, just as long as you are both very, very happy.'

Chapter 9

Liz arrived with Lily and an enormous bag stuffed with baby paraphernalia.

'Baby group starts at eleven,' she said, untangling herself from multiple straps and buckles. 'That means you have about ten minutes before you have to set off.'

'Baby group?' said George. 'With *babies*?'

'Just this baby,' Liz said, handing over Lily. 'And whatever other babies are there obviously. The Friday group does get quite busy actually so it's definitely a good idea to get there early or you won't get a seat in the circle for rhyme time and then you'll have to sit on the outside of the circle and it will look all weird and it makes people cross.'

'What's *rhyme time*?' Maggie asked.

Liz sighed loudly. 'Everyone sits in a circle and sings nursery rhymes, of course. What else would it be, Maggie?'

'I don't know,' Maggie shrugged.

'It's a good thing, Maggie,' Liz said pointedly. 'A good thing.'

'Ah, right,' Maggie said, nodding her head in acknowledgment.

'Babies ... *singing songs?*' George asked, looking increasingly perturbed.

'No, George. Just the adults.'

'I'm not sure this is going to be very suitable, darling,' he said as Lily started to struggle in his arms, desperate to get back to her mother. 'I'm not very good at babies and whatnot.'

'Don't be so ridiculous, George,' Liz said. 'Just put your coat on and get a grip. Grandparents do this sort of thing all the time.'

'Do they?' he asked. 'Why?'

'Because they want to spend time with their grand-children. And they also want to help their daughters who really, really want to go back to work but childcare costs far more than most people earn and if they just stayed at home all day when they had a really, really good career, they might start to go a little bit mad!'

George nodded slowly as the words sunk in. He was inscrutable at the best of times, the baseline emotions smothered in layers of theatrics, but Liz thought that she might just have just seen a flicker of understanding, or at the very least, an acceptance of his situation.

'I have written all the instructions down on this piece of paper,' Liz said, producing a piece of typed A4 from her pocket. 'It's all very straightforward. It's easy, in fact.'

Maggie and George exchanged quick glances but didn't dare speak.

'Oh and I would rather you didn't talk to the woman with the red hair. You'll know which one she is because she's got the baby who looks like Gary Barlow and she's always banging on and on about how *amazing* her husband is. It's as if she wants us all to be jealous.'

Liz had already decided that she loathed the receptionist at the dentist's office.

She had a son in Sophie's year, a fact that Liz found unfathomable as it meant that they shared the same space somehow. They had the same weekly spelling tests and phonics sheets and reading books on their kitchen tables, the same request slips for cardboard boxes or one-pound coins or old T-shirts for messy play, the endless school admin roping them together, their names sitting alongside each other on the bcc line of school emails. You can choose your friends but not the other mothers in the Class 2 WhatsApp group, Liz thought.

Or your family, of course. You can't choose your family.

How could this twenty-something woman with the long, orange nails filed into those pointy spikes and the thick stuck-on eyelashes and blindingly terrifying white teeth have anything in common with Liz? Liz, Elizabeth, Elizabeth Vivacity Addison Farley, mother of three, fully qualified accountant, county hockey player of the year 2012 and owner of an Executive Family Dwelling could not possibly be in the same circumference as *Alfie's mum*. The world was not made that way. It had order. It had structure and it had purpose and she, Elizabeth Farley, had just as much right to be at the dentist as anyone else in that waiting room, even if it was the third time that month.

It was acceptable to judge other women if they were judging you, Liz told herself. It cancelled the judging out, and anyway, Alfie's mum was judging her far harder. She had looked her up and down at least twice when she entered and had given her jeans a hard stare, so as far was Liz was concerned they were equal now.

'Are you here again to see Dr Jackobsen?' she asked, eyebrows attempting to arch.

'Hello, yes, I have an appointment at eleven thirty,' Liz said, smiling and polite as ever, although the woman's pronunciation of 'Jack' and then 'obsen' as though they were two separate words annoyed her intensely, not to mention the pointed use of the 'again'. She picked up a magazine, lowering her face behind it, and wondered if it really was obvious why she was there. Maybe they all knew. Maybe they laughed about it in their staff room, that middle-aged woman in the Executive Family Dwelling who fancies the dentist. Did dentists even have staff rooms? Where did they eat their lunch? There was an article in the magazine about how effective singing along to pop songs was while doing your pelvic floor exercises and for a brief moment, Liz thought she might scream.

She was not one for self-analysis, but she knew it wouldn't have taken much navel-gazing to trace the steps from childhood to where she was currently sat, her face hidden behind *Grazia*, her legs crossed over so tightly on the plastic seat that her muscles had started to ache. She was clever enough to know it went far deeper than just pleasant infatuation, but she preferred not to question it too much as questioning might dig up all sorts of unpleasantness that she couldn't quite fit in at the moment. The fact was that her teeth and gums had been a little sore. There had been a little bit of bleeding. One of her back teeth felt a little sensitive. Perhaps not quite sore enough to warrant an emergency appointment but she had been clenching them, a sign that she was bothered by something. The problem was that there were so many somethings, a whole inventory of small and medium and occasionally big somethings, and somethings that were actually nothing at all.

'Sophie's mum, you can go in now,' the receptionist said, and Liz shot up sharply from behind her magazine and walked, head down, into the consulting room where she slid quickly onto the long black chair and tried very hard not to start apologising.

Dr Jackobsen had his back to her, looking at something on the computer screen in the corner of the room, and the nurse, a different one this time and ostensibly around seventeen, was refilling the white plastic cup with aqua mouthwash. Dr Jackobsen was half Norwegian – the tidy, precise half – and seemed to Liz as though he had been chipped and lathed out of wood, the strength and solidity and wholesomeness of him so very, very apparent through his crisp white medical jacket. He was intensely masculine, broad and tall and fair, and Liz had imagined him many times nimbly throwing her over his shoulder in a fireman's lift as they escaped a fire somewhere; at the dentist's perhaps, or maybe they were just running happily through a meadow about to have a picnic. It would have to be made by her of course, everything wrapped neatly, all arranged in size order.

'Ah, hello, Liz,' he said, turning around. 'Lovely to see you again.'

'Hello,' she mumbled, and allowed herself to look into his eyes for the first time since entering the room. The liquid blue of them was quite astonishing in the laser brightness of the LED light. Liz thought you might be able to see right to the bottom of them if you were only allowed to look for long enough, and there you might find the answer to everything about the world.

'Not at baby group this morning?' he said. 'I think Sarah's gone along with Monty.'

'Oh, has she?' She knew this, of course. Sarah was always there.

'I think she goes most weeks. Monty seems to love it.'

Fucking Monty. How weird that his baby should look so like Gary Barlow when he looked nothing like him. Perhaps it was actually his wife who looked like Gary Barlow and her red hair was just a distraction, or perhaps it was just one of those things, like babies looking like Winston Churchill. Maybe all babies looked like Gary Barlow. Maybe hers did?

'No, no, I'm not going this morning, no,' she said, and then, more quietly, 'I'm here this morning.'

'So, these teeth then?' he said cheerfully. 'Still feeling uncomfortable?'

'They are a little sensitive. I'm not really sure what's going on.'

'Shall we have a look?' he said, stretching the baby blue latex gloves over his long fingers. God, she had thought endlessly about those fingers. Why the fingers? Perhaps she was some sort of deviant? Was it possible to be a deviant and not even know it? Perhaps she had always been one, right from the very start, and it was

86

only now that it was bursting out of her like that creature in Alien.

'Open wider, wider, well done, well done.'

She tipped her head back further and felt the cold metal of the instruments against her gums and the warmth of his finger hooking softly around the corner of mouth, and as she closed her eyes and fully submitted her body to the recliner, she felt a cool shiver of excitement run up her spine and forgot all about whether it was wrong or not. The exquisite unholiness of it all, the delicious secrecy of those awful, wonderful, terrible thoughts. The wild, wild rebellion of it. What was wrong with her?

The examination was short, cursory almost, and once it was over Dr Jackobsen raised the chair to the upright position and encouraged Liz to rinse with the mouthwash.

'Not much to see I am afraid, Liz. It all looks very healthy in there.'

'Oh? Right.'

'Perhaps we should do an X-ray? What do you think?'

No, no,' she said, quickly, the thought of being quite so exposed, so *naked* in front of him completely horrifying. 'It's fine.'

'It's quite routine and only takes a few seconds.'

'I don't want one. Thank you.'

'We do them every day, Liz. They're very safe.'

'It's really not necessary.'

'Is there a chance you could be pregnant?'

'No! God, no,' she said, jumping off the chair. 'Definitely not. Doug and I, we're, well, not really, no. I'm not pregnant. In any way.'

Dr Jackobsen pulled his face mask down and smiled at her. It was a smile of kindness, of understanding. Or perhaps it was just pity? She felt a sharp punch of shame and wanted to leave.

'A lot of postpartum women experience teeth sensitivity, Liz,' he said. 'It's really very common.'

'That's very kind, thank you,' she said. 'Very, very kind.'

Liz left the dentist feeling restless and slightly empty. Restlessness was a theme these days. A low hum of irritability, which on its own was not unfamiliar territory, but when combined with the newly arrived and far more exotic duo of ambivalence and apathy, Liz did not recognise the woman she had recently become. The postpartum woman. *Sophie's mum.*

She wanted to go home so that she could hoover, but if she went home, she would think about Doug and she didn't want to think about Doug, not while she could still taste mouthwash if she ran her tongue along her teeth. She thought about exercising, going for a jog or a swim even, she used to do that, she used to run for miles. Or maybe just a wander around Sainsbury's, a nice look at the cleaning products, but she found she couldn't even be bothered to do that. Didn't people like her have hobbies, *things* they did with their time, things that helped define them as a person? Who even was she if she wasn't working or tidying or mothering?

She started walking in the other direction, down the hill towards Great Martin, towards George and Lily, towards the new village hall and the baby group, back towards everything she knew.

'Elizabeth! Elizabeth! Elizabeth!'

That voice, at times both high-pitched and manly, could travel an astonishing distance. Liz sighed and turned to face the oncoming noise.

'Elizabeth, are you all right? What on earth's happened?'

She was crossing the road now, her face set in an expression of horror and panic.

'I'm fine, Mrs Wilson. Nothing's happened.'

'Where is everybody?'

'Who?'

'*The children*! Where are the children?'

'They're at school, Mrs Wilson. Two of them are at school, and Lily is at baby group.'

'Oh, thank God. Thank God!'

'I do sometimes venture out without them. I do have things to do.'

'Oh, goodness me!' Mrs Wilson began to chuckle. 'You gave me an awful fright then.'

'I've been at the dentist, Mrs Wilson.'

'Did you have the lovely Dr Jackobsen? Very hard to get an appointment with him I hear. He's booked up until the summer, apparently!'

'He fitted me this in this morning,' Liz said, feeling ever so slightly smug.

'I do prefer to see Dr Halfpenny though. She's got the experience, you see. You can't put a price on experience.'

'Dr Jackobsen squeezed me in last minute,' Liz said again, unsure if she had been heard the first time.

'Are you on your way to Great Martin then, Elizabeth? I will just pop in to see Verity I think, if you're heading that way. Do you know Verity Broom? She's had a stent put in recently. Lovely lady, lives in the Old Bakehouse, has a schnauzer, son is a lawyer, so I might just come along with you if you don't mind?'

Liz minded enormously but smiled anyway and offered her arm for support as they walked on down the hill discussing dentist availability and NHS waiting lists and reusing teabags and how many houses in Little Martin had entered the National Garden Scheme this year. As Liz's irritation faded, she found something pleasantly soothing about the gentle back and forth of mild conversation, the slow pace of their feet. If only she could just stop being so bothered by everything. If only everything could just stop being so bothering.

As the hall came into view, all shiny and smart in the winter sunshine with its timber cladding and enormous bifold doors, Mrs Wilson let out a small gasp. There was something quite striking about it. It was so defiantly modern against its ancient backdrop.

'It's very *new*, isn't it?' she said, the 'new' sounding like something to be hated or feared, and Liz knew that the word not only meant the building itself, but the money that had paid for it.

The hall had been entirely funded by a wealthy Great Martin resident, the sort who had recently moved into the area, so while the money was appreciated, it was also different, flawed even, as though it had been handled by the wrong sort of people. The other Martins, yet to flush out a community-minded resident with sufficient funds, new or otherwise, were all still making do with their chilly, church rooms or cricket club huts for their bingo and baby gatherings while grumbling about council planning decisions. It was funny how new buildings, domestic or public, could alter the psyche of a whole community, Liz thought. Change caused such a commotion, despite it being the only consistent, reliable thing in life.

'It's very loud,' Mrs Wilson said, and Liz agreed, as music could be heard from all the way down the street. Hip-hop, she thought as they got closer, something fun and happy, something that suddenly took her by the hand and led her back to when she was younger, drinks after work and dancing in sticky nightclubs on Friday nights, neon-coloured shots and those first sweet kisses with Doug, her arms looped around his sweaty neck. She fell in love with Doug so quickly, almost from the moment they kissed, and it was so wonderful because she never expected it, not then anyway, when she hadn't even really made a start on life.

'They have offered the hall for play rehearsals this year, but I don't think we will take them up on it,' Mrs Wilson said.

'Why not?' Liz enquired.

'Well, we are fine with the way things are, aren't we? If it isn't broken, Elizabeth, there is no need to fix it.'

Liz thought about mentioning all the many repairs that needed fixing in the various community buildings dotted throughout Little Martin but decided against it. Mrs Wilson wasn't the type of person to listen to something she didn't want to hear.

As they got closer to the hall the music seemed almost comically loud, the bass reverberating up through the ground and into their bodies and while Mrs Wilson started muttering something about disturbing the peace, Liz walked around to the side window to have a peek inside through the vertical blinds. Baby group must be over, she thought. Baby group must have ended early and aerobics had started and George must have taken Lily back to the Manor; except no, there he was, dancing in the middle of the room, Lily lifted high in his arms, and there were women, dozens of women and babies surrounding him and they were all dancing too.

The song, 'Boom! Shake the Room', then finished and there was huge cheer followed by clapping and whooping and everyone laughing together. Another song came on, something by Abba, and another enormous cheer went up as everyone started to dance again. Liz was transfixed. The joy in seeing Lily smiling and giggling and twirling around was only tempered by the sight of George, seventy-five-year-old George, who was gyrating around in a circle in a burgundy roll-neck, his hips swinging back and forth towards a small crowd of whooping women, one of whom was red-haired Sarah with her Gary Barlow baby, Monty. Everyone, literally everyone, was having so much fun, and Liz had the distinct and very familiar feeling of being left out, of not being brave enough or fun enough, of watching life from the sidelines.

'What on earth is happening in there?' Mrs Wilson flapped, as she joined Liz at the window. 'Good God, has there been a break in?'

'No, Mrs Wilson. There are babies in there,' Liz said. 'It's baby group.'

'*Baby group?*' she yelped, squinting through the glass. 'Dear God!' She then started to knock loudly on the window, her knuckles rapping so hard against the panes that Liz thought they might break.

'They can't hear you, Mrs Wilson. Mrs Wilson, MRS WILSON! Can you stop that!'

'You should go in then, Elizabeth, and tell them to turn that racket down. Those poor babies will be deafened!'

'They're fine,' Liz said, in spite of herself. 'They're having fun.' And they stared silently through the glass for a few minutes, transfixed by the music and the dancing. The confusion of desperately wanting to be in the room, of wanting to be there, with everyone, dancing, but also to not be there at all, was completely hypnotic.

'Good gracious, is that *George*?' Mrs Wilson said, her wide nose pressed against the glass.

'Yes,' Liz sighed. 'It is.'

'George Addison. I don't believe my eyes. He has returned!'

The song then ended, and the mothers and babies were gathering their things and filing out of the hall, laughing and chatting together over their prams about what a great time they'd all had. George was slowly bringing up the rear, the old shepherd herding his giddy flock, with Lily under his arm, all pink-cheeked and gummy and blinking in the daylight.

Mrs Wilson, trembling with excitement, straightened her skirt and glided over to say hello, a strange, almost girlish fluidity seeming to take over her body. Liz watched as George greeted her with kisses on both cheeks and a huge embrace (much to Mrs Wilson's delight) and then continued with the cheerios and hugs with the other women as they said goodbye. The ease with which he moved among them all, the way they seemed to orbit around him, was not unfamiliar to Liz, but it was somehow always surprising. What was it about him that drew everyone in? Why was he so comfortable, so *happy* around others, when she found it so hard? Liz thought that if she could just understand that, then all of life might make more sense.

Sarah approached then, and after kissing George on both cheeks, threw her head back in laughter as he said something in her ear. She noticed Liz then and waved at her, and Liz, of course, waved straight back. Liz wanted to hate Sarah almost as much as she wanted Sarah to really, really like her.

'What a marvellous group of ladies,' George said as he eventually sauntered over. 'You didn't tell me it was going to be quite so much fun, Elizabeth.'

'Didn't I?' she replied casually, reaching out to take Lily, and she had felt a surge of relief and joy so intense on holding her that she had to swallow a few times to stop a tear from forming.

Chapter 10

After the success of the baby group, Liz's focus on the Good Things list moved up a gear.

'We're doing a family meal,' she announced to Maggie on the phone. 'Sunday lunch, like proper families do. Board games, a brisk walk, chatting around the table, that sort of thing. Can you make some food?'

It was Saturday morning, early, and Maggie was curled up on the wrinkled black sheets of Callum Collins's bed.

'Sure. What sort of thing do you want?'

'Nothing too weird.'

'What's weird?'

'Spicy. Moroccan.'

'That was a tagine, Liz, and it wasn't weird.'

'Well, just typical Sunday lunch things this time, please. You know, English.'

'Is that what *proper families* eat?'

'It's what *this* proper family is going to eat.'

Maggie sighed. 'Fine. I'll do all the side bits.'

'Right. So, this is what else I have on the list so far:

Sunday lunch . . . tick

Baby group . . . tick

Wood chopping.'

'What *wood*?'

'Shhh. Just wood, OK?

DIY

Picking us up from somewhere late at night

Driving us places, dropping us off, that sort of thing

Board games, lots of board games

Golf.'

'Who plays *golf*?'

'Mowing the lawn

School stuff, plays, sports days, etcetera

Playing catch, or any ball game for that matter

Camping, or abseiling, or both, could be both

Cinema trip

Bowling trip, any sort of trip really

McDonalds

Family walks

Building a bonfire or foraging, possibly together as a weekend bonding type thing

Reading stories . . . err . . . I think that's it for the moment. What have you got?'

'That's . . . quite a lot, Liz.'

'This is only the start, really. Tell me yours?"

'I'm still working on mine, Liz,' Maggie said.

'Right, well there's plenty of time. I can print this one out for you if you like and then we can just add to it.'

They were silent for a moment. Maggie stretched her legs out in the bed before turning on to her other side. 'Is there anything else?' she said. 'Otherwise I might go back to sleep.'

'We're starting to wean Lily,' Liz said, with some purpose.

'Oh?'

'Just purée to start with, carrot and parsnip, that sort of thing, although I am going to try fruit soon too. Banana, maybe. Or is it mango? I can't remember if that's the one you are meant to start with or not—'

'—I'm not sure I'm really the right person for this chat, Liz—'

'—No, no, just listen please. There is a point to this.'

'OK.'

'So, Lily has always been a good sleeper, right from the start, she was miles better than the other two and I thought it might be because she was the third child and you are supposedly not as stressed with the third, but recently she kept waking up and crying and I couldn't work out what was going on. The GP, some locum I saw in Deddington, she suggested that we start food a bit earlier, even though most people say you have to wait until they are at least five or even six months. They change their mind *all the time* about baby stuff so from one baby to the next you have a completely different set of advice on what you are meant to be doing and how you are meant to be doing it and you think, well the babies survived last time so surely whatever you said then can't be *that* bad and why can't we just have one set of rules about everything because it's hard enough to just keep track of day-to-day stuff, let alone the latest advice on when to feed your baby. So, I went to get all the jars and spoons anyway as we'd got rid of all that stuff ages and ages ago, and to cut a long story short, she didn't want it. She wouldn't have any of it. Spat it all out.'

'And the point is . . .?'

'The point *is* that it just took a bit of persuading. A bit of patience. Perseverance. All the ps. It was just a new taste. Something different. And now, *now* she loves it, she can't get enough of it and she sleeps amazingly again. Right through the night!'

'So . . . George is Lily?'

'George is Lily. He just needs a bit of persuading. Perseverance. Patience.'

'All the ps.'

'All the ps.'

'I'm not sure we can compare Lily eating baby food to George being a father, can we? Or maybe we can.'

'Sometimes people don't know what's good for them. They need to be told what to do.'

'But shouldn't he just want to be a parent though? Isn't that the problem?'

'But he's never actually *done it*, has he? He needs to give it a go. He needs to try it.'

'So, we're the purée?'

'What?'

'You and me, we're the carrot purée?'

'It doesn't matter who the purée is, Maggie. We just need to do this Sunday lunch, OK?'

Callum rolled over and coughed sharply. He had the worst cough, shrill and strangulated and fake sounding, and Maggie shut her eyes and braced for the inevitable.

'Who's that?' Liz barked.

'No one.'

'Someone coughed. I heard someone cough.'

'It's nobody, Liz.'

'Oh, God, Maggie, you're not with Callum again are you?'

'How do you know it's Callum?'

'Well, isn't it?'

'I don't want to talk about it, Liz, OK? I don't ask who you're with.'

'You know who I am with!'

'Fine. Fine. I just don't think it's any of your business.'

Liz contemplated saying that of course it was her business and who else was going to tell her what a shit Callum Collins is, how many women he has been with, how he never picks his son up from school or goes to sports day or goes to anything for that matter, but they'd had this type of argument so many times before and she didn't quite have the stomach for it.

'Are you OK?' she said instead.

'I'm fine. I am an adult, remember? I'm a fully functioning, self-employed adult. I'm just not married with kids, Liz.'

'It's OK to have someone looking out for you, you know.' Liz said in her well-worn, older sister voice. 'It's generally considered to be a good thing in life that someone worries about you. *Me.* I am the someone. I worry about you.'

'But you're not looking out for me, Liz,' Maggie replied. 'You're just giving me a hard time. You're on your "I'm married, and everything is perfect" high horse and it's the same fucking horse you have been riding your whole life.'

'What *horse*?'

'The Liz horse! The Princess Elizabeth, Cheltenham Gold Cup, prize-winning fucking horse. I can't be sorted out like George, Liz. I don't want to be. I am different. *We* are different. We always have been.'

'I'm not a horse, Maggie.'

'I didn't say you *were* a horse, Liz. I said you were *riding* the horse. It's a very different thing.'

There was a pause and it was long enough for Maggie to start to wonder why she was back in Callum's bed again, why she put herself in these ridiculous situations, why she never listened to anyone, ever. But then she knew that Liz had always been jealous of Maggie's boyfriends, a jealousy so ingrained that Liz didn't even know she was feeling it anymore as it was just filtered out as disapproval and blame.

'Maggie?' Liz said quietly after a while.

'Yes?'

'Do you think Lily looks like Gary Barlow?'

'*What?*'

'Gary Barlow. The singer.'

'Gary—'

'—GARY BARLOW! From Take That! Gary bloody Barlow!'

'No,' Maggie said. Then, more confidently, 'No.'

'You paused. Why did you pause?'

'I don't know.'

'You paused, Maggie.'

'It's just not what you expect to be asked first thing in the morning, all right?'

'Right. Well, I'll see you tomorrow.'

'See you tomorrow, Liz.'

Maggie knew how unsuitable Callum was. It was part of the appeal. She had known all about him for over twenty-five years, back when they sat next to each other in Mrs Deane's class and he'd invited her to his house for tea and given her a grasshopper in a matchbox as if it was a wedding ring. Callum's dad was the local pest-control man and he used to drive a large white van with flashing orange lights and a plastic rat that span around on the roof when you pressed a button on the dashboard, and that sort of thing just doesn't go unnoticed in primary school. When Mr Collins picked Callum up from school on a Friday afternoon, he sometimes beeped the horn and spun the rat around, and for that brief minute or two, Callum was the only boy you wanted to know in the whole entire world.

Maggie knew that Callum was selfish and cocky and often bad-tempered. She knew that he often put his own needs ahead of those of his son and called his ex-wife a bitch. She knew that he should eat better food, wear better clothes, wash the toothpaste off the side of his sink and start liking dogs. She knew that he had never really left the area, or even hoped that there might be more to life than what existed within his own five-mile radius. She knew that they had so little in common that if she had to spend more than a few days with him she would struggle to be in his company, and yet this too was part of the appeal.

She also knew that he only saw a small segment of Maggie, that he wasn't really interested or even capable of seeing any more, and that she wasn't interested in showing it. To show anyone the whole of her meant that the whole of her could be rejected, so she dished herself out in segments, one at a time.

Callum and Maggie went out for a short while at secondary school. He was the first boy she introduced to

Queen Vic. Liz was always getting praise for her achievements. She won endless prizes, certificates, rosettes and silver cups on little felt covered plinths, all backed up with as many 'well done' and 'clever girl' pronouncements as she could have possibly needed, but she loathed the attention Maggie got about Callum. Even when Maggie came home late and tipsy one evening after drinking a bottle of wine that Callum had stolen from his parents' cupboard, she came through the door so nonchalantly, triumphantly Liz had thought, and Queen Vic just laughed and said, 'I told you she was a Margaret,' and it had seemed like something to admire.

Their adult relationship was based purely on timing. It was based on the principle that every few weeks or so, Maggie would inevitably find herself disappointed or bored or angry and Callum would somehow be without female company or at a loose end, and their worlds would temporarily collide. Just one night here or there, the evenings when they would be the last people left at the pub with the same number of drinks inside them, just sex and alcohol and sparse conversation, and always at Callum's house, and if Maggie hadn't been drunk or sad and Callum had been even a little bit more stimulating, then it would never ever have happened.

Aside from Liz, it had been the most consistent relationship in her life.

'What does Her Highness want, then?' Callum was tall, wiry and pale with a somewhat startled expression and short brown hair that he dyed regularly. When he turned over in bed to wrap his arm around Maggie's waist, his sharp elbows and knees jabbed into her.

'Nothing really,' Maggie said, moving his elbow out of the way. 'Just family plans. My dad's here.'

'Oh, yeah?'

'He's staying with me. Just until the sale goes through.'

'What's he doing here, then?'

'He was dumped,' Maggie said, matter-of-factly.

'*Dumped?*' Callum laughed for a good ten seconds and stretched his long arms up behind him so that he could rest his head in his hands. 'Bit of a legend your dad, isn't he?'

'In what way?' Maggie asked, and she turned onto her back so that they were both looking up at the ceiling. She noticed a squashed bug, a mosquito probably, and felt a small stirring of pleasure in the irony of its life being exterminated in such a primitive fashion when Callum's family business prided itself on being at the 'cutting edge' of pest control.

'Bit of a shagger, isn't he?'

'He's seventy-five,' she said. 'Do we still say 'shagger' at seventy-five?'

'We say shagger if he is a shagger,' he replied with a grin.

'Jesus, Callum.'

'What? He's not *making love*, is he?'

Maggie thought for a moment about which one was worse. 'You can't say either. They're both awful.'

'How many women has he got on the go at the minute?' continued Callum. 'Come on, how many?'

'I don't know. None, I think.'

'Is he on the apps? Which apps is he on?'

'How would I know?'

'Bet he's on the little blue pills. Bet you fifty quid he is.'

'Can we not—'

'—He'd have to be at his age, I reckon. He's probably knocking them back—'

'—Callum—'

'—Do you reckon he's going to be one of those blokes who dies on the job? You know, having like a heart attack while he's banging some granny?'

'Fucksake, Callum,' Maggie snapped, as she jumped out of bed and started to rummage about on the floor for her things.

Callum's house, a sixties two-up two-down had always been sparsely decorated and had a blank, grey studenty feel about it that made Maggie feel intensely glum. His bedroom was dark and bare walled, the floor always covered with plates or mugs or damp towels, and as Maggie tried to find her clothes in the half-light, she wondered, and not for the first time, if she might be sensible enough to let this visit be the last.

'What? *What*? It's a good way to die. It's what I'd want.'

She found her jumper and skirt and began to put them on, her irritability rising with every pull and tug.

'What are you doing, Callum? What are you *actually* doing?' she said.

'What do you mean?' he replied, gawping back at her. She tried not to muddle him if she could possibly help it, as she couldn't bear the way his face looked when he was confused, all slack-jawed and boggle-eyed like a Victorian child staring through a sweet-shop window.

'What do you want out of your life? What do you want to achieve?'

'I don't know what you mean?'

'You don't *do* anything, Callum. You sit on your arse all the time, drinking in the pub or playing video games. You kill the odd rat for a living. What do you actually want out of life?'

'I don't know,' he shrugged. 'What does it matter?'

'Don't you have any ambitions? Don't you want to go anywhere or do anything different *at all*? Don't you want to fall in love? Or go and see something in the world? Don't you want a dream that's a little bit better than dying while you're having sex with someone?'

'It's not a bad dream,' he said quietly.

'You have to actually live life, Callum. You have to get up and be present and do things. You have to throw yourself into it all and not look back. I mean, are you really just going to sit here and do the same thing over and over again for the rest of your life?'

'I don't bloody know, do I?' he said as he swung his legs off the side of the bed. 'I haven't got there yet!'

'And you're not going to, are you? You're just sat there, in your pants.'

'All right. What about *you* then?' Callum sneered. 'What are *you* going to do? You're hardly throwing yourself about, are you? You're stuck indoors most of the time, moping about.'

'No, I am not!'

'Yes, you are. You hide away in that big stupid house making quiche.'

'I don't make *quiche*.'

'Whatever it is then. Pie, cake, sauce, I dunno! But you're not out there changing the world, are you? You're not doing anything good. You're just some stupid fucking posh girl who puts stuff in an oven.'

The words hit her hard, and for a moment she felt almost winded, as though he had slapped every last bit of life out of her.

'This isn't about *me*, Callum,' she then said quietly as she headed for the door, and it was such a ridiculous, naked lie that that the thought of it almost made her laugh.

Chapter 11

It was early on in his marriage to Liz that Doug decided he should become so skilled in cooking meat that he would not only be left alone for a good hour or two on a Sunday, possibly even once or twice during the week, but he would also be spared the quiet agitation of competitiveness that sometimes bothered him around his wife.

He could deal with the back seat most of the time. He liked the back seat. It was where he felt most comfortable, it's where he stretched out and watched the world go by, but at the weekend, with all his family around him, he liked to occasionally move to the front and take charge, even if it was just with a chicken. He was safest with a chicken. While he'd had some success with pork and lamb, Liz had thought it best to play safe for the family lunch and had bought the largest and most expensive organic bird she could find at their local farm shop, imagining it all tanned and steaming as it sailed out of her integrated oven and onto the lunch table. She then panicked on Sunday morning and asked Doug to get a backup rotisserie bird from the supermarket, just in case.

'Only one cooked chicken left, Liz,' he said on his return.

'Where did you go?' she asked, without looking up from laying the table.

'Sainsbury's.'

'They always sell out quickly. You should have gone to Morrisons.'

'And they have moved the spice aisle over to the *other side* of the pasta,' Doug said, as he unpacked the shopping. 'It doesn't make any sense though. And the fruit and veg are all mixed up again. I found the lemons next to bananas. The bananas, Liz! I mean, who is in charge of these places?'

'I don't know, Doug,' Liz said, lining up the forks.

'Citrus fruit goes with other citrus fruit, doesn't it? I mean lemons and limes and you know, all those other vitamin C guys. Otherwise we may as well put, I don't know, horses in with sheep and just give up on life.'

'They do put horses in with sheep, Doug.'

'Oh, do they?'

'Yes. All the time.'

'And do they get on OK?'

Doug Farley had the same lunch every single day (tuna sandwich, apple, salt and vinegar crisps). He had the same hobbies that he'd had as a child (aeroplanes, bicycles, Lego). He told the same jokes (one-liners, wordplay, repeated often), had the same laugh (guttural), the same hair (wiry, short) the same awful mother (judgemental, cold) and the same gentle father (bookish, shy). But it was his predictability and steadfastness that Liz had fallen for, his contentment to be routine and reliable, to get married and have children and work his way through life's adult milestones without question or deviation and in the acceptable order.

He was also patient and kind, he listened, and he nodded, and he said the right things when the right things
needed to be said, and they shared a deep commitment
to order and precision and numbers that Liz knew would
be so hard to find in another. He was, most importantly,
almost entirely content (and often very grateful) to be
led by her, to be held by her hand and guided through
marriage and parenthood and all the big decisions in life.
He knew that in return he would be in charge of meat
and be the best husband and father he could be.

'Hey, Doug,' Maggie said as she walked into the
kitchen with a large tray of potatoes. 'Can you help with
the rest of the veg? It's in the back of the car.'

He was also an excellent brother-in-law, and Maggie
cherished her relationship with Doug more than she could
ever admit to Liz. Having someone who understood her
sister as deeply as she did often made up for the fact that
Maggie was without present or competent parents. There
was a look that the two of them had given each other at
the engagement drinks, the room full of distant cousins
and family tension and everyone showing off in one way
or another, a look of recognition in what it meant to be
someone who could only really endure a fraction of an
event like that, and they had looked out for each other
ever since.

Doug followed Maggie out to the driveway where her
old red Fiat Panda was parked. It was a crisp, bright
day, the late frost determinedly sparkling on the lawn
into mid-morning, and in the sky a full spring moon was
hovering over the tree line, silver and cold against the
sharp blue sky.

GOOD THINGS

'Everything OK?' she asked him as she stacked foil-covered dishes of carrots, peas and cauliflower cheese into his arms.

'Oh, yes, definitely.'

'Every*one* OK?'

'Um, she's a little nervous, I think. You know how it goes.'

'How many times has she rearranged the table?'

'Err, four times maybe? We have a backup chicken.'

'Oh, thank God. I completely forgot to get one.'

'And she's hoovered a lot.'

'Standard.'

'And the parenting books have all been out.'

Maggie sighed. 'Oh, God. Are we going to have to *do* anything?'

'It's not too bad,' Doug said, as they headed into the house. 'It's icebreaker questions, I think. Getting to know each other again stuff. "How to reconnect with your loved ones".'

'That sounds awful,' Maggie said with a sigh.

'That's what I thought.'

'I guess the next question is, do we have enough wine?'

'Plenty.'

'And do you need any help with the chicken?'

'All under control,' Doug said with a salute, and Maggie gave him a kiss on the cheek.

George arrived shortly after, having walked across the village with Albert. He wore a pair of milk chocolate coloured tweed trousers, a navy cashmere V-neck jumper over a pale blue shirt, an olive silk scarf tucked in at the collar and his old Jaeger camel coat. He looked impeccably smart. Liz would be happy, Maggie thought as she saw him crossing over the communal green space in front of the house, Albert lolloping along contentedly beside him. He had dressed for an occasion of some importance.

'Bit of a bloody expedition, Elizabeth,' he said, gripping the doorframe for dramatic effect as she greeted him. 'I might need a little sit down after that.'

'It's not that far,' she huffed. 'It would have done you both some good. Albert has obviously been eating all the tapas.'

'Does the postman come out this far?'

'Yes! Of course he does.'

'And it's stable, isn't it?' he said, shielding his eyes with his hand as he looked up to the roof. 'It's not going to fall down?'

'Are you coming in or not?'

'Yes, yes,' he said as he stepped the hallway. 'It's very nice. Very nice and very, very new.'

'You'll have to put Albert in the garden,' Liz said, taking his coat.

'Good lord, it's a bit *brisk* for that, isn't it? He's just come from Spain. He'll be feeling the cold.'

'Fine. He can go in the utility room, next to the kitchen, but he's not to get in the way.'

'You won't get in the way, will you Albert?'

Albert looked as though he would quite happily not get in anyone's way ever again, and he heaved an enormous sigh before settling himself on to the floor.

'Hello, George,' Doug said cheerfully, stepping out of the kitchen with Maggie behind him to shake George's hand. 'You are looking very well, very well indeed. That Spanish climate must suit you.'

'That's very kind, Doug,' he said. 'But that's all in the past now.'

'Well, it's lovely to have you here. How are you faring?'

'I am clinging on,' George said, grim-faced and squeezing Doug on the shoulder. 'Clinging on to hope. And to family, of course.'

'Good,' Doug said, looking slightly startled. 'That's very good.'

'Do you know, girls, if it hadn't been for Albert, I don't know how I would have continued.'

'What's Albert done?' Maggie asked, genuinely curious.

'He's been here for me. He's been my rock.'

Albert looked up, wondering if he was required to do anything. It appeared not, and he gratefully rested his head back onto his paws.

'I've been here,' Maggie said quietly. 'We've all been here.'

'Dogs don't ask anything of you, don't you find? They just want to be by your side. Quite remarkable really.'

Maggie was going to say that she hadn't asked anything of him either, but decided against it.

'Do you think they sense something, Doug? Do you think they know what's going on?'

'I really couldn't say, George. But how about a drink?' Doug chirped. 'Who would like a drink?'

'Yes, please,' Maggie said.

'A drink would be just what the doctor ordered. Ah, and there's my dance partner,' George said, pointing to Lily in her baby bouncer. 'Looking delightful, as always.'

'And not at all like Gary,' Maggie said to Liz with a small nudge.

'She needs putting down for her nap actually,' Liz said, looking at her watch. 'Do you mind, Doug?'

'Not at all,' Doug said, with a small salute. 'I'll be right back with drinks,' and he scooped Lily out of her bouncer and carried her upstairs just as Tom and Sophie came running in, laughing and squealing.

'Dear God, what an awful noise. Who are you?' George said, peering down at a wriggling Sophie, his hands clamped over his ears.

'That's Sophie,' Liz said. 'You have met her before. She's six and Tom is eight, and yes, Lily was a surprise.'

'You're very small, aren't you?' George said, peering down at Sophie. 'Do you think you might grow anymore or is that it?'

'I'm going to be as tall as The Rock,' Sophie said, scrunching up her face in determination.

'Sounds very reasonable,' George said, patting her on the head.

'Tom, can you shake grandpa's hand like a big boy?' Liz said, guiding him towards George with a hand on his back.

'No,' he said, crossing his arms, his lips pushed out defiantly. 'I don't want to.'

'Come on, Tom. We talked about this, didn't we? We have to remember your manners. What do you say?'

Tom shrugged himself free from his mother and planted his feet stubbornly on the floor. 'Hi,' he said, without looking up.

'He's going through a phase,' Liz said apologetically, which was the way she described anything that couldn't be controlled. Tom looked up at her, hurt.

'I'm going through a phase too,' George said to Tom, his voice low, his hand on the top of his back. 'I'm sure it will pass. In the meantime, we can endure it together.'

By time everyone sat down, Maggie had served the food, the plates all beautifully arranged with the chicken and vegetables; buttered carrots, broccoli, peas and cauliflower cheese, and she had put enormous bowls of golden roast potatoes at each end of the table.

'Never enough roasties,' she said as they all took their places. 'And there's extra gravy too if anyone wants it.'

Liz was delighted. It could not have looked more perfect or more wholesome or more exactly as she had imagined it would be. She gave Maggie a small but very appreciated nod of approval, and Maggie felt a swell of pride.

'Dad, would you like to make a toast?' Liz said. She had placed him at the head of the table.

'Oh, right, yes,' he said, clearing his throat. 'To my beautiful daughters, Elizabeth and Margaret, thank you.' He paused then, looking around the table, as if he might actually be taking it all in, as if being there with all of them was actually something he would want to remember. 'Thank you all very, very much for having me here.'

He raised his glass towards Maggie, and then to Liz who smiled back at him, and for a moment Maggie felt that everything was exactly as it should be, and that life was possibly just a series of complications and misunder-standings, but that every now and then, it all came together the way that recipes sometimes did. Perhaps that was all there was to life and they were no better or no worse than anyone else. Maggie could have believed it right then.

'You're very old, aren't you?' Sophie said, inspecting George from across the table after the main course was done. 'Will you die soon?'

'*Sophie,*' Doug gently chided. 'That's not very polite.'

'You didn't say *please*, Sophie,' Tom said pointedly, while glaring at Liz. 'Or thank you.'

'Please, will you die soon?' Sophie said carefully.

'It won't be long, Sophie,' George replied, gravely. 'I think my kidneys might be failing.'

'That sounds sad,' Sophie replied, her brow all wrin-kled, which seemed to be exactly the sort of response that George was looking for as he beamed across the table at her.

'Isn't it terrible, darling?' he said. 'Just terrible.'

'Why don't we have one of the questions from the pieces of paper,' Liz said, keen to move on. 'Maggie, do you want to start?

Maggie picked up the piece of paper that was folded on her place mat and opened it.

'"What do you think our family motto should be?"' she read.

'Ah, good question,' Doug said. 'Very good question.'

'What's a motto?' Sophie asked.

'Something we believe in,' Liz said. 'As a family. Or something we would like to do more of.'

'Veni, vidi, vici,' George said, raising his glass.

'Kick more butts!' Tom blurted out, raising his fork.

'Come on, Tom,' Liz said, while Sophie giggled help-lessly. 'I'm not sure that's the sort of motto we want, is it?'

'I rather like it,' George said, giving Tom a thumbs up. 'It gets right to the point.'

'Talking of getting to the point, Maggie likes the estate agent, don't you, darling?' George said as he half-heartedly picked up his paper and began fiddling with it in his fingers.

'What?' Maggie said.

'The estate agent who showed her around the other day. Lovely man. Very smart, wears spectacles. I do find men in spectacles to be very trustworthy, don't you?'

'What? Who are we talking about?' Liz said, leaning forward in her chair.

'Dad, can you not?' Maggie said.

'They were out quite late the other night,' George said, winking at Liz. 'And she was a little worse for wear, weren't you, darling?'

'It's nothing,' Maggie said, shaking her head. 'We used to go to school together, that's all.'

'You mean *Joe*?' Liz barked.

'Yes, Joe! Joe from school. Joe the estate agent. We went for a drink, OK? But it's nothing, it's really nothing. Can we just move on?'

'Is he your boyfriend?' Sophie asked, excitedly.

'No, no, just a friend, Sophie.'

'I do like Joe,' Liz mused. 'He seems nice. His dad died not that long ago.'

'Yes, I know, I know,' Maggie said, rolling her eyes.

'What did he die of?' George asked.

'He was ill for a while,' Liz said. 'I'm not sure what it was though.'

'Everyone is dying,' George huffed, taking a large slug of wine. 'It will be me next, girls.'

'Can we *please* talk about something else?' Maggie pleaded.

'Good idea,' Doug said, decisively tapping both hands on the table. 'How about pudding?'

'I'm not sure I have ever mentioned it to you both, but I would like a wicker coffin when the time comes.'

'A what?' Liz said.

'*Wicker*, girls,' George continued, his voice getting louder. 'As in *Alan*.'

'We have apple crumble and ice cream, I think,' Doug said. 'Kids, ice cream?'

'I'll have some, thanks Doug,' Maggie said, and she started to clear the plates from the table.

'Wicker is a more eco-friendly option by all accounts, and rather aesthetically pleasing.'

'Dad!' Maggie said.

'Although I am hoping to hang on till after the summer, girls. I have an audition next week for the Martin Players. They're doing *A Midsummer Night's Dream* this year, and Mrs Wilson said I could get a very decent part, considering my experience.'

'Can we not talk about this now?' Liz hissed at him.

'The play?' George said.

'No. Death!'

'We're all family here, aren't we? Can we not talk about these things with family? You should be able to say anything in front of your family.'

'Coffin options are not really the sort of chats we want at Sunday lunch though, are they?'

'Well, I don't see what the problem is, do you Doug?'

Doug's eyes widened, a deer in the headlights. 'Perhaps we could chat about it after we have had pudding?' he suggested. 'When the kids have got down from the table.'

'Pudding! Yes, let's have pudding,' Maggie said, lifting a large pile of plates and cutlery off the table. 'Ice cream, Tom? Sophie? Why don't you two have yours in front of the telly? Go and put something on and I will bring it over.'

Liz looked horrified for a moment before quickly relenting. Letting Tom and Sophie break the no food in the sitting room rule was a far more palatable prospect than continuing to police George in front of them. However dedicated she was to her house rules, Liz also knew the value of flexibility.

'I'm going to read my question out,' Liz said as the children disappeared. 'Right. Here we go. "What would you tell your twenty-year-old self?"'

'Vanilla ice cream, here we go,' Maggie said, coming back to the table.

'Maggie, twenty-year-old you. What would you tell her?'

Maggie put the tub of ice cream on the table and thought for a moment. 'That you won't know much more by the time you are thirty-five?'

George laughed. Liz looked annoyed. 'You're meant to say something positive,' she said.

'Why is that not positive?' Maggie asked, jamming a spoon into the solid, frozen tub.

'It just doesn't sound very positive.'

'We're all just making it up as we go along, aren't we?' George said. 'The great mystery of life!'

'I'm just existing, I think,' Doug said quietly.

'Well I'm not,' Liz retorted. 'Somebody has to know what's going on. There has to be a plan.'

'My motto is to have more fun!' George said, pouring himself more wine. 'More love, more joy, more of everything.'

'I don't think it's possible for you to have had *more* love, is it, Dad?' Liz said.

'And no regrets. No regrets at all.'

'No regrets?' Liz said, slowly.

'Well, maybe a little bit more time on the telly. I don't think I got a proper swing at it, all things considered.'

'Is that it?' Liz said. 'No regrets about anything else? Nothing at all?'

George narrowed his eyes and he looked up to the ceiling for a few moments as if he was in sifting through a rolodex of memories. 'I don't think so, no,' he said eventually. 'We're not meant to have regrets anyway, are we? We are meant to look to the future, to forge ahead, to push on through.'

'But how do you learn to be a better person if you don't regret things from your past?' Liz pressed. 'If you don't feel bad about *anything*, how are you going to change?'

'Change what?' George asked, his face looking increasingly bewildered.

'*You*, George!' Liz said. 'You!'

'More pudding anyone?' Doug said, suddenly standing up. Maggie shook her head.

'I think it might be a bit late for all of that,' George said. 'Changing I mean, not the pudding, Doug.'

'It is *not* too late,' Liz said. 'Anybody can change. That's the whole point of everything, isn't it? The whole point of what we are doing! That we keep learning, we keep improving? Otherwise what's the bloody point?'

'You get to an age when you just want a bit of a sit down actually, darling,' he said with a smile to Doug and Maggie.

'You have to take accountability. You have to take accountability for what you have done wrong. What about the business, George? What about all the money you lost?"

'I can't change the past, Elizabeth,' George said, somewhat firmly, before gulping down the rest of his wine.

'No, no you can't, but you could feel a bit more shit about it.'

There was a brief silence as the sentence hung in the air. George's face contorted slightly, a scowl or possibly a burp, and he suddenly looked quite old and tired.

'How about some coffee? Dad, coffee?' Maggie said.

'None for me,' George replied, pushing his wine glass away and placing his hand on his stomach. 'Rather overindulged, I fear.'

'Ha! The story of your life,' Liz scoffed. 'That's *your* motto, right there!'

'Coffee, Liz?' Maggie said, as she stood up from the table.

'I'm sorry I am such a terrible disappointment to you, Elizabeth,' George said, sitting back in his chair. 'I'll be dead soon.'

'You won't be,' Liz sighed. 'I have a list of DIY things for you to do.'

'And believe it or not, there are things about this family that I find quite upsetting too.'

'You are joking?' Liz said, leaning forward across the table.

'Not being left the house was a terrible, *terrible* shock girls. Just terrible. You'll be sad to hear that I was in a significant amount of distress. *Significant.* Realising that your own mother doesn't love you enough is not something I would wish anyone to go through.'

'She loved you, Dad,' Liz said. 'She always loved you, despite everything you did. She didn't leave you the house because you didn't deserve it. She didn't leave you the house because she knew you would just fritter it away just like you do with everything else!'

Maggie could feel that she was holding her breath, although she couldn't remember deciding to. She glanced over at George who was now clutching his chest, a look of horror and panic across his face.

'And we do know what having a mother who doesn't love you enough is like. Maggie and I know that better than anybody.'

'Dad, are you all right?' Maggie said, moving around the table to where he was sitting. George had begun to slump forward in his chair, his arm now wrapped around his chest, his face a flushed grimace.

'I'm not sure I am, no,' he spluttered.

'Oh, God, here we go!' Liz said, throwing her hands up in the air, but Doug had jumped up from his chair and was around the other side of the table too.

121

'George? George? Is everything OK?' Doug said.

'He's fine, Doug. He's more than fine.'

'I think we better call an ambulance.'

'*What*?' Liz said. 'An ambulance? He's just had too many potatoes! Too many potatoes and too much wine and one too many home truths.'

'LIZ!' Doug bellowed. 'Call an ambulance!'

So Liz went to call the ambulance, and she wasn't sure whether it was because she so rarely heard Doug shout, or because the woman who answered her 999 call said that they should be ready to start CPR, or the sight of ice cream spilt all over the carpet in the sitting room, but her legs began to shake. She realised then that the sky had gone dark. The day had somehow slipped away without her even noticing, and as Maggie came over to squeeze her hand, Liz thought how lovely it had been, all of them together. The sisters looked at each other, their eyes as wide and as round as the spring moon, and even as they heard the sirens approaching in the distance, they didn't believe that they were going to lose him, did they? They had only just begun.

PART TWO
Summer

Chapter 12

The summer that Pat left, George threw an enormous party.

There were always parties at the Manor House, the garden ones being the most memorable. There was always someone to welcome or to wave off or celebrate and no end of charities which Queen Vic chipped in with. While the garden at the Manor was certainly not the largest in the village, it was generally considered to be the most beautiful, the hosts the most generous and welcoming; and after all those years of cups of tea and weak Pimm's on the striped emerald lawn, the summer parties felt like a Little Martin institution. Queen Vic liked to show off her roses and George liked to show off his charms, and there was still something gentle and English about it all, the scones balanced on china plates, the girls handing round cucumber sandwiches, corgis weaving in and out of old sturdy legs, the comfy shoes and best Sunday dresses, the straw hats and gardening chat and then everyone home by six.

But the summer that Pat left, the summer he moved down to the basement, George hired a jazz band from Cheltenham and the guests drank cocktails and white wine and ate canapés served up by waiters in crisp white suits. George had wanted everyone to know that while his suffering was heartfelt and really rather moving if you wanted to see it up close, it could also be packed away quite easily after a glass or two and he was very much available for dinners, barbeques or picnics, as and when the invitations arrived. The ladies of the village would then come to the Manor House, one by one, dress by dress, just 'checking in' with a potato salad and a sponge cake and offers of a little light supper; and when George took everything into consideration, it really wasn't a bad summer after all.

The summer of George's return to Little Martin, there was another party at the Manor House.

It had been three years since Queen Vic's death, and while the roses still looked glorious, the local gardener hadn't quite got her expert eye for pruning. There was a feeling of wildness about the garden that Maggie loved, and she imagined the flowers and plants taking over the whole house and letting her hide inside it forever until the countryside swallowed her whole.

The spring had been wet and grey, but summer sashayed in at the start of June with a blousy flourish of blush peonies and sweet peas and endless sunny days that warmed everything to life. The house still needed to be sold, but when the first buyer fell through not long before the contracts were exchanged, Maggie didn't think it was an entirely awful thing.

Joe had then suggested an open day.

'We'll get everybody in, all in one go, and we can have a few drinks and nibbles in the garden,' George had said to Maggie as he rubbed his hands together excitedly.

'I don't think the vendors are meant to be at an open house, are they?' Maggie said. 'Don't the estate agents do all of that?'

'Joe said it was fine. In fact, Joe said the more the merrier as it will look like everybody wants to buy the house and it might push the price up a bit.'

'Oh, right.'

Maggie had not seen much of Joe. They had spoken about the house sale, tedious administrative conversations that Maggie didn't have to try to sound bored on, but there had been no mention of that night. Liz had told her it was because she 'transmitted hostile signals' and it was precisely those signals that attracted someone like Callum and repelled someone like Joe, and they had then argued about Liz's hostile signals and not spoken to each other for over a week. Maggie then heard that Joe had a girlfriend, someone from his office, and while she had felt relieved to know that everything had moved on, there was also a dull melancholy that she found hard to shake.

'Just a few extra in the garden, you know, milling around, making all the right noises,' George continued, his enthusiasm growing by the minute. 'I could get the cast to come along. We could do a bit of improv!'

'What?'

'Improv. Improvisation! You know, as potential buyers.'

'No,' she said, smiling, but firm.

'Just a few friends then. I thought you might want to do some of your delicious food, darling, get your name out there.'

Maggie thought for a moment. 'I could do,' she said, the ideas already forming, the ingredients lining up in front of her, the food she liked to make in summer; strawberries and basil and tomatoes, grilled asparagus, fresh mozzarella, lavender and figs, cucumber sliced so thinly you could see right through it.

'Marvellous. What was that chicken dish you made the other day? We had it on toast, I think, and it was truly spectacular.'

'It was a sort of coronation chicken thing,' she said, with a shrug. 'With a few extra bits added in.'

'It was the best thing I have ever eaten,' he said slowly, hand placed on his heart. 'The very best.'

There was, without a doubt, something quite different about George. The dark clouds of Rhonda had seemed to finally clear, and as spring fluttered down on Little Martin, George reported that he was feeling like a whole new man. Depending on who he was speaking to, it was either Maggie's cooking, amateur dramatics, his grandchildren, the English climate, Albert, or the rejuvenation of a good old-fashioned heartbreak that was responsible for the sprightly spring in his step. There was also the small matter of his 'near death experience', the recounting of which Maggie had heard so many times she could recite it word for word in all its many renditions. His funny turn at lunch that day had been nothing more than indigestion and wind, but George was not one to let a blue light dash to hospital go unembellished, particularly if he had a female audience.

His casting in the Martin Players summer production of *A Midsummer Night's Dream* had given him near daily access to a devoted female audience of fellow cast members, and had seemed to rouse long forgotten reserves of energy, enthusiasm and bonhomie. While it was easy to believe, as Liz did, that having a constant supply of attention was all that George really wanted or needed in life, Maggie hoped that their spending time together also had something to do with his transformation. As the weeks had gone by and items on the list of good things had slowly been ticked off, Maggie and George had settled into life together at the Manor House very well. Gone was the leg cancer and the dementia and the rusty kidneys. Gone was the talk of death and disease and heartbreak, and in came optimism and laughter and an eagerness to be with his family.

There he was, in the garden of the Manor House as the open day unfolded, fetching drinks and chairs and compliments with ease and grace and a smile so infectious that the event felt far more like a party than a house sale, which was exactly how George had wanted it to be. He wore a pale salmon cotton shirt tucked into cream linen trousers and a cricket sweater tied loosely around his neck as if he had just been called away from a lawn game somewhere. The boxes in the attic labelled 'Summer, George' had managed to provide the perfect wardrobe for the senior gentleman having a later than usual life renaissance: timeless, tidy and ever hopeful of fair weather.

Maggie and Liz were sitting on the garden steps that led down from the French doors in the Blue Room, and they had been carefully observing the comings and goings of the day for quite some time, the memories of all those garden parties sidling up alongside them. They had sat there as children, Maggie on the left and Liz on the right, as Queen Vic pottered around the garden, tinkering with her plants and flowers while George entertained ladies in the basement.

'Headline, please,' Liz said.

Maggie thought for a moment. '"English gent clings on to the last days of his crumbling empire."'

Liz smiled. 'Or, "Old man pretends large house belongs to him."'

Maggie laughed. 'Nice. I like it.'

'All those days are long, long gone,' Liz said with a sigh. 'There'll be a hot tub in here this time next year.'

'There's nothing wrong with a hot tub, Liz.'

'You only say that because you've been in one. With *Callum*, or whoever.'

'Exactly. There's nothing wrong with them!'

'Well I haven't been in one, so I can be as rude as I like. That's the rule.'

Maggie frowned at her sister before turning back to the garden. A woman in a long floral dress was trailing her hand along a row of daisies while chatting to another guest and Maggie watched the soft, wave-like motion as her long fingers gently bent the flowers back before they waved into position again.

'*God*, do you remember Persephone?' Maggie said, nudging her sister's arm. 'Skipping around the garden, completely smashed on gin?'

'*Persephone*? Yes! Wait, was that during Anne, or Diana?'

'Diana, I think. I must have been about ten. And wasn't she really called Sue or Sarah or something like that?'

'I think it was Dawn,' Liz said.

'Queen Vic said she was Persephone because she had daisies in her hair.'

'It was because she was completely naked!' Liz said.

'Naked and pissed!'

'Poor Queen Vic. What a job she had.'

'We believed everything she said back then, didn't we?'

'No, we didn't!' Liz scoffed. 'I didn't, anyway. I knew it was one of dad's flings. I saw him chasing her out of the basement!'

'"How does Daddy know the Goddess of spring?" you said. And didn't she say something like, "Your father knows everyone in the Cotswolds."'

Liz laughed. 'She never said a bad word about him. How did she put up with it all? He always had such bad taste in women.'

'There was only one of him,' Maggie said. 'And she loved him. Like we do, I suppose.'

'You know what *this* means though, don't you?' Liz said, pointing to the middle of the garden.

'What?'

'He's not going anywhere. Look at him.'

George was in the centre of a large group of guests telling a story about something or other, his arms gesticulating vigorously as he shifted back and forth on his suede loafers, and every single person was completely enraptured by what he was saying. At points the crowd seemed to collectively draw in towards him before pulling back again, a murmuration of sorts, the flock all moving as one. The story ended, a punchline, and then more laughter, the crowd still suspended in his orbit and keen to hear more and more.

It was not the first time Maggie and Liz had seen his command of an audience before, but every time they did, they found it utterly mesmerising.

'I'm pretty sure the prodigal son didn't organise his own homecoming party, did he?' Liz said. 'Who are they all? I don't recognise any of them.'

'Some of the cast of the play, I think,' Maggie said. 'I've hardly seen him the last few weeks to be honest. He's been rehearsing most nights.'

'I think some of the school mums are in there,' Liz said, squinting at the crowd in the bright summer light. '*God*, maybe I should have done the play. Do you think I should have done the play?'

'*Really?*' Maggie said.

'Why not? I did my LAMDA exams at school. Top of the class, if I recall.'

'That doesn't mean anything! You were top of the class at *everything*!'

'It looks quite fun, doesn't it?' Liz said quietly, as they watched the cast all mingling together, the ease and familiarity between them, the laughing.

'Not sure it's for me,' Maggie said.

'Bloody hell, Maggie, do any of these people actually want to buy a house?' Liz said, throwing her hands up in a sudden burst of frustration. 'Why are they all here?'

'Padding,' Maggie said. 'It's a marketing ploy. Are the kids going to come over?'

'No. Doug's got them. His mother's here.'

'Well, they could all come couldn't they? The more the merrier! Isn't that what George said?'

'There is nothing merry about my mother-in-law.'

'Fair enough,' Maggie said. 'The kids at least though?'

'No. Tom hates me at the moment. He'll be happy to not be here.'

'What? Don't be silly. He loves you.'

'He definitely thinks I am an idiot.'

'All kids think their parents are idiots, don't they?'

'He used to think I was great. He used to think I was the best person in the whole wide world.'

'Oh Liz, he still does. Of course he does. It's just a phase or whatever you call it. He's probably just trying to be cool or weird or whatever it is eight-year-olds do.'

'My birthday card from him this year said, "Dear Liz" on it,' she said, before sighing deeply. '"Dear Liz, happy birthday, love from Tom".'

'Shit, we really should stop calling George, George I suppose.'

'But he's always been George. He told us to call him that when we were about two!'

'I know, but it's confusing.'

There was another loud laugh from the garden, and Liz had had enough.

'We do *actually* need to sell the house, Maggie. This is actually meant to be an open day.' Maggie had noticed that Liz said 'actually' or 'literally' a lot when she was discussing George-related matters, feeling the need, she supposed, to hammer home some truth.

'I know,' Maggie said. 'There are some real buyers too, somewhere.'

'Where's Joe?' Liz asked, turning to look back at the house.

'He's inside, showing people around with *Susie*.'

'Why did you say it like that?'

'Like what?

'Like you were ten!'

'I didn't realise I did,' Maggie said.

'Well, you did. Can you just go and talk to him?'

'Why?'

'Because you *like him*?'

'He's got a girlfriend, Liz.'

'That's never been a problem before, has it? Surely that's an added incentive – the nice, normal, available ones have never been your style, have they?'

Maggie glared at her but was too hot and bothered to reply. They turned back to face the garden, their eyes drawn again towards George as he led a blonde curly-haired woman in a red and pink dress away from the crowd and over to the edge of the garden, his hand on the small of her back.

'Uh-oh, he's doing the corgi graves,' Liz said, as they watched him point down to the tiny wooden crosses underneath the pink polyanthas. 'That old trick.'

'How many are there?' Maggie asked.

'Seven? Eight?' Liz said, as they saw George retrieve a handkerchief from his trousers and dab at his eyes while the woman made sad faces and sympathetically rubbed his arm. It didn't seem that long ago that they'd buried Diana, the three of them standing by the freshly dug grave as Queen Vic looked on from the window and George recited the lyrics to *The Littlest Hobo* theme song.

'I think he's interested in her,' Maggie said as they watched the grave vigil unfold. 'He's different with her. Look, the way he leans slightly in when he's talking, the focus, the concentration, the touching her arm.'

'He's always touching some woman's arm, isn't he?' Liz said.

'He's more attentive somehow. He likes her.'

'Oh, *God*,' Liz said, rolling her eyes. 'Not again!'

'It's a good thing! The fewer old ladies coming to the door with cakes the better. Your pal Mrs Wilson has been over at least five times.'

'*Mrs Wilson*? What does she want?'

'George! She wants George!'

Liz smiled and congratulated herself again on picking a house on the other side of the village. Across the garden, George whispered something into the woman's ear, and she seemed to find it very funny, shaking her curls and playfully batting him as she laughed.

'As long as she knows what she's getting into,' Liz said, standing up. She brushed herself down and put her hand on Maggie's shoulder. 'I'll have a quiet word.'

Chapter 13

Even if Pamela Hamilton III had not been cast as Titania in *A Midsummer Night's Dream*, she would have bobbed to the surface sooner rather than later, being a bright and bubbly sort in a sea that was mostly quiet and grey. She was American, divorced, atheist, rich, extravagant, blonde and Anglophilic, and therefore perfect for George in every possible way.

Liz had to wait to see her in the hallway while George finished showing her the house, the sounds of, 'oh, wowee,' and 'gee, whizz,' and 'that's so cute,' drifting somewhat gratingly down the stairwell.

'Ah, there she is,' George said, as they finally came down the stairs, Pamela's arm looped through his as though they were descending into a ballroom dinner dance. 'Elizabeth, my eldest daughter. And one of my two landladies.'

'Hello,' Liz said coolly, offering Pamela her hand. Pamela ignored it and went straight for a hug, covering Liz's face with her large mass of yellow curls.

'Well this really is something, Elizabeth. What a palace you got here! I'm just waiting for the jolly little butler to come along and get me a cup of old English tea!'

Pamela laughed at her own joke. At least Liz thought it was a laugh, the sound appearing as a series of sharply expelled 'Ss', as if a small child was practicing the letter in a phonics class.

'There is food and drink about, if you want something,' Liz said.

'Oh, no, just a little joke. But really, it's one heck of a place. So much history. So much *drama*! I mean, God, what a place to own. Really.'

'Well, it is for sale!' Liz chirped. 'Isn't it, George?'

'Yes, yes. Very much so. Time for the old girl to take on a new captain.'

'Well doesn't that make two of us!' quipped Pamela, and then she laughed again, louder this time. 'S,s,s,s,s,s,s,s,s,s,s!'

'Oh. Ha ha! Very funny,' said George, cottoning on to the joke slightly late, and then they both laughed. Liz began to feel distinctly uncomfortable.

'George here is my Bottom, aren't you, George?' Pamela purred, leaning into his arm and gazing up at him adoringly. On closer inspection, the red and pink dress was more of a kaftan, floaty and voluminous, and on her feet she wore gold sandals with straps that criss-crossed tightly up her calves like butcher's string. She was mid-sixties Liz thought, clearly quite wealthy and gave off the impression that she had been put on earth solely to have a good time. They could not have been more different.

'I am your Bottom,' George replied, his grin wide and slightly drunk looking.

'This is the play?' Liz asked, hopefully.

'Are you coming to see it, Elizabeth? It's going to be wonderful. George is fabulous in it, just fabulous.'

'You can call me Liz,' Liz said.

'*Liz*! Oh, I love that. So casual.'

Liz cleared her throat. 'Have you seen the basement yet, Pamela? It's where George used to live after our mother divorced him due to his many infidelities.'

'Oh? No, we hadn't made it down there yet. Sounds lovely.'

'Why don't I give you a quick tour? You can spare her, can't you, George?'

After the heat and noise of the garden, the basement felt pleasantly cool and quiet and Liz wondered how long she could get away with sitting down there before she was needed. How long had it been since anyone had actually been down the stairs? Had Maggie even bothered to open the windows? The rooms had a thick stillness to them, the air long undisturbed by human presence.

'The problem with Florida is that there's just too many fat Americans,' Pamela Hamilton III sighed as she ran her finger along the windowsill of the George's old bedroom. 'Too many Floridians anyway.'

'And your ex-husband?' Liz asked.

'Jeff was pretty trim actually but they're mostly fat and stupid down south and you can't get past their enormous asses in the supermarket.' The way she said 'ass', the American way, seemed exotic to Liz somehow. Everything about Pamela was exotic: the way she flicked her hair, the way she lifted her chin in the air when she was thinking about something, the way she laughed. Her confidence. Her *sexiness*.

'Jeff was trim *and* tight-fisted! He played *a lot* of tennis. *A lot* of tennis. And he went on and on and on about what I was spending. Let's hope the Atlantic is big enough for me not to hear him moaning about how much my moisturiser costs!'

'So it wasn't very amicable then?' Liz asked. 'The split?' She found herself utterly transfixed by Pamela's teeth, absentmindedly counting them while she talked. They were enormous and incredibly white and there seemed to be so many of them.

'It wasn't *that* bad,' Pamela said. 'It's all in the past now, anyway. Jeff's all right. *Total* church nut. I fell for him because I thought he must be a good person, being a Jesus fan and all of that crap, but we weren't compatible, not really. It took me ten years to realise. Can you believe it? Ten goddam years, because we were so busy playing tennis or hosting endless brunch parties for Republicans or making stupid salads. All I seemed to do was make salad. For like a decade, I made salad. I barbequed bits of meat for people who believe that evolution doesn't exist. Can you believe it?'

'No,' Liz said, wondering if that was the right answer.

'It's OK. I guess that's why I came here anyway. Change of scene and all that . . .' she tailed off before letting out a few gentle 'Ss'.

'Listen, Pamela, my dad doesn't have the best track record with women,' Liz said. 'I thought, *we* thought, my sister and I, that you should probably know a few things before you decide if you want to go out with him.'

'Oh geez, he's not a weirdo, is he?' Pamela said, spinning around to face Liz.

'No, no, he's very sane and normal, actually. He's charming. Very charming.'

'I'm not into kinky stuff. Not anymore.'

Liz swallowed and hoped that her face wasn't showing how utterly uncomfortable she was. 'It's nothing like that. It's more that he's not very . . . responsible. Consistent. *Faithful.*'

'Oh? I see,' Pamela said, as she took a seat on the four-poster bed. Liz looked down at the bedding and wondered how long since it had been changed. If a bed hadn't been slept in but the sheets were fresh when they went on, how long is it technically clean for? Liz knew she would be thinking about it for a long time to come.

'We are sort of looking after him at the moment,' she said. 'He's staying here with my sister, until we've sold the house anyway, and he's just had this whole thing happen in Spain, and he doesn't have much money, so I don't know if he's going to be the most reliable of partners.'

'OK.'

'He's also supposed to be spending some time with us as well. With Maggie and me. Father and daughters. *Just* father and daughters. We haven't really had him around very much, so . . .'

Pamela let out a small 'S' and looked down at her hands. She began to twizzle the ring on her finger, a huge magenta stone with gold claws that bulged out of her hand like an angry boil.

'Listen, Liz, I appreciate the concern, I really do, but I've been around the block many times now and I am not looking for anything serious or heavy. It would be nice to grab a glass of wine with someone on a Saturday night. It would be nice to go and see a movie with someone who isn't, you know, old and decrepit or can't remember who the hell you are. I have my own money, my own house, I don't need to be looked after and I don't want to get in the way. I just want to, you know, have a bit of fun. Shits and giggles, isn't that what we say here?'

In the kitchen, Maggie was arranging strawberries and meringues on to a plate when Joe came in.

'Hi,' he said, standing just beyond the door. 'Can I do anything at all to help?'

'No, no, you're OK,' Maggie replied, barely looking up.

'There was a, um, woman outside asking about the food. She wondered if you had a business card? I think she has a party or something that she'd like you to cater.'

'A *business card*?' Maggie said, as though Joe had just asked for something pharmaceutical.

'With your details on?'

'Oh. No, but I can write down my number, I guess?'

She wiped her hands on her apron and rummaged around in one of the drawers for a pen and paper.

'The food was really amazing, Maggie,' Joe said, stepping a little further into the kitchen. 'You should be really, really proud. Everyone is talking about it.'

'Oh, really?'

'Definitely. A man from London who was looking around asked if the house could come with the chef. He said he'd offer a lot more if it did!'

'What did you say?'

'I said that you would only consider eight figures, minimum.'

Maggie laughed. 'Thanks, Joe. What did you think?'

'Me? Well, I probably won't be able to eat again for at least another three, four years, but it was absolutely worth it.'

'That's great. I'm really pleased,' she said, handing him the scrap of paper with her number on. 'How's things?'

'Good, good. All good.'

'How's *Susie*?' She had not meant to say it like that.

'She's fine. She's showing someone around upstairs, I think.'

'Sorry, I didn't mean to say it like that.'

'Like what?'

'Like I was ten?'

He smiled at her. 'You're fine,' he said. 'It was more like . . . fifteen.'

'Oh, right. Marginally better, then!'

'A lot can happen in five years,' Joe said. 'Five weeks even. Five minutes.'

She smiled back at him across the kitchen table. 'It's good to see you, Joe,' she said. 'I'm sorry it's been so long.'

'You've been busy.'

'*You've* been busy.'

He shrugged. 'We're all busy.'

'Some of us are definitely *more* busy.'

He laughed. There was the dimple again. She had forgotten about the dimple. How could she have? It was so completely strange and yet so perfect.

'It's good to see you too, Maggie,' he said. 'And I'm really happy it went well today. There's definitely a few interested buyers, so I'm sure we'll get some good offers.'

'You're a wonderful estate agent, Joe, so I have no doubt.'

'Well, it's a wonderful house,' he was looking down at his shoes and fidgeting around, like he had done when he had asked her out for a drink all those months ago.

Footsteps could be heard in the hallway, high heels on the flagstone floor, and Susie marched into the kitchen, house brochures under one arm, glossy lipstick freshly applied. She was young, petite and excessively smiley and she wore her pink skirt suit and cream stilettos in a way that made it very clear this was just a starter job in a long and very successful career somewhere else.

'Hi! How are we all doing? Everyone OK?' she said abruptly, grinning back and forth at Joe and Maggie.

'Hi, Susie,' Maggie said, very carefully.

'What a day! It's all going so well, isn't it? So many people! Yes?'

'So many!' Maggie said, nodding politely.

'I don't think we have ever known an open house to be *so* busy, have we, Joe?'

'Oh, I'm not sure really,' Joe said shaking his head. 'I've not done that many.'

'It's been lovely,' Maggie said. 'Thank you for all your hard work, Susie.'

'Oh, I've hardly lifted a finger really,' she demurred. '*Joe* has been amazing. He's so brilliant, he'd be able to sell anything.'

'Both of you. Thank you,' Maggie said, placing both hands on her heart for emphasis.

'This must be a sad, sad day though, isn't it? You must be *so* devastated to be losing the house. What a loss!'

Susie's face scrunched with imagined pain, her delicate, tiny features all squished up. Maggie took a deep breath in. She had seen many similar facial expressions when the topic of the house sale came up, although all were somehow far less annoying than Susie's.

'It's OK,' she said. 'We've had a long time to come to terms with it. It's just a building, after all. It's just bricks and mortar, whatever mortar is.'

'And you've been so busy in here,' Susie said, indicating the kitchen, the plates, the growing mess of it all. 'Working *so* hard!'

'I'm happier in the kitchen really,' Maggie shrugged. 'Much happier.'

'Good for you,' Susie said, smiling broadly at her. 'Good for you.'

She then turned to Joe and, placing her hand on his chest, said 'Baby, Mrs Cotton, the one from London in the green dress, she has a few questions about the central heating. Can you have the chat with her? She's in the hallway.'

She tiptoed up to his face and then kissed him on the lips and Maggie felt her cheeks suddenly get very hot and achey and her throat begin to close up. She turned back to the kitchen drawer and half-heartedly picked at some rubber bands in it.

'Right. No problem. I will go and have a word,' she heard Joe say behind her. There was a moment of silence, a hesitation perhaps, before Susie said, 'She's waiting, Joe,' and then she heard two pairs of footsteps walk back down the hall.

Chapter 14

When Maggie finally emerged from the kitchen at the end of the evening, everyone had gone home.

'Dad?' she called in the hallway. 'Dad, are you here?'

The house was silent, the sort of silence she'd known when she lived there by herself, the sort of silence that hangs in the air after people have recently left. It felt strange, unfamiliar, uncomfortable even. She'd got used to people being around. She had got used to the background noise, the visitors that now came and went, George rehearsing his lines, his bathroom singing. She wandered into the Blue Room and fell back onto the cream sofa. The French doors were still wide open and an evening breeze was fluttering the fringes of the curtains and Maggie had that particular feeling of pleasant weariness when you know you have worked hard and the rest you are going to take is well deserved.

She closed her eyes for a moment and pulled her legs up on to the sofa and it wouldn't have been very long before she drifted off to sleep when she suddenly heard footsteps in the hallway.

'Hello?' a voice said. 'Hello?'

'Hello?,' Maggie replied, sitting bolt upright.

A figure appeared in the doorway. It was Joe.

'Holy shit! You scared me!'

'I'm so sorry, Maggie. I didn't mean to scare you. Are you OK?'

'What are you doing here?'

'Your dad asked me to stay for a bit. He said he wanted to chat to me about something, but I think he just left.'

'When did everyone else go?'

'I don't know. Not that long ago. Ten, fifteen minutes maybe?'

'Shit, I thought I was here on my own!'

'I was just sorting through all the brochures and stuff from today. Your dad gave me a beer, so . . .'

He had unbuttoned his shirt, the tail of it hanging out from the top of his suit trousers, and there was a gentle, end-of-the-day scruffiness about him.

'I was just going to sit out in the garden actually,' Maggie said. 'Do you want another drink?'

'OK. Sure. That would be nice.'

Maggie got a bottle of wine from the fridge and two glasses from the dresser and they walked out of the French doors and down the steps to the lawn. Lights from the house were warming squares of the grass in dark burnt orange and Maggie lay down on her back and exhaled deeply. It was a clear night and the stars were so bright and beautiful that she wondered if she should mention them, despite them both looking up at the same sky.

'Can you smell that?' she said.

'What?'

'It's the smell of summer.'

Joe inhaled and then breathed out slowly a few times before resting his hands on the back of his head, elbows out wide. 'Is it the roses?' he said.

'It's every village lawn after it's been mown,' Maggie said. 'It hangs in the air when it's warm like this. It drifts right across England. Right across the world.'

'Of course, it's the weekend,' Joe chuckled. 'That's when everyone mows their lawns.'

'It's what summer smells like. And hope. Don't you think? Hope that it won't rain, hope for just lying about with the sun on your face. It's a very English thing, all that rain and grey and cold and then the amazingness of summer when it comes. We appreciate it so much more because of what has come before.'

He turned his face to look at her. 'You'll still be you without this house, Maggie. You know that, don't you?'

She blinked back at him, astonished at how he boldly and brilliantly he had just cut straight to the heart of it all. 'Oh, sure,' she said, although she knew quite well that she wasn't.

'What was it like to grow up here?'

'Um, it was chaos mainly,' she said, with a small laugh. 'All the antiques, the furniture piled up, the rugs and statues and paintings. It was amazing, really, to be surrounded by so many beautiful things.'

'I bet.'

'We had a lot of taxidermy for a while, my grandmother was really interested in it for years, so we had all these huge bears and foxes and weasels everywhere. Liz and I used to give them all names and Queen Vic, she was my grandmother, used to rearrange them when people came over just to freak them out. She'd put them behind doors or in cupboards or in the downstairs loo. A lot of them are still in the attic, I think. There's a whole weird, crazy zoo up there.'

Joe smiled at her. 'She sounds like a pretty amazing woman.'

'She really was. She was my favourite person. She brought us up really, Liz and me. My mum left then my dad moved down to the basement and he had all these different girlfriends coming over and parties and she was the only one who kept us all together. She was the one who taught me how to cook. It was a distraction really, so I wouldn't get too caught up in what was going on around me. Liz found it harder, I think.'

'How come?'

'She likes things to be ordered. Tidy. Precise. It was all a bit too hectic for her and she just decided to move in a very straight line towards the finish. I never really knew where the finish was. Still don't.'

Joe breathed deeply for a few moments looking up at the sky. 'My dad always used to say when I was younger and struggling with something, "keep going, you'll get there," and I would ask him where "there" was. "Where's there?" I would say, and he would say, "you'll know when you get there. You'll know."'

'Solid dad advice. I like it.'

'Yep, he was pretty good like that.'

'You must miss him a lot, Joe.'

'It gets easier. You find ways of managing it, of putting it to one side.'

'How?'

'What country do you really, really want to go to? Think of somewhere that you have always wanted to visit, somewhere you know you would love. For me it's Japan. I've always wanted to go, and I just imagine that he's gone ahead of me. He's on the Izu Peninsula and it's cherry blossom season and he's put his feet up for a moment and he's drinking tea in his pale blue suit and he's breathing it all in. The sun is shining and there are people on bicycles and children playing. When I really miss him, I just think of him there and what an amazing adventure he must be having. It doesn't matter where he is really. I just like to think of him out there, somewhere.'

'I'm sure he is, Joe,' Maggie said, and she leant over to squeeze his hand.

'The tricky bit is that he was our buffer person,' Joe said. 'The one between me and Mum. We only really got on, we only really talked, when he was around. There isn't anything to say to each other anymore. She just kind of looks at me and doesn't know what to say.'

'I'm sure she's just grieving. Give it time, Joe. You'll figure out how to be with each other. It might just take a bit of working out, that's all.'

They were quiet for a moment, both stretched out on the grass as the air slowly cooled around them.

'Do you think we're losers?' Joe said.

Maggie laughed. 'Quite possibly! What made you say that?'

'Didn't you used to look at the adults who lived here when we were at school and think, "What are you doing here? There's a whole world out there!"'

'We get pulled back in. It's like gravity.'

'Maybe I'm just stuck,' he said with a sigh.

'I'm stuck too,' she said. 'I keep waiting for real life to start, like a klaxon is going to go off somewhere and I will suddenly know exactly what to do.'

'You know what you're doing, Maggie Addison.'

'Do I?'

'I think you do.'

Maggie looked up at the stars. A plane was crossing far overhead, its tail-light blinking noiselessly across the sky. She thought of Joe's dad, and the many imagined trips that Joe had sent him on, and felt an enormous swell of warmth and love.

'I'm really sorry if I was rude earlier, Joe' she said. 'Susie seems really nice.'

'She is. She is nice.'

'And she's young, you know? She's got youth. She's ambitious, she's got goals, she's properly dressed, she's got suits and shoes and all of those things. You should be really, really proud.'

'Are you taking the piss?'

'No! No, not at all.'

'How do you know she's got *goals*?'

'She's definitely got goals. She's probably even written them down. She'll have a new notebook somewhere and the on the front page it will say 'Goals' and it will be underlined.'

'Really?'

'I don't know what men like you are really after these days, but I would say, you know, from an objective point of view, that Susie has it all. You can just list off all of those qualities so easily on your hand. They just come out, don't they? A full list!'

'I haven't actually counted them,' Joe said, taking a sip of his wine.

'Two hands, even! She definitely goes on to the next hand.'

Joe thought for a moment. 'We all go on to the next hand, don't we?'

'I don't know if we do, Joe. I worry that I might be a one-hand person, sometimes.'

'You are not a one-hand person, Maggie.'

'Most people are awful though, aren't they? Well, maybe not all of them. Eighty per cent maybe. Seventy when the sun is out.'

'It's just a list of *things*, isn't it? Anyone can come up with a list of *things*. Good things, bad things.'

'I definitely know some one-handers,' Maggie said. 'One or two fingers, even, and Susie is definitely a two-hander.'

Joe propped himself up on his elbows and looked across at her in the dark. 'Why are you saying all this?' he said. 'You don't like her, Maggie.'

'Of course I do!' she protested. 'You should be happy, Joe. I want you to be happy.'

'She said she wants to keep it casual anyway.'

'Oh. Right. Is that a thing these days?'

'I don't know,' Joe said, rubbing his chin. 'I really don't know.'

Maggie lay back again and stared up at the sky. The stars suddenly looked closer somehow, as though they had been leaning in to listen. It was so easy to be with Joe, even in silence.

'Did you ever go to Mrs Jericho's house?' she said eventually.

'*Who?*'

'Mrs Jericho. When you were at school, did you ever go to her house?'

'No, I don't think so. Why would I go to her house?'

'She has this beautiful old house on Oak Lane, just set back from the road. It's behind a wall mostly so you can't really see it, but it's amazing, with this huge garden and box hedges and a fountain. She's some sort of chocolate heiress, apparently, although I don't think anyone has actually had a conversation with her. She's a bit of a recluse.'

'OK.'

'Do you remember when Google Earth came out and everyone was trying to find where they lived? It would take ages and ages to load on your computer and when you finally got to Britain and then to the Midlands and then somehow managed to find the village on the map, you'd try to zoom in and see if you could see your house. But right there, almost right in the middle of the village, before you can even be bothered to look for where you live, you see this rectangle of bright, bright blue. It's right in the middle of the village, right there, just down the road.'

'A pool.'

'A pool! And nobody knew it was there because it's behind this big wall and nobody ever goes over to see her.'

'So . . . you went over there?'

'We went all the time. When it was hot anyway, and late at night, *so* late, when everyone was asleep and there wasn't anyone about. Sometimes she would have a pool cover on and you'd have to roll it back *so* quietly.'

'You went swimming?'

'Loads of times.'

'Did Liz know?'

'No, God no. She would have been horrified. It was with some of the school lot. I don't really remember who now. Some of those guys I used to hang out with.'

Joe then sat up, his eyes wide and jaw tight. He looked down at Maggie.

'Let's go,' he said.

'What?'

'Let's go. You and me. Let's go now.'

'*Swimming?*'

'Yes! Why not? It's warm. It's late. We should go. *I* want to go.'

Maggie sat up next to him, and for a moment they were very close, peering at each other through the dark.

'Really?' she said quietly. 'You want to?'

'Definitely.'

'I didn't think it would really be your thing.'

'I'm going to make it my thing,' he said.

They went silently out of the front door, holding hands as they made their way down the steps in the dark. As they went down Church Street and towards Oak Lane, there was an urgency in their footsteps, a need to get there before they changed their minds.

'We have to climb over this bit,' Maggie said, pointing to a low hedge at the edge of the property.

'OK. Shall I go first?'

Maggie nodded at him and he swung his leg over before bringing the other one to meet it. He held his hand out.

'Come on, I'll help you.'

She climbed over and then led him down a long, very narrow path alongside a wall before the garden opened up into an enormous lawn flanked with flower-beds on each side, large box-hedge borders, a pond with a fountain and the house at the back, large and vaguely gothic-looking in the half light. Rippling softly at the end of the grass was a large aquamarine swimming pool, a light steam rising from the water and lit from underneath. The whole thing looked alien somehow, exotic, ridiculous.

'Shit,' Joe said. 'I don't think I've ever seen anything quite so beautiful!'

Maggie laughed. 'I haven't been here in so long,' she said. 'I forgot how amazing it is.'

'Why did I never come here?' he said.

'Why *didn't* you? Everyone knew about it.'

'I never wanted to get in trouble,' he said simply, and then turned to smile at her.

Maggie took his hand and walked him silently across the lawn, the dew wet beneath their toes. As she got to the edge of the pool, she took her T-shirt off, throwing it down onto the concrete by the side of the water before undoing the top button on her jeans. Joe watched her, uncertain for a moment, his hands hesitating over his clothes.

'Are you OK?' she said. 'What's wrong? Nobody is going to come, I promise. And I'm going to keep my pants and bra on, just in case.'

'No, it's not that, it's just that I think I have *SpongeBob Squarepants* boxers on today,' he said sheepishly. 'They've got Patrick the starfish on them.'

'Patrick the starfish?'

'Yes. I think so.'

'OK,' she said, the smallest of laughs escaping. 'That's perfect.'

She held out her hand for him, and he walked over to her as she pulled her jeans over her feet and then tiptoed over to the pool to lower herself into the water, dipping under the surface before coming up with a small gasp. Joe stood on the side, watching her for a moment, before unbuttoning his shirt and trousers and sitting down on the edge, his feet dangling into the water.

'It's OK,' she said, smiling encouragingly at him, and he took his glasses off and quickly pushed himself in.

'Wow,' he said as he re-emerged. 'It's warm! It's actually quite warm!'

Maggie giggled. She was treading water at the side. 'She's old. And rich!'

'I know, I just wasn't expecting it to be quite so warm.'

'Is that why you were nervous about getting in?' she laughed.

'No! It's because it's England!' he exclaimed, and they both laughed again. 'Aren't pools always freezing in England?'

'Not this one.'

They swam along together for a bit, just smiling at each other, with only the noise of the water lapping around them, and Maggie wondered how she could have ever thought she'd had fun in that pool when she now knew what it *could* be like. They reached the far end, their eyes following each other, unblinking, and Maggie shuddered a little as she steadied herself on the side.

'Are you cold?' Joe asked.

'No. No, just . . . happy,' she said smiling at him, the fullest, widest smile she thought she'd ever felt. He leant over and pushed a tangle of wet hair away from her eyes.

'Me too,' he said.

'Can you see anything without your glasses on?'

'Not really,' he laughed. 'I can see you though, so that's OK.'

'I can see you too. Hi, Joe.'

'Hi, Maggie. Thank you for tonight.'

'It was your idea.'

'Was it?'

'Yes. You rebel!'

'I like it. I like being with you,' he said, and he reached underwater to find her hand, linking her fingers through his. 'I like who I am with you, Maggie.'

'I . . . don't want to make things difficult for you with Susie, Joe. Really, I don't.'

'You're not,' he said. 'You're making it much easier.'

He put his arm around her then and pulled her in towards him, their chests pressed into each other again, and it felt comfortable and familiar in a way that Maggie wasn't expecting. Her whole body felt like it was part of his, like they were one thing together in the water.

'We've been here before,' he said with a smile.

'I know,' she sighed. 'I'm so sorry, Joe.'

'No, no, it's fine. I just wanted to make sure this was what you wanted, after last time.'

'It is what I want,' she said, but she was looking down then, her eyes turning away from his.

'But . . .?'

'But I don't want to get in the middle of anything or upset anybody, Joe. I really don't.'

He was quiet and still for a moment but something in her must have changed as his body stiffened and then he suddenly pulled away from her.

'We should probably get out,' he said. 'Are you cold?'

'A little bit. I'll warm up quickly though.'

'OK,' he said, and then, more confidently, 'OK.'

They swam back in silence to where their clothes were lying on the ground and Maggie wondered if she had upset him or confused him or led him on in some way and the thought of it made her feel physically sick.

'We didn't bring a towel, did we?' he said as they reached the far side of the pool.

'Oh, shit!' she said. 'I'm sorry, Joe.'

'Come on, then,' he said. 'We'll just have to run.'

He hauled himself out of the pool and then leant down with his arm outstretched to help her out too, pulling her out of the water in one swift, strong move. They ran over to where their clothes had been discarded, and then they were jumping and giggling and swearing through the cold as they pulled on shirts and trousers, and Maggie thought that she might have just done the first truly sensible thing in her life.

Chapter 15

In hindsight, Maggie thought Liz should really have worked with people and not numbers. She should have been a saleswoman of sorts, or a politician perhaps, a lawyer, or one of those terrifying women they bring into police cells when they really need the prisoner to talk. Liz had always said that numbers were easier than people: they didn't answer back, they did what they were meant to do and there was never any uncertainty with adding up and taking away. She could rely on numbers, she could rely on the outcome, whereas people were unpredictable and let you down and did endlessly stupid things.

Maggie understood, in a way. She liked to return to recipes occasionally, the more complicated the better, to turn off the more rambling side of her brain and to just follow the instructions, the exact weights and measurements, the rules of it all. It was reassuring to be reminded that life could work that way. Not that she usually cooked like that. She tended to be more spontaneous and free-form, and it had seemed to work for the most part, but she never lost sight of the need for a good set of scales.

But Liz was also good at getting people to do what she wanted, at least she had been in recent years. Maggie wondered if her powers of persuasion had been honed during parenthood, the endless evenings spent coaxing small bodies to eat broccoli and get into baths and go to sleep. Liz's gentle (and sometimes not so gentle) persuasion had, over the last six months, successfully turned George into something resembling a grandfather. He knew his grandchildren's names, he remembered some of their likes and dislikes, he could engage in short conversation with them and not make them cry, and he had collected them enough times to not be viewed with suspicion at the school gates. When all was said and done, it was a miraculous turn of events.

Liz had suggested that the three of them meet in The Owl for a debrief on the open day. She wanted to discuss 'next steps.' There had been a number of offers on the house in the days that followed and decisions needed to be made, alongside what Liz had described as an 'appraisal' of George's fathering contributions. While he had certainly fulfilled his duties as far as Liz's quota was concerned, Maggie had yet to really add to the list. When it came to her powers of persuasion, Liz found her sister stubbornly uncompliant.

'Maggie,' Liz said, sharply. 'We were going to talk to George about dad stuff, weren't we?'

They were sitting outside in the pub garden. George had a fawn coloured pug on his lap which he stroked intermittently while it panted feebly in the mid-afternoon heat. Lily lay fast asleep in her buggy, and it was one of those perfect summer afternoons where the warmth of the sun was cooled just a little by a thin, cloudy haze. Maggie found her mind pleasantly lethargic, a combination of the heat and the wine and passing thoughts of

Joe. He had called a few days after their swim to say that things with Susie were now over and she could barely think of anything else.

'Maggie?'

'Yes?'

'Good things?'

'Oh, right,' she said, shifting awkwardly in her seat.

'Are these my *tasks*?' George asked.

'This is *parenting*, George. 'And rent payment.'

'Jolly good,' he said with a grin. 'I'm enjoying this!'

Liz scowled. It was clear that he was not meant to be enjoying it one bit. 'You'll probably be leaving soon,' she said firmly. 'Who knows where you'll end up next? Or if we'll even see you again? I am sure Maggie would like something to remember you by before you swan off again. Wouldn't you, Maggie?'

Maggie nodded vaguely.

'What have you come up with for George?' she asked, getting the list out from her pocket. Maggie noticed how crumpled it looked, the sharpness of the folded lines, as though it had been opened and closed hundreds of times.

The truth was that Maggie had thought about the list endlessly, but whenever she had tried to turn those thoughts into a practical action, she had failed. Liz did practical action, not Maggie. But there was more to it than that, a deep-rooted lack of motivation, and she wondered why she didn't have the same urge to make George atone for being an absent father as Liz did. Was it as simple as Liz being a parent? Did having your own children give you a chance to see the mistakes of your own parents in a clearer, less forgiving light? Did having a partner like Doug, so stable and dependable, amplify George's failings?

Or was it because she just didn't remember as much as Liz? The five years between them seemed to be nothing now, a handful of lifestyle anomalies at most, but had she just been too young to recall the many different layers of dysfunction at the Manor House all those years ago? Persephone had been the Goddess of spring after all, not Dawn from Bicester.

Or perhaps it was just that having George live alongside her at the Manor House had made her feel, what was it exactly, contentment? Equilibrium? *Peacefulness*? When everything else is stripped away, surely just being present is the most vital part of being a parent?

'What about work?' Liz said impatiently. 'What about the jobs you got off the back of the open day? Can he help you with anything?'

'Well, I have one next week in Great Martin,' Maggie said. 'I could, do with an extra pair of hands with moving the food, I suppose?'

'There we go,' Liz said, clapping her hands together then scribbling it down on her list. 'Dads put things in cars, don't they? They put things in cars and they carry things inside from cars.'

For all of Liz's practicality, there was something endearing about her thinking that moving some scones and sandwiches from A to B was going to somehow make everything all right. But what were you meant to ask a father to do for you when you were thirty-five, single, with no children, half a job and soon to be homeless?

'And don't forget that you are going to Tom and Sophie's summer fête thing next week. I have a keeping-in-touch day at work.'

'What's that?' Maggie asked.

'It's when you have been on maternity leave forever and you get so fed up with it all that you want to visit your old workplace to remind them that you exist. Or maybe it's to remind yourself that you exist.'

'Are you going to go back to work soon, then?'

'I don't know,' Liz said with a large sigh. She looked in the buggy and gave it a little rock. 'There's so many of them it might be impossible.'

'What about the house, then?' George said, quickly moving on. 'These offers, Liz? What's the news?'

'It's a bit complicated, actually,' Liz replied as she tucked the list away in her pocket and got out her note-book. 'We've had a few offers, so we need to decide who to go with. There are two lots from London, one an investor (although he was a bit vague apparently), another a couple wanting a second home, then a family from Martin St John looking to upsize, and someone from up north somewhere, not sure who they are.'

'*London*,' George snorted.

'They have to come from somewhere, George,' Liz said.

'Who has offered the most?' he asked.

'The investor.'

'There we go, then,' George shrugged.

'Do we not feel some sort of responsibility as to who is going to take over the house?' Maggie asked. 'It feels like such a huge thing to be handing over doesn't it?'

She couldn't imagine a time when it wasn't going to feel like their house. It was who they were, it was their whole history, it was everything about them. If it had to be someone else's, she wanted to hand it over gently, carefully, and to someone who understood what it meant.

'It's not our house, Maggie,' Liz said quietly. 'It hasn't really been since Queen Vic died. The bank owns a little bit of it for a start.'

'It will always feel like our house to me,' Maggie said.

'It's just business, isn't it, darling?' George said, looking slightly confused. 'Business is business is business.'

'And *your* business failed,' Liz snipped. 'That's why we're all here, after all.'

'What about the local family?' Maggie asked. 'How does their offer compare?'

'Just because they live locally, Maggie, it doesn't mean they're not going to dig up the garden or paint the whole thing orange.'

'It just sounds nicer, somehow,' Maggie said. 'Someone local.'

'Any thoughts on where you are going to go, Dad?' Liz asked. 'You can't hang around for too long now.'

George cleared his throat. 'Err, not yet, no, darling. I have been *deep* into rehearsals over the last few weeks, as you know.'

'What about you, Maggie? There are a few houses in Fair Meadows up for sale if you want to come and have a look?'

'Oh? Right,' Maggie said. 'Might be a bit a little close for comfort, don't you think?'

George said nothing but began to stroke the pug again. The panting had turned to more of a wheeze, a deep rasping sound like a small saw hacking through a piece of wood, and it was timed with precision to the flapping of its pink tongue in the soft summer breeze.

'Why do you have that dog?' Liz eventually said. She had hoped that she could get away with ignoring it, but the growing noise had made it impossible.

'Pamela is at the hairdressers,' George said. 'And Hermione does not like to be left alone. She has separation anxiety.'

'*Hermione*?'

'Hermione Granger, I believe.'

Hermione stopped panting and lifted her head for a moment, seeming to recognise her name. Maggie and Liz exchanged glances.

'Is she a Harry Potter fan, then?' Liz asked with a smirk.

'I think she might be, yes.'

'Wow. I wouldn't have guessed that,' she said. 'Not at all.'

'It's all a bit of an eye-opener to be honest, girls,' George said, looking slightly pained. 'Just when you think you know everything you need to about life, or even women for that matter, along comes all this.'

He pointed down to Hermione, but then extended his arm out to a wider sphere which presumably included wizards, magic and dark lords.

'You look good with a pug, Dad,' Maggie said. 'She matches your linen suit.'

'We've actually become rather close,' he said as he picked up the plastic pub menu and began to fan

Hermione's dark, wrinkled face. 'She's a new chapter, girls, a fresh start for Albert and I. He has a whole new lease of life now he's met Hermione. A whole new lease. He skips now, girls. *Skips*.'

'That's very sweet,' Maggie said. 'Lucky old Albert.'

'The power of love, girls. It rejuvenates even the most haggard among us.'

Liz scowled. 'Does she want any water or something?' she said, as the wheezing began to turn into more of a death rattle.

'Yes, yes, she might well do,' George replied. 'I do rather suspect she will be better company when the weather is a touch cooler.'

'So, it's quite serious with you and Pamela then?' Maggie asked. 'If you and Hermione are . . . *close*.'

'We're having rather a lovely time,' George said, beaming. 'Very lovely indeed.'

'That's all quite quick, isn't it?' Maggie said.

'She's rich,' Liz said. 'It adds speed.'

'You don't have time to mess around at our age, Elizabeth. You have to strike when the iron is *hot*.'

Liz grimaced and took a gulp of her drink.

'That's great, Dad,' Maggie said. 'I'm really happy for you.'

'Thank you, darling. We do make rather a good team in one way or another. And she's invited us all over for dinner next week, girls. Doug too, of course. And Joe.'

'*Joe?*' Liz said, turning sharply to look at Maggie. Maggie couldn't tell if Liz's expression was one of disapproval or delight. They often overlapped.

'Yes, if he'd like to come,' George said, smiling at her.

Maggie smiled back at him, and it was at that exact moment that she realised George had asked Joe to stay late after the open day for her, for the two of them, and she couldn't believe that she hadn't worked it out before. It all seemed so obvious now, so glaringly obvious, and her heart swelled in her chest like a rose in bloom.

'I'll ask him,' Maggie said, and that was that.

Chapter 16

It was Doug who was the most reluctant to go to dinner at Pamela's. He wanted to watch something on the telly about the housing market, and he found eating in front of people he didn't know very troubling.

'You know George and you know Maggie and you know me, and you sort of know Joe. It's really only Pamela you don't know, and I wouldn't worry about her,' Liz said dismissively.

'Why?' Doug and Maggie asked at the same time. They had all met at Liz and Doug's house for a pre-dinner drink, Maggie and Joe sat on the sofa next to each other, their hands entwined, while Liz was hunting crumbs with the mini vac.

'You won't have to see her again because she'll only be temporary,' she said, giving a spot on the carpet a quick vacuum blast.

'Really?' Maggie questioned.

'Aren't they all?' Liz snipped.

'This feels different, somehow,' Maggie said. 'He seems really keen.'

'She's got tonnes of money, Maggie. Of course he's keen.'

Doug chuckled and Joe squeezed her hand.

'He hasn't said he's dying for weeks now,' Maggie said.

'The healing power of hard cash,' replied Liz, and they set off for Martin St John.

Pamela had bought a house in 'Martin's Rest', just outside Martin St John, an extremely exclusive development of just six houses that were designed by a neo-traditionalist eco architect from London and cost well over seven figures each. Unlike Fair Meadows, Martin's Rest hadn't seemed to cause too many issues within the local community, possibly because it was such a small development, or possibly because it was bringing in a large amount of money. Liz didn't need to see it to know that she was going to determinedly hate it.

Pamela opened the enormous black door wearing an orange silk kimono and a necklace with large pink turtles on it, her sunflower-yellow hair tied up with a scarf. Her make-up was bold and characteristically bright, pink glossy lips, eyelashes long, black and polyester, shoes high and glittery. The martini in her hand had to have been her second or third as she seemed to sway slightly on her heels, a pink blossom tree in the wind. Under her other arm she gripped Hermione who was grunting contentedly in a Gryffindor sweater.

'You're here! Welcome, welcome!' she squealed.

'Thank you for having us,' Liz said, and it sounded so formal and stiff that Maggie felt compelled to add, 'Hi, Pamela!'

'Hello everyone, come in, come in!' She beckoned them all into the hallway, and turning back into the house shrieked, 'Georgie, darling, they're here!'

'Christ,' said Liz, a little too loudly.

'Hi, Maggie, hi, Elizabeth,' Pamela said as they all shuffled in. 'You must be Doug, Sensible Doug, and Joe. New Joe.'

'Just Joe,' Joe said, holding his hand out to shake Pamela's, which was perfectly manicured and covered in large gold rings.

'Well come on in, *Just* Joe,' Pamela laughed, the 'Ss' thrust out loudly and with some force. 'Come in everyone. I have cocktails on the go!'

She turned on her heels and sashayed back down the hallway, her kimono wafting behind her like a bright billowing sail as the four of them shuffled tentatively behind. The house was, as expected, emphatically modern; white and shiny, with lighting that rose up from the ground, cupboards and drawers that had to be pushed in or to spoken to nicely to open, and little digital screens everywhere that controlled mood and temperature and humidity. It had a strikingly stark and sterile feel to it, beautiful but cold and functional like an extremely expensive psychiatric ward or a Swiss detox clinic. Maggie wondered how on earth George was coping in such a place, his natural habitat being somewhere far older and more jumbled.

But there he was, standing in the kitchen, stirring something at the huge range cooker as if he had been there all along; and not for the first time Maggie marvelled at his endless capacity to adapt to fit his circumstance, an aged chameleon in a purple and pink paisley shirt, a pair of snugly fitted pale jeans and an apron that said, 'I'd try the sausage' on it. There was music playing, something by

Harry Belafonte, and he was sort of twisting side to side to it, his hips cranking around in circles, looking exactly like he belonged. The four of them all stood there for a moment, acclimatising, as if they had just stepped off a plane into a completely different time zone.

'What are you wearing, Dad?' Liz said, eventually, the words coming out robotically, one by one, as her eyes tried to focus.

'Ah, here they all are!' he exclaimed cheerfully, gliding over to greet them. 'Do you like it, darling? Pamela is jazzing me up a bit.'

'You look like . . . *Wham!*' Liz replied, clearly horrified. She had never been able to hide her disgust at other people's bad choices.

'Who?' George asked.

'*Wham!* They're an 80s band. George Michael and the other guy,' Maggie said. 'You must know *Wham!*?'

'I don't remember much of the 1980s,' George replied with a grin as he kissed the girls on both cheeks.

'Camp popstar is what we mean,' Liz said. 'You look like you're in *Club Tropicana*!'

'Ah ha! There you go, darling!' George said, wrapping his arm around Pamela. 'You said I would look like a diva in this shirt.'

'Golly, I should have brought my sunglasses,' Doug chuckled amiably, shaking George's hand. Doug only ever wore navy and grey, except at Christmas, when he dusted down a pair of faded red chinos that he'd had since sixth form. His blandness was another reason why Liz loved him. Maggie often thought that one of the most wonderful things about Doug was that he took everything just as he saw it on the surface, including George, who he saw as an amusing, affable chap who his wife had some issues with and was now wearing a very bright shirt.

'I feel rather underdressed!' he said.

'You look good, Doug,' Liz said to him, and then more quietly, 'You look normal. I don't feel nauseous looking at you.'

'Nonsense, Sensible Doug, you look very handsome,' Pamela said, drawing him into the kitchen by linking her arm through his. The four of them had been standing in the doorway feeling too awkward to go any further. Maggie nudged Liz and pointed to a large dog bed in the corner of the kitchen where Albert was reclining next to Hermione, licking her ears.

'Plus, *you* are the sensible one, Doug. We need *you* to keep us in line and tell us off when we get a bit naughty. S-s-s-s-s.'

'Gosh, right, okey-dokey,' said Doug, his face immediately flushing as he was led away. As Maggie and Liz followed behind, they caught each other's eye for a moment and Maggie felt a familiar warmth inside, one that she knew from childhood. How brilliant it was to have someone by your side who knew exactly what you were thinking, and how unlucky for those who did not. She knew Liz would be mortified by the clothes but there was more to it than that. She knew Liz would also be wondering if Doug should make more of an effort, be a bit bolder and daring, be funnier, more spontaneous. Then she would be wondering if it was her who should be bolder, funnier, better.

'Right. Drinks! Red or white, girls?' George asked. 'Or this martini thingy that Pammy has made. It's fairly lethal I'm afraid, but I rather like that.'

'It's a *Little Martini*,' Pamela said. 'The *Martini St John* is obviously far stronger, but I wasn't sure you could all handle that.'

'Ooh, controversial!' Doug said with a chuckle.

'What are we eating?' Maggie asked, picking at a bowl of crisps on the kitchen counter.

'Margaret is a chef,' George said to Pamela. 'A *very* good one.'

'She's excellent,' Joe said.

'Of course you are,' Pamela said. 'How could I have forgotten that? I really should have got the caterers in. Do you guys have caterers over here?'

'We have caterers,' Liz said. 'That's what Maggie does.'

'Do you know, I might never have got divorced if I was a better chef?' Pamela continued, oblivious. 'Jeff was too tight to get caterers in most of the time, even though he had a ton of money. He said he liked to see me cook, even though I was usually burning something.'

'Did you get divorced because you were a bad cook?' Doug asked, which made Pamela really laugh, a sort of bark into the air that then morphed seamlessly into the Ss, their volume decreasing like a descending musical scale. Liz had told them all about Pamela's laugh, but even with forewarning, it was still quite a surprise. Doug's jaw dropped slightly, and his face flushed a deep crimson.

'Lord, no,' she said. 'Not just that anyway, Sensible Doug.'

'And Liz is the accountant, aren't you, darling,' George said. 'Tell Pamela how much money you used to make.'

'*What*? No!' Liz said.

'We're eating pasta,' Pamela said to Maggie. 'I hope that's OK? I can't remember how to do anything that isn't on a barbeque or doesn't have a biblical theme going on.'

'That sounds great,' Maggie said. 'I'll have red wine please. Joe?'

'Sounds good.'

'Doug, Doug,' George said excitedly as he bounded over, labrador-like, with the wine. 'What will your bonus be this year?'

'Um . . .' Doug said, looking around nervously.

'Dad!' Liz bellowed. 'Stop talking about money. It's embarrassing.'

'What? I am only proud of you. You can't blame me for being proud.'

'Let's just change the subject,' Liz said, and George muttered something about it being a perfectly normal question and why was everyone in England so buttoned up about money and achievement. Liz and Doug then bickered about who was going to drive home. Doug had done it last time, but Liz needed large amounts of alcohol to get her through the evening, so they deferred the decision and both had a very large glass.

'A toast!' George exclaimed. 'To my beautiful daughters, Elizabeth and Margaret, Maggie and Liz, who I have loved spending time with and who I am so very proud of.' His voice then tailed off, his lower lip starting to tremble a little, and he raised a hand to say he could no longer go on due to the intensity of his emotion. Pamela squeezed his hand, and Doug said, 'Here, here,' and Joe said, 'Cheers!' and Maggie and Liz just smiled politely, not daring to look at each other.

'Thank you all,' George said, composure regained, and he leant over to kiss Pamela, a long one this time, and Doug's cheeks flushed for the third time in as many minutes. He looked down at his shoes while Liz turned to Maggie, her eyes wide and blinking, and mouthed 'TONGUE!'

'I hear you met on the stage, is that right?' Joe asked, sensing that another change of subject was needed.

Pamela nodded. 'It has been a bit of a whirlwind, to be honest. It's rather taken us by surprise, hasn't it, darling?'

'When you get to our age, Joe, you have to make the most of every chance you get,' George said, his arm around Pamela's waist, his hand clearly resting on her bottom. 'There is no time for fannying around anymore. This wonderful, *sexy* woman has given me that chance and I am going to grab it by the horns and take off into the sunset!'

'Yeehaw!' Pamela yelped, which made Liz jump a little.

'What *horns*?' she grumbled.

'It's just an expression, Liz. There are no actual horns,' Maggie hissed back at her, and she leant over to get the bottle of wine to refill Liz's glass.

'I don't think we should be talking about horns,' Liz said. Doug gripped her hand.

There was then some back and forth about the open house and how well it had gone and how much Pamela had loved the day, *loved* the house, but Liz found her mood would not improve, despite the large quantities of wine she was consuming. This house, its owner and the whole evening was so much newer and shinier than Liz expected, and she felt resentment settle on her like a fine dust.

'Is this underfloor heating, Pamela?' she asked as she moved around the large, white kitchen island.

'Oh, I am not really sure to be honest. There's so many buttons in here, I've kind of lost track.'

'And is your oven self-cleaning?'

'Well now you've got me, Liz. *Someone* cleans it and it's not me! That's all I know!'

'Mine is self-cleaning. My dishwasher is integrated.'

'And we're all *very* proud,' Maggie teased, giving Liz a playful shove.

'Our turn to host next!' Doug said, brightly. 'We'll have you all back for a big slap-up, won't we, Liz?'

Liz sniffed and turned away to inspect the hot water tap.

'Golly, what's a *slap-up*?' Pamela asked.

'It's a big meal,' Maggie said. 'Nothing to worry about.'

'In which case, that would be lovely,' Pamela said, and then it was thankfully time to eat.

By the time the main course was over, Liz was clearly drunk. She would never admit to it, but Maggie recognised the surliness in her tone, her meanness to Doug and the way her head wobbled slightly as she spoke. For someone so measured, it was always a novelty for

Maggie to see her with her guard down, regardless of what was lurking underneath.

'Hermione is going to join us for dessert, if that's OK with you all,' Pamela said, very much rhetorically, as she placed the pug on a chair at the end of the dining table. The tip of Hermione's tongue was just poking out of her mouth as if she was halfway through eating a thin piece of ham.

'Ah, there's my girl,' George said. 'Isn't she beautiful?'

'She is quite a looker,' Doug said.

'Pugs are very intelligent animals, did you know that, Doug?'

'I, erm, didn't, actually,' he replied. 'I thought you were more of a corgi man, George?'

'I think I probably swing both ways these days, Doug,' he said, with a wink. 'Hermione has rather turned my head.'

'What's the dog doing there?' Liz said, rather belligerently.

'She likes to feel included,' Pamela replied with a polite smile, as she placed a small slice of cake in front of Hermione. 'And she has me wrapped around her teeny tiny paws I'm afraid.'

'She has a very lovely Harry Potter jumper on,' Doug said cheerfully. 'She looks almost exactly like Hermione Granger.'

'Thank you, Doug,' Pamela said, clearly delighted. 'She reminded me so much of her, all smart and sassy and stubborn.'

Liz made a sort of snorting sound and Maggie glared at her across the table.

'You two girls are both named after someone pretty special, aren't you?' Pamela said.

Liz stiffened in her chair. 'No,' she said quickly, and flapped her napkin in a way that she hoped would flick the conversation on its way.

'It's a long story,' Maggie explained.

'Just the details then,' Pamela said, ignoring Liz's souring face. 'Your father is hopeless at details.'

'Well, the short version is that we are named after Queen Elizabeth and Princess Margaret,' Maggie said. 'Although they are pretty common names here these days, so we're just Maggie and Liz really. Liz and Maggie. Maggie and Liz. Whichever way you want to say it.'

Liz took another large drink of her wine and straightened herself a little in her chair.

'The long version is that our mother, his ex-wife, Pat was her name, she came from the local town and got a job with George, back when the business was doing well and made actual money. She worked very hard, very, very hard, and the company thrived. But she didn't find the Manor House very easy, or parenting for that matter, and she struggled with the madness of it all – Queen Vic, and George being George, and the parties and the silly poshness – and I think she thought that calling us Elizabeth and Margaret was a chance to fit in. To be accepted. To be like the rest of them. So, they're not just names, Pamela, they're armour really.'

George cleared his throat but didn't say anything. Nobody made a noise, even Hermione who sat very still on her cushion and pulled the tip of her tongue back in. Maggie was sure her heart had stopped beating. She had never heard Liz talk about their mother like that. They rarely spoke of her at all and if they did it was in the abstract, someone they had once heard about, someone they knew long ago. Someone who had left them. Liz had never spoken about her as if she had actually been an *ally*.

'But she didn't fit in after all. Who could have? We lived in a mad house. So, she left. She left and she didn't come back and then she died. She died, so she may as well have just called us . . . Sandra or Sharon. Or Pamela!'

After dinner, Maggie helped Pamela take the plates into the kitchen. She was loading them straight into the dishwasher without rinsing, large chunks of lasagne and bread still stuck to them while Hermione and Albert tried to hoist themselves up onto the side to lick the leftovers. Maggie stood for a moment, wondering whether or not she should intervene. Pamela had such confidence with everything she did, you almost began to question yourself.

'I'm sorry about Liz,' Maggie said eventually. 'I think she's had a bit too much to drink.'

'Don't be silly,' Pamela said with a wave of her had. 'I'm sorry about your mother.'

'Thank you,' Maggie said. 'It was a long time ago now. Car accident.'

'Geez,' Pamela said, her head still in the dishwasher.

'It was harder for Liz. She was older, and she gets very protective about things. It's just the way she is.'

Pamela then straightened, her expression suddenly serious.

'You don't need to worry about me and your dad, Maggie,' she said. 'I'm a big girl. I can look out for myself. Your sister has already had a *long* talk with me, and I get it, I really do.'

'Oh. OK,' Maggie said as she turned to the sink and began to rinse some of the wine glasses.

'I mean, we all have some sort of baggage, right? Nobody gets to our age without a whole heap of trash following them around. I'm pretty sure I have seen it *all* in my time!'

'You just seem really close really quickly, and that's brilliant, really, *really* brilliant, it's just, well, I wouldn't want anyone to get hurt.'

'Me, or your dad?' she said.

'Both I suppose.'

Pamela smiled at her, a wry sort of smile that made her lips purse. 'How long have you and Just Joe been dating?' she said.

'Joe? Oh, hardly any time at all,' Maggie said. 'It's very new. But we've known each other since school.'

'Uh-huh, uh-huh,' Pamela said, nodding her head.

'We did PE together.'

'*PE?*'

'Physical Education. Sport. Running.'

'OK,' she said with a smile. She leant in towards Maggie then, her voice almost a whisper. 'Listen, it's probably just the sex, you know? There's been *a lot* of sex. You know how it is when it's like that.'

'Oh. *Sure,*' Maggie said, hoping that her face hadn't fallen short of the casual, easy-going look she was trying to project.

'It's just sex, right? But God did I get in so much trouble with all those Bible bores across the pond. They just couldn't wait to tell me how happy Jesus was to be a virgin. Can you actually believe it? Jesus was *not* a virgin. He was hot and he was muscly and he travelled around a lot with all that gorgeous, long hair and that silly little loincloth thing or whatever it was he was wearing. He was always half naked in the pictures, wasn't he? He must have been at it all the time. I mean, *all* the time.'

They both laughed, for quite a long time, and Maggie felt strangely liberated, a weight she didn't even know she was carrying suddenly lifted.

'And the hands!' Maggie said. 'He had those big, magic, miracle-making hands.'

'Oh, my God, YES! The hands! I didn't even think about the hands. You're right. God, just imagine those all over you.'

'He'd have to cheer up a bit though, don't you think?' Maggie said. 'He always looks so moody and serious in pictures. You'd want him to at least smile occasionally, tell a few jokes.'

'Well, he takes his job very seriously, you know. I like that in a man.'

'That's true,' Maggie said. 'That's true. And he's good with animals and children, which is always a good sign. Never trust a man who doesn't like animals, that's what my grandmother used to say.'

Pamela laughed woozy, contented Ss, and downed a half-drunk martini from the kitchen counter, wiping her mouth with her hand as she finished. There was a dishevelment to her now that Maggie rather liked. The real Pamela seemed to be emerging from underneath the glossy topcoat.

'I keep forgetting I'm in England now and I've got to keep it all zippedy zipped up!'

'No, no, no don't zip up,' Maggie said. 'We need more unzipped people here. We need shaking up a bit.'

'I'll do my best,' she said with a wink, before bending down to pick a whining Hermione up from the floor. She stroked her for a bit, smoothing down the red and gold Gryffindor sweater. Maggie noticed a scroll at the front embroidered with the words, 'Brave at Heart.'

'I'm very rich, Maggie,' Pamela said, looking up at her. 'Did you know that?'

'Oh? I don't think I did, no,' Maggie said, feeling an instant prickle of embarrassment. Queen Vic had instilled in her granddaughters the importance of never discussing money, unless of course you didn't have any, in which case polite conversation on the topic was allowed. This was the loophole that George squeezed himself into in order to have free rein on the subject.

'Well, I am. Very rich. But money isn't everything, Maggie,' she said.

Maggie thought this was probably an easier position to hold if you had a lot of money, but she simply nodded in agreement.

'I mean, we're *all* screwed up, right? All the therapists in the world aren't going to sort our problems out, however much they say they will, however much we pay them. I should know because I have seen *all* of them, done *all* of it, and I can tell you, Maggie, after spending a small goddam fortune, none of it, *none of it* works. The only thing that helps, really the only thing, is just to ride along with the current and have as much fun as you can along the way. I can't worry about what George is going to do. Neither can you, or anyone else for that matter. We'll all have our hearts broken, Maggie, but that's what we're here for. So let's just raise our glasses here and see what tomorrow brings.'

Joe drove everyone home. Liz tried to instigate a row with Doug in the back seat but he was too tired to engage and so she turned her attention to Maggie.

'What were you and Pamela chatting about in the kitchen?' she said.

'Oh, nothing much.'

'You were in there for ages. You must have been talking about *something*.'

'She was saying she thinks Jesus probably had a lot of sex because of his hair. I said it was probably more to do with his hands.'

'*What?*'

'We talked about Jesus having sex,' Maggie said again, louder. 'I think it's the hands that are sexy, but she thought it was the hair.'

'Definitely the hair,' Doug said quickly, his own thinning somewhat at the top.

'For God's sake, she's *obsessed* with sex,' Liz snapped. 'It's disgusting.'

'Come on, Liz,' Maggie said. 'She wasn't *that* bad.'

'She had her hands all over him, didn't you see?'

'Why does it matter?' Maggie said. She caught Liz's eye in the rear-view mirror. She looked flustered and cross, her arms folded tightly across her chest.

'I don't want to have to play happy families over there with them sticking their tongues down each other's throats. They were practically having sex in front of us!'

Maggie laughed, even though she knew it would annoy her sister. 'We don't have to play happy families, Liz. We don't even have to go again. Or at least you don't have to anyway.'

'What's that supposed to mean?' she said, leaning forward in her seat.

'Nothing, Liz. It doesn't mean anything. If you don't like her, you don't have to see her, that's all.'

'He's supposed to be helping *us*, isn't he? Not arsing about over there.'

'I liked her,' said Doug, and Liz told him to shut up.

'Right! Thank you, Doug,' Maggie said, giving him a thumbs up.

'No problemo,' Doug replied, and Liz huffed loudly, turning away to look out of the window.

'Joe, what did you think?' Maggie asked.

'They seemed happy,' Joe said with a simple shrug. 'But she'll probably hate it here after a while. People like that always do.'

Everyone was quiet for a moment, although Maggie was sure she could hear Liz seething in the back seat, and the atmosphere in the car became heavy with drunken frustration.

'How's *Susie*, Joe?' Liz then said, each syllable laced with tipsy bile.

'I'm not sure actually, Liz,' Joe replied, cheerfully. 'I think she's on holiday in Greece, the lucky thing.'

Liz made a tutting sound but didn't speak, and Maggie felt a surge of pride in how astutely, how kindly, Joe had dealt with Liz, whose intention in asking the question was clearly to wind her up. Maggie turned to glare at her sister but saw that Doug had firmly wrapped his arms around her and was gently pulling her towards him. Doug smiled at Maggie, and she knew Liz would not be saying anything else.

Chapter 17

Joe dropped Liz and Doug at Fair Meadows, hopping out of the car to use their bathroom, and Liz stumbled slightly while quarrelling with Doug about who had the house keys. Maggie watched them out of the passenger-seat window, Doug shaking his head as he checked his pockets while Liz put her hands on her hips. She found their squabbles strangely reassuring these days, the domesticity of it all feeling less like a death knell and more like a comfortable sweater. By the time they reached the front door and waved Maggie goodbye, Doug had his arm around her shoulders again and Liz's face seemed to have softened. Even if they hadn't properly made up by bedtime, everything would be all right in the morning.

Maggie had often tried to remember the time that Liz and Doug got together but found she couldn't recollect anything about it. She had wanted to recall Liz's behaviour during that time, to break it down into manageable blocks so that she could follow it, stage by stage, like a recipe. As with most things, Maggie had wanted to measure herself against Liz, to see how it should all be done, but with this, there was nothing at all to latch on to, nothing tangible at all. Liz was in her first job when they met, but she came home regularly and there was no seismic shift, no flicker of electricity, no recognition that this was what life was all about. She was seemingly unchanged by falling in love, life continuing on in its Monday to Friday way as if nothing of consequence had happened. As a couple they had somehow skipped over the giddiness of those first few weeks and months and settled on middle-England, middle-aged contentment.

Maggie thought now, as she sat waiting for Joe in his Vauxhall Corsa, that this might possibly be the best way to approach the messiness of love. By taking out the extremes at either end and staking your claim on the soft middle ground, you may lose the pleasure of some of the sharper edges, but at least you would be spared the pain. There she was again, on that beautiful, silvery edge, just before it all spills over into something else. Here she had often stayed, quite comfortable on that narrow ridge, while men willingly flung themselves over the precipice.

But Maggie was not a middle-ground type of person, not really, and as she saw Joe walk back towards the car, his hand running through his hair, she recognised that woozy, blissful feeling, the earth tilting slightly as your body begins to fall helplessly and heavily into love. The weight of it.

'Do you want to come back?' she said to him. 'To the Manor House? There's nobody there.'

'Are you sure?' he asked, and she smiled and took his hand. She kissed it and then nodded a yes.

Nobody had ever come back to the Manor House. Not with Maggie anyway. She hadn't wanted them to. Doug had often stayed in one of the spare bedrooms in the days before he and Liz were married, and there had been many visiting couples over the years, but the house had always had a hallowed feel about it to Maggie, particularly when Queen Vic was alive. When George moved down to the basement and installed a waterbed, it became quite easy to separate what went on upstairs versus what happened below. But Joe was there now, in her bed, and the house was different once again and Maggie couldn't help thinking that her grandmother would approve.

'I'm sorry about my family,' Maggie said. They were curled around each other, naked, their legs intertwined in the near dark, the only light a cool, grey shard of the moon laid out on the wooden floor.

'Why?' he replied.

'I don't know really.'

'Which bit are you sorry about?'

'Every bit, I guess.'

'I didn't know about your mum dying. I'm really sorry, Maggie.'

'It was ages ago and nobody ever really talked about it.'

'Still . . . it leaves a mark.'

'I suppose it does.'

'Well, I had a good time tonight.'

'*Really?*'

'Yes! It was fun. I loved that I was included.'

'It wasn't too much?'

'I haven't been to a big family dinner thing in ages. It was just nice to be with everyone.'

'*Everyone* is mad though.'

'All families are a bit like that though, aren't they?'

'I don't know. I think there might be grades of mad. Like OK mad and pleasant mad and quirky mad and then just *mad* mad.'

'My mum didn't speak to her sister once for about two, three years. They used to speak to each other every day on the phone, sometimes more than once, and then, just like that, nothing. Not even a Christmas card.'

'How come?'

'They fell out over a cake.'

'A *what*?' she laughed.

'A cake. Well, a cake recipe to be precise.'

'What happened?

'My mum had given my Aunt Lucy this recipe she'd seen in a magazine and said she'd made it hundreds of times. I think Lucy wanted it for an important lunch or tea. She had people coming over that she wanted to impress and it all went wrong and the cake was awful for reasons nobody really knows but are most likely something to do with Lucy being a *terrible* cook. She's always been a terrible cook. Always. Poisoned the lot of us many, many times. Anyway, it was all my mum's fault, somehow. Lucy thought she had given her the wrong recipe, or the wrong instructions and told her that she'd done it all on purpose. They had a big argument about it and that was that.'

'That was *that*?'

'Yep.'

'Cake sabotage. Wow! That's quite an accusation.'

'It wasn't really do to with the cake though. It was more to do with them not listening to each other, my mum being the older one, my aunt thinking she knows best. I think they actually just needed a break from each other. They needed not to talk. Everything is fine now.'

'How did they make up?'

'My dad got ill. My mum wasn't so cross about it after that.'

Maggie wrapped her arms tighter around Joe's chest and inhaled the scent. It was white washing powder and supermarket shower gel and Dylon starch spray around the collar. It was old pine cupboards and dusty comics and framed photographs wiped clean with Pledge. It was the smell of a mother delighted to be looking after her grown-up son, of a man who has unexpectedly returned to their childhood bedroom, but it was also sunshine and red wine and sweat and to Maggie it smelt of everything that was good.

'We hadn't spoken to my dad for over two years before he came back,' she said, resting her head on his arm.

'I didn't realise it had been that long.'

'When my grandmother died and he didn't inherit the house, he just sort of disappeared. He went to Spain and we never heard from him. I don't think he could deal with it all to be honest. He never thought for a minute that the house wouldn't be his in the end, and he'd waited so long for it. I think it was the failure more than anything else. Everyone knowing, having to tell people that he didn't have anything.'

'He had you.'

Maggie smiled and kissed him on the cheek. 'He did.'

'It's more than a lot of people get. You, and your sister and all the kids.'

'I know, I know. I just don't think he knows who he is without the house. It's his whole persona. It's everything he is. He doesn't know how to be someone who doesn't live in a Manor House. I don't even think it would matter which one.'

'What about a modern house?' Joe said simply. 'He looked pretty content this evening.'

'That's true.'

'He'll be fine, Maggie. He's a grown man. We all have to adjust through life, don't we?'

'Liz has been trying to keep him in line. If anyone can do it, she can.'

'Is that why she was giving him such a hard time?'

'She's been trying to get him to do some *fathering* to make up for never being around.'

Joe laughed. 'How do you do that?'

'I don't really know. We have a list. She has been getting him to do all sorts of school pick-ups, babysitting, that sort of thing.'

'So, *grandfathering*, then?'

'I suppose so, yes. I think he's pretty good at it actually.'

Joe exhaled deeply. 'My dad took me to London Zoo every year.'

'When you were little?'

'And when I was not so little. It was a summer holiday thing, and we just sort of kept it going, even when I was at uni and then when I moved to London. He'd get the train down and I would take a day off work and we'd *"meet at twelve at the penguins"*.'

Maggie laughed a little at Joe's impression of his father, a sort of sweet, bumbling academic type that he dropped his voice for.

'That was our thing. *Twelve at the penguins.* We knew all the names of the lions and the hippos and the elephants, when they still had elephants. Some of the animals would have given birth by the time you went back again the following year and there was a sort of a journey to it all, time passing, year on year, some things changing and others feeling the same. There was this giraffe actually, we called him Geraldo.'

'Geraldo?'

'Geraldo Giraffe, that was our name for him, although he was probably called something far more boring. He was very young when we first started going and every year we would go and see him and he would be a little bit bigger and a little bit more independent. We watched him all way through his life until he died about five or six years ago.'

'Oh, no!'

'It was OK. It didn't feel sad really, it just felt like we had watched this lovely, beautiful life together. The last time we went to the zoo was the year before dad died. It's probably my favourite memory of him actually. Favourite last memory, anyway. Sitting on a bench some-where near the camels, drinking a cup of tea, chatting about . . . I don't even know what.'

'That sounds really lovely,' she said, and she had an image then of Joe as a child, what he would have been like, in shorts and a homemade sweater perhaps, scuffed knees and his thick curly hair and first pair of glasses. She thought about him holding his father's hand, his mother waving them off from the door, the adventures they went on together. Then later, as a teenager, the hair slicked back, the glasses looking awkward, the body not yet grown into. She had a flash of him then as he was at school; nervous, quiet, always studious, greeting his father at the car, and even though she was right there with him, lying as close to him as she possibly could be, she also wanted to be alone so she could just lie there and think about him.

'How many good memories do you think is enough?' she said after a while. 'Are one or two good ones OK? Or do we need to keep adding to them to top it all up?'

He thought for a moment and then said, 'I think we have to work with what we have.'

'But how do you think we work out which ones are worth keeping?'

'I think we have to trust that the ones we remember are the right ones.'

Joe came over every night after work for the next two days, and then stayed all weekend, and whether George knew somehow that Maggie had a guest, or whether he was just too busy with Pamela and the play, and all that that entailed, he never came back. The house was a different place to Maggie then, different from when they lived in it as children, different from when she lived there alone and even from when she was there with George. It was a whole new space, somehow; softer, smaller and almost, Maggie felt, suspended in time.

They moved between the kitchen and the bedroom. Maggie made food, simple, easy things for supper: pasta and roasted vegetables and eggs again, and again, and on the days when Joe was not at work, they lay out in the garden on Queen Vic's old tartan picnic rug and Maggie marvelled at the colour and brightness of the world. Being at the Manor House made complete sense to her then, the time she had spent alone, the time with George and now the time with Joe, each stage following the next in an order and a progression that felt like it was all heading towards something bigger and better. She was filling the house with love and more happiness than she had ever known, and then she would let it go.

After four days together, Maggie felt as if they had covered most of the important topics of conversation: whether baked beans were better than spaghetti hoops, Wotsits or Quavers, Dairy Milk or Galaxy, Beatles or the Stones, city or country, biscuits and toast, telly and tea, jobs, travelling, marriage or no marriage, children or no children . . . life in every permeation. Being with Joe felt like picking up a favourite book, one where the best bits had the pages folded over, sentences underlined, familiar passages marked with pencil, as they stepped back into their younger selves over and over again. They talked about school and family, they talked about exes, about Stephanie and then Susie, and he had told her it had been a series of dates and not much more. Then he had asked about her, and she had known that it was coming. He wanted to know what had gone wrong, why had she run away that first time and was she going to do it again?

'I lived in Paris before I moved back here. I did a cooking course. French food, obviously, and I met a man there.'

'French, obviously?'

Maggie nodded. They were sitting on the floor of her bedroom, their backs against the bed in just their underwear, and they did not know what time it was or even what day.

'He was married. He was older. He was the chef, actually. The course leader.'

'Right.'

'I didn't feel very good about it. I felt terrible really, but he said he was unhappy and that he was getting divorced and I believed him.'

'But he didn't?'

'No. No, he didn't. But I hung around for a long time thinking he would. I have a bit of a knack for choosing unavailable men. Or choosing good ones and then fucking it all up. It's a bit of a skill.'

'What was his name?'

'The French guy? Serge.'

'*Serge?*'

'Yep.'

Joe broke into laughter.

'What?' Maggie said. '*What?*'

'Sorry, sorry, I didn't mean to laugh. It's just, well, it's a *very* French name.'

'He was *very* French. He used to stand naked on the balcony, smoking Gauloises.'

'Oh, wow,' Joe said with a chuckle.

'He was horrible really. He was mean.'

'I'm sorry, Maggie,' he said, lifting her hand to kiss it. 'Is that why—?'

'—No. No, not him. It's not really why . . . I don't know. I find it hard to let people in and I had with him. He didn't deserve it.'

'Serge! *Je t'aime Serge, je t'aime! Je t'aime*!' Joe said in a ridiculously exaggerated French accent and Maggie laughed, swivelling over so that she was sitting on top of him, her legs straddling his.

'Stop it!' she giggled, grabbing his hands. 'That's enough!'

'But Serge, you are *so* sexy!'

'Oh, my God, your accent is so terrible!'

'Come here, you,' he said, pulling her in very slowly for a kiss. '*Serge est très, très stupide. Serge est un idiote*!'

'*Serge est un trou du cul*!'

'What does that mean?'

'It means "Serge is a butthole".'

'Ah, *formidable*!'

'Your French really is very, *very* good,' Maggie teased, leaning in to kiss him again, her hands in his hair and then on his face. 'You're practically fluent. What else can you say?'

'I can say "*Je m'appelle Joe, et j'habite à Great Martin*."'

She sat back then, smiling at him, and he wrapped his arms tightly around her waist.

'Rubbish. What else?'

'*Je suis très heureux, madame Maggie*. I am very, very happy.'

'That's very good. Anything else?'

He pulled her in slightly, his eyes fixed steadily on hers. 'I can say "*J'adore*, Maggie",' and then, quieter, almost a whisper. '*Je t'aime de tout mon coeur.*'

'I love you too,' Maggie said, the words tumbling out so effortlessly it felt as if they had just been waiting there all along. It all felt so easy, so *perfect*, that she laughed.

'It feels nice, saying that. I like saying it.'

'I like saying it too,' he said, stroking the hair from her face and pulling her in a little closer. She could feel him sigh then, a heaviness settling in his limbs.

'What is it?' she said. 'You're worried about something. You're worried about me, aren't you?'

'I know it's not been very long, Maggie, and I don't want to scare you, I really don't, but if there's any doubt in your mind about all of this, if you're worried that it's not what you want, can you please tell me? It's just that I have a sort of feeling that I don't think I have ever had before, and it's wonderful and also quite terrifying and I might need to make it stop somehow if you think you might decide that I am in fact very dull and boring and not at all what you were looking for.'

She put her hand on his cheek, the deep, warm brown of his eyes seeming like the safest and most comforting place you could ever wish to be.

'I know it's because you are scared, Maggie. I know you find it hard to trust people, and you look for things to not like about them because you worry they are going to hurt you and they are going to leave, and I understand that, I really do. But I think it's going to be OK. I just have a feeling about it, and I know that sounds mad and you probably want to run away now, but I had to tell you. I'm not going to leave, Maggie. Not unless you want me to.'

She sat quietly for a moment, gathering up his words, and she knew that she would hold on to them for as long as she possibly could. Then she lay her head on his chest. She still did not know what the time was and neither did she care.

Chapter 18

'Look at us,' Maggie said to Liz a few days later, as both sisters were dressed and ready to go to work on the front steps of the Manor House. Liz was in her suit, dropping Lily off with George before catching the train to Oxford, and Maggie was already in her apron, wooden spoon in hand. 'We look like those pictures outside the job centre that advertise fun and exciting career opportunities!'

'I look ridiculous,' Liz huffed, tugging her suit jacket down.

'You're City Girl – smart, professional, got great A-levels – and I'm the one who went to the crap polytechnic and serves school lunches.'

'Can we not do all that today?'

'What?'

'You, moaning, comparing yourself to me.'

'OK. Sorry.'

'I mean, does this skirt even fit me? I've had three children in this stomach since I bought this.'

'You look great,' Maggie said.

'Do people even wear skirts anymore?'

'You look like an accountant.'

'*Really*? Are you sure?' This was possibly the best thing Maggie could have said to her.

'I've forgotten how to do all of this,' she said, her face scrunched up and anxious.

Maggie stepped out of the front door so that she was on the same step as Liz. She took her hand and looked into her eyes. 'It will all be fine once you get there. You know how to do *all* of it, Liz. Better than anyone. They're all idiots and you are amazing.'

'What if I have forgotten everything?' she asked.

'You haven't! Plus, you're only going in to see everyone aren't you? Check back in? Remind them all how bloody brilliant you are?'

Liz nodded and then dipped her chin slightly so she could kiss Lily's head.

'Thanks, Maggie.'

Maggie smiled at her. Liz would never accept impromptu compliments and was seldom vulnerable enough to ask for them, so when Maggie was given the chance to tell Liz how wonderful she was, she wanted to do it as best as she possibly could.

'What time is the train?' she asked.

'I don't know. Soon. Where's Dad?'

'He's having his morning bath.'

'Do you mind taking this then?' she said, passing over Lily. 'I don't want to miss it.'

'OK, no problem,' Maggie said, taking Lily and resting her on her hip. 'Are you sure she can handle the pace of an eightieth-birthday lunch? It might get pretty rowdy!'

Liz smiled at her before a small frown appeared between her eyebrows and she quickly looked away again. She touched her throat and then straightened her skirt, anxiously tugging at its edges. An apology was coming. Either that or she was going to be sick.

'I'm very sorry about the other night, Maggie,' she said, quietly. 'I was very out of sorts and I drank too much wine and I'm really sorry.'

'Oh, don't worry,' Maggie said with a shrug, although she was a little taken aback. Liz rarely apologised for anything.

'Please say sorry to Joe too. I like him.'

'OK.'

'He's great, Maggie. I like him a lot.'

'OK!'

'I hope that he likes me too.'

'*Of course,* he does, Liz. Everything is fine.'

'I should go, shouldn't I?'

Maggie nodded at her, suddenly desperate to give her a hug. 'And Liz,' she said, taking her hand, 'try not to think about her today.'

Liz smiled at her sister, although she would have preferred to cry. 'Everything will be much better when I get back to work,' she said, and she hurried off to get the train.

It did occur to Liz that thoughts of Pat only made an appearance on the train to work because it was one of the few times that she was able to sit very quietly, undisturbed by small voices, and let her mind wander. She had dismissed this notion fairly swiftly as it would mean that Pat was always there, just waiting to be invited in on the back of a daydream, and Liz had never quite been able to give her mother quite that much weight. The journey was only fifteen minutes, twenty at most, but it took just five for her to appear, sat next to her there, on that rare empty seat. She was not surprised that she appeared that morning. She wasn't happy and she wasn't sad, just unsurprised. Pat had been there when she went back after having Tom, and then again with Sophie, a reminder of what they had in common: work.

'Your mother couldn't wait to get back to work,' she remembered George saying over and over again when she was young, sometimes with the emphasis on 'wait' and sometimes on 'work' and Liz not knowing which one was worse or if any of it was her fault. And here was Liz, not waiting to get back to work.

You're not meant to think about people who leave. They don't deserve your time. Liz didn't need to be told that. She had succeeded in not thinking about Pat for most of her adult life, even through weddings and babies and all those tiny beautiful/awful moments in between. But here Pat was again, on the 8.09 to Oxford, and then by her side on the short walk to her office, through the front door and up the stairs, along to corridor to her old desk and still Liz did not know what to do with her.

'She just wasn't meant to be here,' Queen Vic had told her after she left, as though Pat had been a character in a novel or a play who had stumbled into the wrong plot and had to extricate herself so that she could find the right story. They were all just trying to work their way through their own plots, weren't they? Lurching about the stage, looking for the right characters, the right endings. But children were different though. You couldn't rewrite them, and it was only when she became a parent herself that she really understood why Queen Vic had said it. How else do you explain a mother leaving her children? Liz had no idea.

The party for Elsa Gibbs's eightieth-birthday was only a short drive away at the new Martin St John village hall, and although George wasn't officially invited, an extra space was soon made for him at one of the tables. George had helped Maggie load the food into the car, then out of then car, and then he passed round the asparagus fritters and the broad-bean bruschetta while making sure that everyone had drinks. By the time Mrs Wilson, quivering and pink-cheeked from white wine, had asked him to join them, Maggie didn't really need him anymore. She had two part-time servers, Tammy and Kathy, who she occasionally borrowed from The Owl for a few hours, and George was in fact far more useful sitting at the table, explaining what each of the dishes was and how beautifully they had been made. As the main course was cleared and the lemon and lavender posset was passed around, Elsa Gibbs said it was the best food she had ever eaten. Everyone did.

'She's going to open a restaurant you know,' George said, popping a small macaron into his mouth. After a few heavy morning showers, the sun was now pushing through the doors and windows of the hall, lighting up tiny flecks of floating dust as if they were glitter, and there was George, in the centre of it all, warming everyone and everything around him.

'A restaurant? How marvellous,' Mrs Wilson said, her eyes wide and watery. He had at least six elderly women completely captivated, with more on the periphery.

'Oh, yes, yes,' George continued, his arms resting on his chest. 'There's already people enquiring from London.'

'*London*?' Mrs Wilson said. 'Crikey!'

'And offers from further afield.'

'Are there really?' another woman said, as more grey heads leaned in.

'It won't be long before she gets poached. London first, but then who knows where? New York, Paris, Montreal, Miami. If it was me, I would book her in as soon as you can. Tell all your friends. Tell everyone, because mark my words, ladies, mark my words, she's going to be in *very* high demand.'

'Well, I am not surprised in the least,' Mrs Wilson declared. 'Are you Barbara? Are you surprised? No, we're not surprised at all.'

He then began to talk about a meal Maggie had cooked for him at the Manor House one day that had almost made him cry tears of happiness before somehow segueing into his time on the *Antiques Roadshow*. If Elsa Gibbs hadn't been the easy-going type, if she hadn't had an ongoing issue with one of her hearing aids, she might have felt a slight pang of regret that her eightieth-birthday lunch was moving in ever decreasing circles around and around the plug hole of George.

But the sunshine had pushed the remaining rain clouds away and Maggie suggested tea and cake outside in the garden, which Elsa thought was a wonderful idea. Tammy and Kathy helped clear the tables and reset the tablecloths and flowers outside and everyone gathered around her to sing 'Happy Birthday'. George put Lily in the baby carrier and walked around the periphery, arms behind his back like he was surveying the troops, while a series of ladies took turns to float over in their floral frocks to coo and squeeze Lily's pudgy calves. At one point, there was almost a queue.

'You're doing rather well,' Maggie said as she finished tidying up and came outside to join him. 'You've got quite the fan club.'

'I think it's Lily's fan club really, darling,' he said. 'I'm just the chauffeur.'

'Nonsense. They all love you. Mrs Wilson is practically throwing her enormous pants at you.'

'Good lord!' he snorted.

Maggie laughed. 'It's quite something, seeing you in action.'

'Rhubarb! I am vouched for now anyway. Pamela has taken me off the peg and I am a very lucky man. Very lucky indeed.'

'Yes, you are.'

'Things are looking up, Margaret, aren't they?'

'I hope so, Dad,' she said, smiling up at him. 'It might finally be our time.'

George put his arm around her shoulder and squeezed it tight. 'I had a very strange feeling earlier,' he said. 'In my chest.'

'Oh, Dad,' Maggie sighed. 'You've probably just overeaten. Or been petted by too many grannies.'

'I'm very proud of you, Maggie' he said. 'That's what it was, I think. It was pride. It sort of comes up from your toes and rests somewhere here, near your heart.' He placed his hand on Lily's chest, where his heart would be underneath. She smiled and kicked and reached up to meet his hand with hers. 'It's a nice feeling. It's rather wonderful, actually.'

Maggie smiled at him and then playfully batted his arm away.

'Either that or I have stomach cancer.'

'*Dad*! You don't have bloody stomach cancer!' Maggie laughed.

'Well then, it was a lot of pride, all at once.'

'It was only lunch, Dad. You know I do this sort of thing all the time.'

'Well, I thought it was wonderful. Everyone did.'

'Mrs Wilson asked me when 'the restaurant' was opening. I suppose it makes sense now.'

'Well, she's a very canny woman that Mrs Wilson,' he said. 'Very canny.'

'If by canny you mean randy, she's not the only one, Dad. I'd watch out if I was you,' Maggie said, pointing to a group of women who were all looking over at them, beaming.

'I can heartily recommend getting one of these if you want to make friends,' he said, pointing down at Lily.

'Oh, right. I'll just pop down to the shops to get one, shall I?'

He laughed. 'Very funny,' he said, smiling at her.

'Ha ha!'

'Bit harder to get your hands on one as you get older, I hear.'

'Don't write me off quite yet, Dad. I'm not *that* old. Or even against the whole thing. I just haven't met anyone I want to have them with yet.'

'Ah,' he said, nodding his head for a few seconds. 'Are you sure?'

'It's not been that long, Dad. Steady on!'

'Don't let what happened with all of us put you off,' he said. 'I suspect you would do a far better job at parenting than me, darling,'

'I think the bar might be quite low on that one,' she laughed.

'Well, quite!'

George busied himself with the strap on Lily's baby carrier for a minute before checking his watch.

'Well, I'd better get going in a minute. It's the school fête thingy, if you wanted to come along? Tom and Sophie are involved with some dance thing, I think.'

'No, no thank you. I better get everything sorted out here.'

'Yes, of course.'

'You go. Have a good time.'

'Righty-ho.'

He began to walk away and then turned, as if he had suddenly forgotten something. Lily licked her legs hard and made a sort of squawking sound.

'I've really enjoyed today, Maggie. Thank you.'

'No problem, Dad,' she said. 'Me too.'

'I know Liz is keeping me quite busy, but if there's anything else you wanted us to do together—'

'—do you fancy a trip to the zoo?'

'The *zoo*?'

'Yeah, you know, all the animals. Lions, giraffes, fathers and daughters, that sort of thing. It might be fun?'

She was sure he was going to say no, or what a silly idea, but his face lit up, his smile widening almost to the very edge of his face. 'I'd like that,' he said. 'I'd like that very much.'

Chapter 19

Liz was fairly sure that her new line manager, Rachel, was straight out of university. Either that or she just didn't have children, or a husband, or a sister, or a father like the one she had, or a school fête to go to. There was a brightness to Rachel, an energy and alertness that Liz remembered having once but could no longer seem to find, even on days when she'd had a good night's sleep. She was flawlessly turned out, trim and neat and not overdone in any way, her blouse and jacket perfectly matched, her hair cut and dyed impeccably, and as Liz looked across the desk at her, she had the horrible realisation that her own standards had slipped without her even realising it. This was how Liz used to be. This was the Liz she hoped she might be reclaiming but wondered if she ever really could.

The small talk was minimal, thankfully, although after Rachel had asked how her 'time off' had been, Liz immediately felt irritated and defensive and wanted to say that she had spent a lot of it on the sofa with one boob out while her tea got cold, or trying to encourage her son to like her again, or dealing with unexpected corgis or fathers and a sister who kept sleeping with a man with no morals who owned a hot tub. She wanted to say that she hadn't actually needed another baby and would have much rather been at work than having to deal with all of her family, but now that Lily was here and she had just about got used to the whole thing, she was completely, wholeheartedly, unashamedly in love with her. She wanted to tell her that when Lily smiled, her heart felt as if it swelled a little, like it had just been topped up, and that just when she thought she couldn't fill it up anymore, it seemed to grow even bigger and then overflow.

She wanted to tell her that being a parent was the hardest thing she had ever done, the thing she worried every day about not being good enough at, the thing that she was quite possibly better at than anything else. She wanted to say that she worried she only enjoyed work so much because it was just so much easier. She wanted to say all of this, and so much more.

'We really value your knowledge, Elizabeth,' Rachel said at one point, her smile fixed and corporate. 'Not many here have your *decades* of experience.'

'Thank you,' Liz replied, forcing a smile in return.

'I am sure you know that there has been some restructuring with our older, more established customer base. We have had a few clients move abroad which means that we are refocusing our efforts on our UK base.'

'Yes, of course,' Liz said.

'The Taylor account is now based out of Leeds, of all places.'

'Oh? That's an interesting move.'

'It does seem a little odd. Most of their exports go from the south coast, but more and more businesses are moving north these days. The infrastructure is improving all the time and the workforce is very diverse.'

'And everything is online these days, I suppose,' Liz said. 'More and more people are working from home.'

'They are, yes, and we are going to be introducing some hybrid working. However, we do like to think of ourselves as a traditional company who offer a hands-on service. We think that really does help us to stand out from our competitors, as I am sure you know from your time here. We feel our clients choose us because we retain some of the older, more conventional work practices. They like to see our faces, as well as talk to us on Zoom.'

Liz could feel her teeth begin to clamp shut. How was Rachel a '*we*'? Rachel was probably still using plastic cutlery when Liz started accountancy. She was probably in school pinafores when Liz started at that very firm. Did having another maternity leave really necessitate Liz being talked to as if she was some sort of apprentice? Had it become some awful game of Snakes and Ladders and she had slipped down that horrible big one just as she was about to get near the top?

'So, with all of that in mind, Elizabeth, the good news is that when you return, you will be able to spend two or three days a week in Leeds getting some real hands-on experience again.'

'*Me?*' Liz said, her eyes blinking fast, her hands tightening on that ill-fitting skirt that she now wanted to rip apart and trample on.

'Yes,' Rachel said. 'We know you like to be right in the thick of it all.'

'I'm not sure that would actually be right for me,' she said, leaning forward so that her arms could rest on the desk. 'It might be difficult with the children.'

'We can talk about it again, but it would be a very good opportunity for you, Elizabeth. Your core competencies really are in that face-to-face interaction that clients look to us for.'

'But Leeds is quite a distance, isn't it; and with all the travel I wouldn't be around at home very much, would I?'

Rachel smiled. Clearly this was not something that she cared about. 'We can talk about the details another time. It really is such a great opportunity.'

As Liz approached the school gates, she felt her legs begin to inexplicably slow, her arms feeling heavy, her body stagnating and turning into something solid and immovable. It was, she realised, the sensation of returning to the rest of her life.

Even from some distance, she could hear the music from the fête, the school's ancient stereo system stretched out into the playground on its long extension lead, its sound tinny and muffled as if partially submerged in water. She could see as she approached the entrance that the turnout was better than the school had expected, the playground almost full with children, parents and grandparents. As she got to the railings alongside the main gates, the red and white bunting buffeting in the breeze, she squinted slightly in the late afternoon sun as she looked for Tom, Sophie, George and Lily.

Across the tarmac she saw a man waving to her, his face painted thickly in orange and black stripes like a tiger, and he had a child on his shoulders. He was talking to a small group of people, six or seven, one of whom she immediately recognised as Sarah Jackobsen, looking beautiful in an apple-green dress, her red hair warmed to peach melba in the sunshine. Then there was a toddler, Monty, looking pink and robust and even more like Gary bloody Barlow in a navy and white sailors outfit. As her eyes scanned the group Liz felt her cheeks begin to get hot as she realised that the man next to Monty was Dr Jackobsen, Dr Erik Jackobsen, in shorts and a white linen shirt with a glorious early summer tan. She took a sharp intake of breath and immediately felt sick with regret that she was wearing the awful, hideous work skirt and ugly, flat black shoes when she could be in something soft and floaty and gorgeous.

The man waved again, and just as she was about to turn around run home she realised that it was George, George and Sophie. There was Pamela too, wearing a pink catsuit, her distinctive curls bouncing in the breeze as she chatted to a group of mums, and then Lily, beautiful, sweet Lily in her buggy with a packet of crisps, her blonde hair almost white in the sun, and Sophie, now on the ground and skipping around, dressed as a fairy with wings and a wand. Tom stood nearby in his Morris dancing costume, looking remarkably good-humoured, despite saying he would never, ever put the outfit on as it made him look like an idiot. She watched them from across the playground, their dancing and chatting and laughing, and felt such an instant rush of love for them all that she gasped a little, placing her hand onto her chest so that she could feel her heart start to beat faster.

'Hello, darling,' George beamed as she walked over, trying not to tug at her skirt. 'How was it all at the office?'

'It was awful, actually,' Liz said with a smile.

'Those idiots,' George said, pulling her towards him for a hug. 'What happened?'

'It's all fine, Dad. I'm here now.'

'Well, this one has been missing you terribly,' he said, wheeling Lily over in her buggy. 'She's been quite agitated, really. I did tell her that you had a very important meeting but you know what these babies are like. It's all me, me, me!'

'*Really*?' Liz said, as she leant down to pick her up. 'She's been missing *me*?'

'We all have,' George said. 'Haven't we, Sophie?'

Sophie skipped over and wrapped herself around Liz's legs, and Tom lifted his hand briefly in a wave and Liz found herself laughing, the relief of being with them again feeling almost euphoric. 'You've been missing me? Really?'

'I've been telling them some of my very best jokes, but I am afraid it's not cutting the mustard.'

'You just need to chat to them really, Dad. They don't need a big song and dance.'

'Speaking of, we have had some wonderful dancing, haven't we, Tom?' George ruffled Tom's hair, and he smiled up at his grandfather. 'They said I can join the troupe next year if I am very, very good.'

'Mrs Jones said he could be the *lead* Morris dancer, Mum,' Tom said. She's going to get him a costume and everything!'

'Gosh, did she? Liz said, feeling slightly alarmed at the prospect.

'We'll see, Tom,' George said, smiling at Liz. 'We'll see.

'Another thing ticked off the list though, Dad,' she said. 'The school event! You probably get some bonus points for this one.'

While they had been talking, the group of mums who had been chatting to Pamela had begun to gather around, at least seven or eight of them, most of whom Liz recognised from the school gates but no one she knew very well. Sarah was there, along with some of her friends, and they were all smiling at Liz and saying hello and she suddenly worried that there was a joke that she wasn't in on.

'Hello,' Liz said back. 'How is everyone?'

'Hi, Liz,' Sarah said. 'It's great to see you. You look wonderful.'

'Oh? Wow. *Me*? Thank you. It's just a boring work outfit really. I didn't have time to get changed.'

'You dad was telling us all about it, and everything before. It sounds so interesting.'

'*So* interesting,' another one said, and suddenly it seemed as if there were three or four more of them, all standing around Liz and looking interested. Interested in *her*. George sidled up to her then, proudly putting his arm around her shoulder, and Liz found herself leaning into it, leaning into all of it.

'Well, it can be, yes,' she said. 'It can also be a bit shit.'

The women all laughed. George laughed, and it was as if she had said something exceptionally funny, and Liz had a sudden vivid memory of childhood birthday parties at the Manor, of being surrounded by classmates that she didn't really know, and the awful worry about whether they were going to have a good time. Perhaps it was because George was there, his face painted like a tiger, that they had gone back to the days when the other girls were only nice to Liz when parents were in the room. These women did not usually give her this much attention. They didn't give her any attention at all.

'We must get Lily and Toby together soon,' said one of the mothers. She had a baby around Lily's age in her arms. 'I'll set something up.'

'Great, great,' Liz said.

'And we must get you and Doug over for dinner,' Sarah said.

'That would be lovely, thank you.'

'Doug's into his running, isn't he?' Sarah said. 'He and Erick can bore each other about protein shakes and personal bests.'

And then the conversation turned to summer holiday clubs and sports day and the ice-pop stall running out of ice pops again and why a mum called Louise always swiped the leftover cakes from the cake sale, and Liz was stood in the middle of it all, right in the middle, quite happily joining in.

Chapter 20

They started at the penguins.

'Look, they're feeding them at eleven,' Maggie said. They were standing at a large zoo map with the 'YOU ARE HERE' sticker on it. Maggie wondered if it was also a marker of where she was in her relationship with George. This was the day-trip stage. This was bonding over animals and eating ice creams and talking about life. This was progress.

'Penguins it is then,' he said, and they walked the short distance to a walled garden area with a number of smaller enclosures in it. A group of children in high-vis jackets were milling around a low barrier and in front of them, on the other side, stood a young man with mousy hair and a goatee, wearing a green uniform and holding a bucket.

'Who can tell me how old our oldest penguin is?' the man said, before pulling a small silver fish out of the bucket and tossing it behind him. Maggie stood on her tiptoes to see a small crowd of penguins in their rocky enclosure, all eagerly awaiting a snack.

'One-hundred and fifty,' a child said, his arm waving for attention while another yelled, 'One-thousand and ten!'

'No, no, that's a bit too old, I think,' the man said, gently. 'How about something a little bit younger?'

'Three!' a small girl shouted out.

'A bit older than that. How old do you think I am?'

'Err, fifty?' a small boy asked, to which the man pulled a funny horrified face.

'Oh dear, oh dear,' he said laughing and shaking his head. 'Do I really look *that* old?'

The children laughed. 'Ten!' someone then said. 'Twenty!'

'That's close, *very* close. It's twenty-eight, and he's very old now. Most penguins only make it to their late teens, some a lot younger when they live in the wild. There are all sorts of predators who might kill them before they can reach maturity. Killer whales, sharks . . .'

The children took a collective intake of breath before breaking into some general nudging and there was an audible whisper of 'Sharks, sharks, sharks!' among them all. Maggie could hear George quietly chuckling beside her.

'What?' she said, smiling up at him. The children were moving en masse towards the meerkats so she and George had been able to move right up to the barrier to get a closer look. The penguins were rearranging themselves onto the rocks after their snack, a couple diving in and out of the enclosure's pool while another lay prostrate on a small wooden pontoon.

'Isn't it absurd that penguins only get to twenty, twenty-eight, tops, and we all have to plod on until our eighties or nineties? Why *us* for goodness sake? Look how ridiculous we are!'

'It's just brain size, isn't it?' she said with a shrug, thinking that this really should be the time to mention his tinned-tuna coloured safari suit, if only she could find the right words.

'A mistake has been made somewhere. None of it makes any sense.'

'Maybe twenty years of being a penguin is enough?' Maggie said. 'Maybe they don't want any more than that? Life is probably quite repetitive for a penguin, don't you think?'

They watched as one of the smaller penguins happily waddled along a ridge beside the pool, completely oblivious to the gawping visitors who were trying to take a photo of him. He shook his tail-feathers out and then dived under the water, re-emerging on the other side of the pool about half a second later.

'I don't know. Looks rather fun to me. Quite a bit of lounging about.'

'They're complete posers. You'd fit right in!'

'It's more that they don't have much to worry about, do they? There are the sharks and whales and what have you, but they're not worried about money or bills or remembering their bloody lines. They're not worried about *death*. A long life should be like that, shouldn't it? Not filled with endless worry.'

'What's brought all this on?' Maggie said. He had not been himself all day.

George stared into the penguin enclosure, his face blank. 'I'm not sure really, darling,' he said, trying to rally himself. 'I'm just getting on a bit now, aren't I? Poor old George, the elderly penguin at the local zoo.'

'Oh, come on, Dad, you're not *elderly*. Look at you! You're fine. You're more than fine. You're having a second wind, a whole other go at life.'

'I have been pondering and I don't think I want to be buried after all, if that's all right?'

'OK.'

'What if I don't like the person they put me next to?'

'I'm not sure it will matter by then, will it, Dad?'

'But the people who are buried with their loved ones have each other, don't they? The single ones, like me, they just have to muck in together.'

'Perhaps you should go for cremation. Less complicated all round.'

'Yes, yes I think you're right. And scatter me over the hills at the back of the village, will you?'

'OK,' Maggie said.

'You see, if I'd only had twenty years, like the penguins, I might have got all of it right a bit sooner.'

'What do you mean?'

'You never think you'll get old, not really, but then one day you are and it's all too late. I should have done it all earlier, Maggie. You know, being a parent, spending time with you all. I should have done it from the start like everyone else. I just didn't realise it could be so . . . *right*.'

Maggie laughed, in spite of George's pained expression. What an unusual choice of word she thought. 'Right', not good, or great or wonderful. She looked at his face, the deep lines creased inwards as if he was waiting for a blow to the stomach. What could she possibly say to make it better? What can you possibly say that would sum up a lifetime?

'It's OK,' she said, eventually. 'Vic did a great job.'

He smiled at her and nodded his head.

'I just don't think I was very suited to being asked for things,' he said, and it seemed so honest, so matter of fact and mundane, like a type of food he didn't like, that Maggie wondered for a moment if he genuinely wasn't capable of reciprocation, at least not in the long term. A design flaw, like a chip that was missing from a circuit board, rather than something he just couldn't be bothered to do because it was hard and messy and sometimes you put more in than you got back. If only they could study men like George under a microscope, dissect and examine them, discover that there was a defect, then Maggie would realise that everything she had ever hoped to receive from him, from other men like him, was always going to be futile. It wouldn't have been her fault.

'You're good at other stuff, Dad,' she said. 'I mean, we can't be good at *everything*, can we?'

George sighed heavily and gripped the railing to the enclosure before moving off to sit on a nearby bench.

'Come on, Dad,' Maggie said, following him. 'Let's cheer up, shall we? This is meant to be a fun father and daughter thing. My one thing from the list! Why don't we go and say hello to the meerkats?'

'I have to tell you something very disappointing I'm afraid,' he said, his head bowed.

'Oh?'

'I've done a bad thing.'

'How bad?'

'I would say, quite bad.'

'Right.'

'There is no Rhonda,' he said, slowly. 'No Rhonda at all.'

'What does that mean?' Maggie asked.

'I made her up.'

'You *made Rhonda up*?'

'Yes. I made all of it up. I wanted you to feel sorry for me, so I told you that I'd had my heart broken.'

'Why?'

'Because I wanted money. I knew the house sale was going through and I thought you might take pity on me.'

'I don't understand, Dad.'

'It doesn't make any sense to me now either.'

'Wait, so none of it was true? All that stuff about her sister and her being a good cook and the wild boars and the Skoda Yeti?'

George shook his head and Maggie sat quietly for a moment, trying to gauge what her reaction should be. She knew that she should be angry, or even hurt, but all she could feel was confused.

'Why would you do that?'

'Because I am a fool,' he said, quite simply.

'But it's so *stupid*,' Maggie said. 'Why didn't you just ask for money? Tell us what was going on? We would have given it to you. Of course we would.'

George shrugged. 'I like a good story, I suppose,' he said.

'And you're telling me this now because you found Pamela and she's filthy rich and you don't need our help anymore?'

'No. No! I am telling you now because I feel terrible about it and I have realised over the last few months that it's not important anymore. Money, I mean. It never did me any good, Maggie, and I was always hopeless with it. Completely hopeless. I have a small amount from my pension and I don't want anymore. I don't *need* anymore. It's *this* that I want, if I am allowed, this whole thing of being here, with you and your sister. This is what makes me happy.'

Maggie stood up and wandered over to the next enclosure where the meerkats were. There were a dozen or so of them on a rock, some standing guard, some eating and some just lying about, and it was all so easy and amiable that Maggie thought how completely ridiculous humans are in the way they mess everything up.

'You're *not* to tell Liz,' she said as George came to stand alongside her.

'Righty-ho,' he said.

'She's far more anal about everything than me.'

'She blames me for your mother.'

'I know,' Maggie said.

'How is she, do you think? In general?'

'Liz? I think she's OK.'

George nodded his head.

'She's busy, you know, the kids. It makes her a bit grumpy and tense.'

'I gave her a bit of a talking up the other day at that fête thing. Just a bit of a polish and shine, a few added details here and there. You know, a bit more sparkle and pizzazz.'

'*Pizzazz*'?

'PR, then. Rebranding. I think I would have been rather good at that.'

'You're rather good at doing it for yourself.'

He chuckled to himself, in recognition, Maggie hoped.

'Liz needs a bit of a boost, don't you think?'

'I think she probably does, yes.'

They were quiet for a lot of the journey home. George hummed along to the radio and Maggie watched the hills and fields roll by and thought about how, with the passing of each one, she was getting closer and closer to Joe. When they approached the Martins, George was about to turn towards Little Martin when Maggie asked if she could be dropped off at Joe's house in Great Martin. The sun was low in the sky by the time they arrived, a beautiful tangerine orange, and George's tuna coloured suit was now an elegant, warm terracotta. She had only needed to see it in a different light.

'How are you two getting on then?' George asked as they pulled up outside the Church's cottage.

'It's good. I like him. I like him a lot, actually,' she said, feeling the sudden release of butterflies in her stomach.

'He's a good man, Joe. I like him very much.'

'You asked him to stay on after the open day, didn't you?'

'*Me*? Well, I don't know, I might have said something.'

'Thanks, Dad,' she said, smiling at him.

'I don't think he needed much persuading, darling,' George said.

'Well, I don't know about that. I'm not the easiest.'

'You do know, don't you, that all the good things in you are not from me?'

'What do you mean?'

'They're not from anyone. They're not from me, or your mother, or even your grandmother. They're from the stars, the trees, the flowers, from the air all around us. They've been there all along, just waiting to bloom. You don't have to be like me, Maggie. Nothing in the world says that you have to be like anyone other than yourself.'

Maggie laughed, although she wasn't quite sure why. The two of them outside Joe's house, the whole day at the zoo, his words, it all seemed so otherworldly.

'Off you go then,' George said gently, tipping his head towards the passenger seat door.

'Right. Well, nighty night. Thanks for a great day.'

She looked out of the window for a moment, not quite ready to leave.

'Rhonda though, Dad. *Rhonda*?'

George laughed then, loudly. 'I know, I know,' he said, shaking his head. 'The Beach Boys, I suppose.'

'Oh, yes! "Help me Rhonda, help, help me, Rhonda",' Maggie sang softly.

'"Help me, Rhonda, get her out of my heart."'

'But can we not do that again, Dad?' she said, suddenly feeling all the mirth evaporate. 'Can we just be upfront with each other from now on? That's all I really want from you. For the list. No more lies. No more stories. That's it. I don't need anything else.'

'Of course,' he said.

She smiled and kissed him on the cheek.

'I love you, Dad.'

'I love you too, Maggie.'

'Well, bye.'

'Goodbye, darling. And don't do anything that I wouldn't do.'

Maggie laughed. 'No chance of that, Dad,' she said, getting out of the car and shutting the door behind her and George blew her a kiss through the window before driving off into the dusky evening light.

Chapter 21

The weather had been on everyone's minds in the run up to opening night. After weeks of sunshine, the temperature dropped and the rain washed in and plans were made to move the performance from Martin St John's large village green to the school hall. This was an enormous disappointment, not just because the hall always smelt strongly of mince, but because they didn't really have a set.

Liz thought that if she had to listen to one more conversation about whether the play should be held outside in the school gardens as originally planned, or inside in the school hall, she might actually cry. After weeks of sunshine and warmth, the clouds arrived on the August bank holiday weekend, sitting stubbornly over the Martins and spitting intermittently onto the outdoor set. If there was a competition for the longest and most protracted discourse on the weather – and being England, there surely must be – then Liz believed that those involved with The Martin Players production of *A Midsummer Night's Dream* would win.

Did Liz feel that the BBC had the most accurate weather, or was it in fact the Met Office? Did the Met Office supply the BBC with their weather reports, or did they have their own information, and if so, was it government sponsored? How much rain was *too* much rain and what type of rain might be acceptable? Would a light mist be tolerable, and was mist the same as mizzle or even the same as drizzle? Did they need to provide disposable plastic ponchos like the ones you wore on a log flume, and how was the management of umbrellas going to work? On which day and exactly what hour would the decision be made, and should it be a joint one, or just the director? And if the rain was too heavy, was the set from the school's recent production of *Oh! What A Lovely War* suitable for *A Midsummer Night's Dream*, and if not, could some foliage be draped over it to make it a bit more 'woodlandy'?

The discussion could have gone on and on, but the director was fortunately a nervous man and decided to step in and move the whole thing inside. Members of the parish council, of which Liz was still a key player, formed the Village Advancement Group (or VAG, strictly to rhyme with 'bag' as Mrs Wilson found herself explaining), and they had been put in charge of the weather monitoring as well as the opening night party. This was to be a large event incorporating all of the Martin villages and would also be held in the school hall to raise money for a local hospice.

Mrs Wilson, giddy with excitement about the upcoming festivities, had needed to pop round to Fair Meadows at least once a day for reassurance and tea and the endless listing of problems and tasks, never once failing to mention how long it had taken her to get there. Liz wondered if she actually knew how to work her mobile phone, or even her landline for that matter, but suspected that these were the type of conversations that Mrs Wilson needed to do in person, preferably with someone who smiled and nodded and had finally learnt to restrain herself when the aching of tired feet and the great distance travelled to the Executive Family Dwelling was inevitably brought up.

'We need young, strong, healthy men to man the bar. Who do you know, Elizabeth? I would say we need at least four or five,' or 'How many eats will your sister be bringing and will they be an equal mix of savoury and sweet?' Or 'What soft drinks do the young drink these days?' And 'How many people do we need for the coat check?' And over and over again about how many raffle tickets they had sold. The top raffle prize, and probably the only reason that so many tickets had been sold, was an enormous box of meat donated by Mr Wiggins, the butcher, which included a whole side of beef, twenty chickens and enough pork chops to build a another village hall.

Liz often found her mind getting fuzzy and she tried to remember exactly why it was that she had decided to join any village committees in the first place. There was the Liz who wanted to be involved, the Liz who wanted to flex her organisational muscles and be in the thick of village life, and there was the Liz who wanted to burn the whole place down. In recent years, it was the second Liz who really came to the fore.

For reasons that nobody was entirely sure about, the after-party was to be a black-tie affair which meant that everyone had to sit through two hours of Shakespeare in old crunchy taffeta, smelling like moth balls. Liz fumed about the dress code, claiming it was blatantly discriminatory and that mothers of three children didn't own ball gowns or have the money, time or inclination to buy one. Instead she wore one of her work dresses and accessorised it with a pashmina and flesh coloured tights, while Maggie wore a long black satin slip dress she had once bought in Rome to impress a man. Sat side by side on the third row, they had never looked more different, never looked more uniquely themselves and yet they had never been more close. Joe and his mother sat to Maggie's left, Doug and Tom to Liz's right, and as they took their seats next to each other and saw George dressed as the donkey on the front of the programme, Maggie and Liz squeezed each other's hands so tightly that their skin turned white.

'Did you bring any booze?' Liz asked.

'No!'

'That was an error.'

'When does the bar open?' Maggie asked.

'Not till after.'

'*That* was an error.'

Sarah and Erik Jackobsen took their seats on their chairs in the next row, Sarah's red hair hanging down in front of them like a beautiful auburn curtain. Liz reached up to touch her own hair, feeling its short, blunt ends.

'Do you think I should grow my hair?' she whispered to Maggie.

'Why?'

'I don't know. Just for a change.'

Maggie looked ahead of her to where Sarah was sitting and sighed. 'You're not meant to have long and wavy hair, Liz.'

'Why not?'

'You're just not! I am not meant to have a neat bob or be an accountant. It's just the way things are.'

'But what if you want to change things? Do things differently?'

'Are we just talking about hair, Liz?' Maggie said.

Liz frowned. 'Yes, Maggie.'

'Get a fringe instead.'

'I don't want a fringe.'

'You can't have long hair, Liz. Did you forget about the hair tongs?'

Liz paused for a moment, thinking, before her face crumpled. 'Oh, my God,' she said, covering her head with her hands. 'The hair tongs!'

'They were stuck in your hair *all day* Liz, and you carried that thing around at school by the handle because Queen Vic said there wasn't time to untangle it before we had to go and it served you right for wanting curly hair when God gave you straight!'

'She didn't even believe in God.'

'She did when it suited her!'

'Jesus, that's when I cut my hair short, wasn't it? It was so tangled that Vic just hacked it all off with the kitchen scissors!'

Maggie started to laugh while Liz tried to shush her. 'You had the flex and the plug around your neck like a scarf, just hanging there, all day, swinging back and forth around your face.'

Then Liz started to laugh. 'I had to do PE with it, holding the handle while I tried to catch a netball!'

Then they were both laughing, the kind of uncontrollable, aching giggles that only happen when you are sat in a row somewhere, hemmed in by other people, and everyone else is politely whispering. Maggie leant over, her chest heaving, while Liz crossed her legs and said she was going to wet herself, which then only made them both laugh more.

Sarah, sitting straighter and straighter as the laughter erupted behind her, turned around then, smiling coolly, her eyes slightly narrowed and suspicious-looking as Maggie and Liz tried to compose themselves.

'Oh hi, Liz. How are you?' she said.

'Hi, Sarah, sorry, my sister made me laugh. *Stop it* Maggie! Sorry. How are you?'

'We're good, thank you. Hi, Maggie, hi, Doug.'

Maggie had just about managed to pull herself together and she smiled and waved hello before introducing Joe and his mum, who it turned out already knew Erick as he was their dentist.

'Hi, Erick,' Liz said as he turned around, his eyes as blue as the late afternoon sky above them, and she worried again that her face did things she wasn't aware of when she saw him, things that everyone else could see. Erick smiled at her before shaking hands with Doug, who immediately went red as if he was blushing on behalf of his wife.

'How's the dentist world?' Doug asked.

'Not too bad, thank you. How's accountancy?'

'Oh, you know, laugh a minute,' Doug chuckled.

'Your dad is in the play, isn't he?' Sarah said as the husbands settled into a conversation about work and then moved on to running.

'Yes, yes he is,' Liz said.

'Your dad's so great,' she said. 'We *all* love him so much.'

'Oh? Thanks,' Liz replied.

'He makes us all laugh *so* much in baby group. He's hilarious. I wish my dad was more like that.'

'Oh? That's great.'

'Some of us are actually going out for some drinks in Chipping Norton next week if you wanted to come? I've been meaning to text you, but Monty's been teething this week and it's been a total nightmare.'

'Me?'

'Yeah, if you're free.'

'Oh, right,' she replied, briefly glancing at Maggie. 'Yes. That would be great, thank you.'

'There's about eight or nine of us, I think. Should be fun.'

'I'd love to, thanks, Sarah.'

'Great. I'll text you,' Sarah said, before turning back to face the front. Maggie nudged Liz and mouthed, 'mum friends,' at her while Liz settled back in her seat, beaming.

It seemed as if the whole village was there that night, either on stage, or backstage or just sitting in the audience; and as Maggie looked over the faces, she recognised almost everyone around her. There were teachers and school support staff, neighbours from her road, the woman who occasionally babysat for Liz, Ted from the newsagents, their postman, Bill, and the man with a lisp who sometimes worked on reception at the GP. There were the staff from the pub, lots of local farmers, the man who came to their house to sell eggs from his smallholding at the edge of the village and the woman who used to give her and Liz piano lessons when they were younger.

There were a lot of people she used to know from school, some even from her year, and at least two or three boys she had kissed once upon a time, Callum being one of them. She had hardly seen him that summer, although he seemed to know about Joe. He had texted her the nerd emoji, the round face with the glasses, and she had texted back the raised middle finger. She smiled at him now and he winked back at her, and she realised that being there, in the thick of it and surrounded by her past, did not feel awkward or strange or even irritating. Was this what being a settled, well-adjusted adult felt like, Maggie wondered, the first inklings of middle-aged indifference combined with a deep familiarity of your surroundings? Maggie could not have imagined, even a year ago, that she would feel comfortable, that she would feel *happy*, to be so embedded in her community, that she could sit among her fellow villagers and feel so at home. Or maybe it was just what love felt like, when the only person you really care about is the one by your side.

The play had been condensed into an almost palatable length, although Maggie felt that it could have still done with a bit more tightening in places as one or two audience members had successfully napped through some of the longer acts. In hindsight, it seemed so painfully obvious that George should be on a stage, his natural inclination towards theatrics only increasing with age, not to mention his lifelong tendency to say most things as though being watched by a devoted audience. He had, in his eighth decade, found exactly the right place to be, which Maggie thought was quite encouraging, all in all.

There were a number of forgotten lines, the prompt working particularly hard from a chair just off stage, and the man playing Lysander skipped an entire section meaning that he ended up with Helena instead of Hermia. Nobody seemed to mind or to even notice, and when a toddler began to sing the entire *Peppa Pig* theme tune from the second row, there was an enthusiastic round of applause. This is what they came for, Maggie thought. The mistakes are always the good bits.

But the scenes set in the woods were particularly magical, the stage suddenly lit up with hundreds of fairy lights, the actors all dressed in shades of cream and white with daisies in their hair. Pamela looked magnificent in a long silver dress, and George as dapper and handsome as ever in one of his old tweeds, and even though they might have been a little biased, Maggie and Liz thought the two of them were the best by far. Maggie held Joe's hand as Titania and Bottom declared their love for each other, not just because George was trotting around on stage dressed as a donkey, but because the words and the lights and Joe were all so beautiful, that she didn't think she had ever been quite so happy in her whole life.

When it finally ended, both Maggie and Liz got up from their seats and headed to the bar at the back of the hall to help serve drinks. The cast all filed out to take the first of many curtain calls, George taking centre stage for most of them, and as they both poured themselves a drink and waited for the adulation to come to an end, Maggie and Liz were suddenly aware of a presence next to them. A small, barely audible voice said, 'That is George Addison, isn't it?'

The sisters both turned to see a petite, delicate-looking woman with tightly cropped, jet black hair and tired blue eyes, wearing jeans and a navy blazer. She must have been close to seventy, her face a patchwork of lines and sunspots, but there was an elfin beauty to her, despite the obvious nerves.

'Yes, it is,' Liz said. 'He's just doing his tenth, or is it eleventh, bow. We might never get him off the stage to be honest.'

'Is he . . . *sick?*' the woman said, her eyes darting back and forth between Liz and the stage.

'No, no,' Maggie chuckled. 'It's just am-dram.'

'*A Midsummer Night's Dream*,' Liz added.

'George was the donkey. Bottom. He was actually pretty good, don't you think Liz?'

'He was great!'

The woman smiled weakly as she looked back towards the stage. 'It's seems silly really, now that I am standing here,' she said, her voice now shaking a little. 'But I really thought he might be dead.'

Maggie noticed her hands were balled tightly together to make one tangled fist, the knuckles pointed and pale.

'No, no, he's fine,' she said, taking a step towards her. 'He's doing really well, actually. He might have found his *thing*. Oh, and a girlfriend. That's Pamela, up there in the silver dress.'

'Oh,' she said. 'I see.'

'Do you . . . know him well?' Maggie asked.

The woman looked up, her eyes searching Maggie's face, her lips pressed firmly together.

'I used to,' she said, her hands then reaching up to her throat as if she couldn't say anymore. George was looking towards them from the stage, his eyes squinting in the bright white stage lights as recognition began to muddy his face. His jaw dropped first, very slowly, while the rest of his face moved in the opposite direction, eyes widening and forehead raising into tight wrinkles as the colour drained from his cheeks.

'Can we help you with anything?' Liz said. 'We're his daughters. I'm Liz, this is Maggie.'

The smallest of smiles then appeared on the woman's face and she stepped forward to take both of their hands in hers.

'I've heard so much about you both,' she said. 'I'm Rhonda.'

Chapter 22

It was quite a thing to see George so completely undone. Even in his lowest moments he had always retained some level of composure, even if it was laced with theatrics. It took him a good few minutes to regain any sense of poise, and even then, he was not at all himself. He was fidgety and pale, which didn't seem too unusual considering the situation, but there was also heaviness to him, as though he was weighed down and pulled under.

After finally making his way off stage and inside the school to get changed, he had met Liz, Maggie and Rhonda in the headmaster's office, Liz positioned behind the desk with Maggie perched on a stool next to her, while George and Rhonda took the two chairs in front.

'That's where the naughty children normally sit,' Liz said, for lack of a better opening. She had suggested that George and Rhonda have a quiet conversation by themselves, but Rhonda was keen for the four of them do it together, and now they were all sat there, the low beat of the opening-night disco vibrating through the plasterboard walls, the atmosphere felt tense and sickly. Maggie felt a familiar nervousness start to bloom in her stomach. The incumbent headmaster, the youngest the school had ever hired, had filled the once bare and bleak office with pot plants and pictures and what looked like a new rug, but the room was as distinctive to Maggie as it was when she was a student and had been hauled in to talk to Mrs Weatherby. It was the smell that hadn't changed, the grey mince and boiled potatoes and little bottles of Tipp-Ex, and Maggie wondered why on earth she had chosen to be quite so defiant back then. Why hadn't she just made everything easier?

'I certainly picked the wrong day to come, didn't I?' Rhonda said. 'I wouldn't have come if I had known all this was happening. I don't want to be a nuisance, really I don't.'

'Yes, you do,' George said, crossing his arms tightly over his chest. 'That's exactly what you want to do.'

'How did you find us here, Rhonda?' Liz asked.

'Oh, I went to the pub, a lovely little place, and there was a man there who said everyone was here and so I just wandered on over.'

'And can we help you in any way?' Liz asked, her words slow and calm. Maggie recognised the tone of voice as the one she used with her children when she was trying to reason with them.

'She doesn't need help,' George said, rather petulantly. 'She's very capable.'

'You two broke up a while ago now, didn't you? Liz asked.

Maggie looked over to George. She had found herself unable to speak, not just because of the setting and because of what was unfolding in front of her, but because her thoughts felt too tangled and unruly, a messy cartoon scribble in her head. George glanced back at her before quickly looking down at the floor.

'Broke up?' Rhonda stuttered, turning to George. 'I—'

'—Yes,' George said firmly. 'A long while ago now. Things have moved on.'

'Perhaps it would make sense for you to chat alone?' Liz asked gently. 'We can leave you to catch up.'

'No,' snapped George, turning around in his chair so that his back was facing Rhonda. 'I don't have anything to say.'

'Is there anything you . . . *want*, Rhonda?' Liz asked. 'Or something that needs to be sorted out? We're not quite sure why you have come to see us.'

'I don't really know myself now that I am sat here,' she replied. 'Now I see that George is all right.'

'You know that I am more than fine,' George said, throwing his arms up into the air. 'I am fit as a bloody fiddle!'

'When I hadn't heard from you in all those months,' Rhonda sniffed, shaking her head back and forth. 'I thought the worst you see, the very, very worst.'

Nobody spoke then for a second or two as Rhonda sobbed quietly into a hanky that she had retrieved from under her sleeve and George tutted and sighed as though the situation was all incredibly tedious and he had far better places to be.

'We didn't think we would ever see you, Rhonda,' Maggie then said. 'Isn't that right, George? We're all very, *very* surprised that you are here.'

'She shouldn't have come,' George said. 'I did tell her not to.'

'I suppose I should have guessed when you left Albert behind,' Rhonda said. 'What a silly, silly fool I have been.'

'Leave Albert out of it, please,' George said. 'This has nothing to do with him.'

'Who left Albert where?' Liz said.

'Although I did get in an awful muddle with the addresses, didn't I? Did I send him to you, Elizabeth?' Rhonda asked.

'Albert?' Liz nodded. 'Yes.'

'I kept forgetting what the plan was! Poor Albert. Has he been all right?'

'He's been fine,' Maggie said. 'He's doing very well.'

'What *plan*?' Liz said. 'What plan?'

'I am so sorry,' Rhonda said, her voice cracking slightly.

'Can someone *please* explain what this is all about?' Liz continued, her patience now all but gone. This was the voice she used when the reasoning had failed. 'What is going on, George?'

George stood up with a large 'huff' and began to pace around the small room. Rhonda began to sniffle again and seeing that her hanky was now looking rather bedraggled, Maggie handed her a tissue from the box that the headmaster kept on his desk for distressed pupils and staff.

'It seems as if we are *all* owed an explanation,' Maggie said. 'Dad, do you want to tell us what's going on?'

They had met in a bar in Alicante, not long after George had arrived. It would have been hard not to notice him, dressed in his pale linen suit and Panama hat with a jug of Pimms and a corgi by his side. That wardrobe had served him so well over the years. Rhonda was homesick for England and there George was, the living embodiment, looking like he had just stepped out of a Graham Greene novel and feeling sorry for himself. He told her all about the Manor House, about Queen Vic and his two lovely daughters, about the garden, the antiques and life in Little Martin and Rhonda had been intrigued. How could she not have been?

They rented a flat near the sea. They walked Albert on the beach and drank sangria and life was as good as it possibly can be – except for the fact that George did not have the house. He thought about little else, even as the months rolled by and the sun stayed in the sky. He dreamt about it, dreams where he would walk through the Manor's many coloured rooms and corridors searching for something, although he did not know what. Rhonda told him the house should have been his. That was the way things worked, the way things had *always* worked, and he had been mistreated. He had been wronged.

Before long there was a plan. When the house was under offer George would return, heartbroken, lost and needing help. His daughters would take him in and look after him and George would keep an eye on the sale until it had all gone through. Rhonda would then return, armed with the best lawyers and the best paperwork, and even if they didn't get the full amount, they would certainly get something. They would settle somewhere nearby and everything would be repaired and mended in the end because he wasn't a bad person, after all. Not really. He'd just had bad things happen to him.

'We were going to try and get the house,' George said, sitting back down in his chair, his face pale and twitchy. 'Once the sale had gone through and probate was all wrapped up. We were going to contest the will.'

'He told me that it would all be all right, you see,' Rhonda said, turning to Maggie and Liz. '*He* told me that it was the right thing to do. It was all his idea.'

'What do you mean?' Liz said. '*How?*'

George cleared his throat and shifted on his seat. 'We were going to say . . . we were going to say that your grandmother had told me that she wanted *me* to have the house. We had documents. We had fake documents.'

'You don't honestly think you would have *won*, do you?' Liz said, half laughing at the absurdity of it all. 'You don't honestly think anyone would have believed you?'

'No,' George said firmly, and Rhonda's head snapped around sharply to look at him. 'No, I did not. But I thought we might come to a financial arrangement. A settlement.'

'I would come over from Spain,' Rhonda said. 'And we would live here, and it would all be all right by then. That's what he said, girls.'

'Why didn't you tell me?' Maggie said to George. 'Why didn't you just say all of that?'

'But then I didn't hear from him, you see,' Rhonda said. 'I didn't hear a thing.'

'You thought you could get money from *the house*?' Liz said. 'From the house that Queen Vic left us? The house that we have to sell because of *your debts*?'

'Yes,' George said. 'But not anymore.'

'Not anymore?' Rhonda said.

'No. Not anymore.'

'Not anymore?' Liz repeated. 'You don't *need it* anymore?'

'No!' George said, leaping up to his feet again. 'I don't want it. I don't want any of this.'

'So, this whole thing has been a lie?' Liz said, standing up from behind the desk. 'You were going to *scam* us?'

'I wanted to tell you,' George said, looking then at Maggie. 'I just wasn't sure how to.'

'That's why you wanted to push the sale through. That's why you wanted to do the open day and to take the highest offer.'

'Not just that, no.'

'You were going to take the money and then just leave? Just like that?'

George shook his head.

'So what's changed, George?' Liz continued, her voice getting louder. 'It couldn't possibly be multimillionaire Pamela Hamilton III, could it?'

'No, Elizabeth!'

'I mean it's not going to be the list, is it? It's not going to be the fact that you've been a father for the first time in your life. That would mean you actually had a heart, and I don't believe you do!'

'I don't want the money. I don't want any of it. It's not important to me anymore.'

'Well that is lucky, because you certainly aren't getting any!'

There was a pause then as the words sunk in, followed by a sudden loud knock, and Mrs Wilson poked her large head around the office door.

'Cooee,' she said, before sailing into the room. 'I'm not interrupting, am I? No?'

'Not at all, Mrs Wilson,' George said moving over to greet her, his composure remarkably restored. 'We've just been having a little family catch up.'

'Ah, how lovely,' Mrs Wilson said, clasping her hands up to her chest. 'Family time is so important, don't you agree?'

Everyone nodded obediently, and Mrs Wilson stepped forward to shake Rhonda's hand.

'Hello there, how do you do. I'm Mrs Wilson. I am on the VAG committee. Vag as in bag. Or flag!'

'Or hag,' Liz muttered.

'Hello,' Rhonda said, quietly. 'Rhonda Jones.'

'Not the Jones' from Martin St John? Bill and Julie and little Verity?'

'No,' said Rhonda.

'Oh. And did you enjoy the play? Wasn't it just marvellous? We have been so unlucky with the weather, haven't we Elizabeth, but none of that mattered one bit in the end.'

'She didn't see it, Mrs Wilson,' George said. 'She's had much more important things to worry about.'

'Oh, I see. That sounds exciting. Well, I will leave you to it, then. Whenever you are ready, George, the raffle is waiting to be announced. Cheerio, then.'

Mrs Wilson backed out of the door, grinning, and Rhonda stood up, pushing her hanky into her sleeve again and straightening her blazer. The tears were gone then, and she looked almost calm.

'Well, I must be getting on,' she said to Maggie and Liz, as if she had just popped in from next door for a cup of tea. 'It was lovely to meet you both. It really was. You look exactly as George described. That part, at least, was true.'

'Goodbye,' Maggie said, and shook her hand. Rhonda held it for a second, looking between the two sisters, and then she smiled, just a little.

'Never trust men, girls. They're all animals. Spineless, pathetic animals.'

Chapter 23

Almost as soon as Rhonda arrived she left again, back to Spain and the life that George had once been so happy in. Maggie woke every morning with the thought that it had all been a very strange dream, this small, jittery Welsh woman with the very short hair who casually threw a grenade into their lives. Perhaps everything since George arrived had been a dream? Or maybe just that long, magical summer, the garden so wild and beautiful, the warm sunny days and everyone seemingly in love. Because now, in that early-morning milky half-light, it all seemed completely impossible.

Why was the second lie more painful than the first? Was it that a lie laid on top of another lie is so much worse, the second one somehow amplifying the first? She had forgiven him for the first betrayal almost immediately. It had been no more than a fib really, a small crease that had been so easily smoothed out. George had always been hustling for money in one way or another, and often by making someone somewhere feel sorry for him.

Or was it that the confession at the zoo had felt like a special secret between them, something for just the two of them, and her forgiveness, her sympathy for him that day had felt like a reset on their relationship. Maggie

247

had thought that there was an understanding between them, an understanding that they were both flawed but they would try to do their best in life for the sake of not hurting other people. For the sake of not hurting each other. It had been a pact, in a way, a promise.

But that was broken now, and what she had feared most in her life had come true – that the ones you love the most will always let you down.

Liz said she had always known he was morally as well as physically bankrupt, and they should all be grateful that he didn't actually have any money as he would probably be a monster of a human being, someone so terrible that they would have all had to change their names and move to another continent.

'Just imagine, *just imagine*, Maggie, if he was actually rich!' she said down the phone a few days after Rhonda had left. 'Thank God for greed and stupidity, Maggie. Thank God!'

Maggie had been silent as sounds of the kids screaming in the background had vibrated down the receiver.

'What's going on over there?' she said. 'It sounds quite noisy.'

'Um, Tom and Sophie are sort of kicking each other and Lily is chewing on the leg of the kitchen table. I think Doug might actually be in another country with work but I can't remember which one.'

'Are you OK?'

'I am great! I have drunk a lot of wine, Maggie. *A lot* of wine. It makes everything much, much better. I presume you already know all about this, but wine is very, *very* good at sorting things out, and sometimes, *sometime*s, if you have a large shot of gin before you start the whole wine thing, it sort of helps everything along a bit.'

George was at the front door of the Manor House a few days later, Albert at his feet. He was in one of his old work suits, royal blue with a crisp white shirt underneath and a silk scarf tied loosely around his neck. Even in times of strife, he was still as well turned out as ever.

'He can't stay with Pamela any longer,' he said. 'Hermione has rejected him.'

'Oh?'

'She senses something is wrong with *me*, of course,' George said. 'That's why she's lashing out at Albert. Pugs are very sensitive to change. Very sensitive.'

'Right,' Maggie said, sharply, before taking Albert's lead. 'I'll look after him.'

He looked down at his feet, brushing away a small piece of grit with his shoe.

'I am very, very sorry, for what it's worth,' he said, peering up at Maggie, his blue eyes all milky and tired.

'It would have been worth more if you'd been honest.'

'I understand that,' he said, and they stood there for a minute not looking at each other, neither of them knowing what to say.

'Why did you leave him behind?' Maggie finally said, pointing down to Albert. He had settled down onto her feet and was resting his head on her toe.

'Albert? Oh, he was terribly travel sick when I took him to Spain. I didn't want to put him through that again . . . although that's obviously what happened in the end.'

'So, you were just going to leave him there? With her?'

'I thought I would get some money together and then fly him over. It sounds ridiculous now, I know.'

'It sounds . . . quite sensible,' Maggie said.

'Righty-ho,' George said. 'Well, I had better get going.'

He put Albert's small bag of belongings by the door and then, turning to leave, stumbled slightly, losing his footing on the top step and then falling down. He landed with a thud onto his elbow and his knee and yelped loudly.

'Dad! Dad, are you all right?' Maggie said as she jumped down to give him a hand. He lay there for a moment, blinking up at the sky, all bent and wrinkled and suddenly looking so old. 'Are you hurt? Dad?'

'I'm OK, I'm OK,' he said, slowly straightening up. 'Just a bit rickety.'

'You need to be careful. You need to be more careful.'

He nodded at her. 'I know that, Maggie,' he said, smiling weakly as he brushed himself down, the blue suit all crumpled now. 'The absolute horror of being a human being, hey?'

It was only an hour or two later that Maggie, lying on her back in Tea with two large gins inside her, rolled over to take Albert's greying head in her hands.

'I'm going to do something bad, Albert,' she said to him, George's voice at the zoo ticker taping across her mind.

'How bad?' Her Albert voice was low and silly and almost made her smile.

'I would say quite bad,' she replied to herself, then she got to her feet and went to get her jacket.

Just as George had arrived at Maggie's doorstep, Maggie arrived at Callum's. He answered the door so quickly, so spontaneously, it was as if he knew that she was going to come all along.

Chapter 24

The children had finally gone back to school when Maggie and Liz met in The Owl a few days later. Liz would soon be returning to work, and before long the whole summer would just be a series of events that had happened a long time ago.

'I've had a few drinks already,' Liz announced on arrival, sounding slightly loose and breathy. 'Three-quarters of a bottle I would say. The wine line was sort of towards the bottom of the label.'

She took off her jacket and thumped a large plastic bag onto the table in front of them.

'The *wine line*?'

'If the line of wine is above the label you haven't had very much, but if it's below, you have probably had the right amount. It's not a scientific system.'

'Right. Well, good for you,' Maggie said, pouring her another glass.

'That's for you,' Liz said, pointing to the bag.

'What is it?'

'It's meat. Two chickens and five pork chops, to be precise. I have dozens more at home.'

'Why is it here though, Liz?'

Liz sighed. 'I won the bloody meat prize at the raffle. I am having to negotiate for space in my mother-in-law's chest freezer until the new one I've ordered arrives. It's all going in the Manor House by the way, in the back.'

'OK.'

'You can then, you know, cook it.'

'Right.'

Liz took a large swig from her glass and then, just as it looked as if she might say something, she flopped her head down into her hands.

'Headline, please,' she mumbled through the side of her arm.

'Now? *Really*?'

'Yes!'

'All right then . . . "Forty-something mum of three finally discovers the numbing qualities of alcohol".'

'Oh,' Liz said, her head popping up. 'I wasn't expecting that.'

'What were you expecting?'

'"Having finally reconnected with their father . . . excellent daughters realise that father is a shit after all"?'

'Hmm, not hugely catchy,' Maggie said, pouring out more wine.

'"Middle-aged woman discovers to her ENORMOUS (in capital letters) disappointment that working very hard and always trying to do the right thing is not a guarantee that life will work out the way she hopes it will".'

'Bit long.'

'Fine,' Liz snapped, and then, with a sigh, '"Middle-aged woman feels lost"?'

Maggie laughed. 'Well, you'd sell out with that one!'

'I thought I knew what I was doing, but it turns out I really don't. Can't we just press pause for a bit until we figure everything out? We should be able to, shouldn't we? At least once or twice in our lives should be able to stop it all and just check that we know what we are doing in life, and then when we realise that we don't, do an Open University course on how to be an adult. Or a parent.'

Or a daughter, Maggie thought. Or a girlfriend.

'But that's it now, isn't it?' Liz continues. 'That's it for me anyway, forty years old, covered in children, still wearing shit jeans. We just tick along now, don't we, waiting for things to sag. I already can't face looking at my boobs in the mirror anymore. God knows why anyone else would want to look at them.'

'Oh, come on, Liz. Your boobs are fine. Your boobs are great! Everything is great. The kids, Doug, your lovely new home, your job'.

'*Not* my job.'

'Well everything else then. We've just had a bad week. You have *everything*, Liz! You always have done. You're clever and kind and generous and patient, you work hard, you're funny. You're funny, Liz. You're really funny!'

'I'm not funny. I'm a mother!' she scoffed, as if the two things could not possibly coexist.

'I think you're funny. I think you're great. I think you are more than great.'

'I think about having sex with some of the school dads sometimes,' Liz said quietly, before taking a large gulp of wine.

Maggie put down her drink and stared at her sister. 'Really?'

'Well, one in particular. That man Erick who we sat behind at the play. Married to the wavy hair, floaty-dress woman.'

'The dentist? Gary Barlow's dad? The one that's married to your friend?'

'I don't know her *that* well.'

'Oh, OK.'

'I was going to see him quite regularly, at the dentist, just so he could touch my mouth. He has the most beautiful blue eyes.' Her voice had taken on a sort of dreamy, meandering tone, as though she was floating gently away with her thoughts.

'Right,' Maggie said, trying to sound casual.

'My teeth were perfect though, of course, so I had to stop going in the end. I think it's over now anyway. I haven't dreamt about him for a while.'

'It's just a crush, Liz. Everyone has crushes.'

'It's a symptom though, isn't it? That's what the books say. It *means* something.'

'Or maybe you just need a shag? It's not a big deal, Liz.'

'What about Joe?' she said.

'What about Joe?'

'I really like him, Maggie. You should be with him. He's good for you. He's a nice guy, really nice.'

'I'm not sure I'm nice though.'

'You're just having a wobble,' Liz said, swigging more wine.

'I told him I couldn't see him at the moment, Liz. That's a pretty massive wobble.'

'What the hell did you do that for?'

'I don't know really,' Maggie said, as a feeling of panic began to creep up her limbs and tighten around her neck. 'I just wanted to close all the doors and not let anyone else in.'

'But not for definite, right? Just for now?'

'I don't know. He looked so, so sad, Liz.'

'Shit,' Liz said, and Maggie closed her eyes tightly for a moment and tried to push the thought of him as far away as she could, his face when she had told him, the way it had sort of buckled. Maggie was sure she hadn't seen anything quite as terrible in her whole life.

'Look,' said Liz, as she put down her wine glass and pulled herself upright in her chair. 'We can't let what happened with Dad mess everything up, Maggie. We just can't. I am not going to let that happen.'

'I think it might be too late for that.'

'Well, I am not going to let it be too late. We are going to pick ourselves up and we are going to get back on track. Right? *Right*?'

'Oh, God, Liz, it's all been decided already, hasn't it? It was decided years and years ago! Our parents, the house, Queen Vic, the stupid names. It was all written out before we even had a chance to find out who we really were. Look at you, Elizabeth, perfect and wonderful and so brilliant, and I am Margaret and I mess it all up.'

'For fuck's sake, Maggie, this is hardly the time to be feeling sorry for yourself.'

'When else then, Liz?' Maggie protested, her hands flying up into the air. 'I would say it's a pretty good time to feel sorry for myself!'

'You think because you are *Margaret* that you are the only one affected by how we were brought up?'

'No. I don't know. Being Elizabeth is a whole other thing.'

'Why do you think I was so good all the time? Why do you think I worked so hard?'

Maggie shrugged. She had never really questioned it. It was just the way it was. They were different, they always had been.

'I thought that if I did well, *really* well, if I was perfect, if I won prizes and came first, then she might have come back.'

'*Mum?*'

'It was different for you, Maggie. You didn't have her around for as long as I did. You don't remember her the same way.'

'But she left us, Liz. She walked out!'

'Do you know why I wanted George to do all these things we have been making him do? All this father stuff?'

'You wanted to punish him, for Mum.'

'No,' she said, shaking her head. 'No. I wanted you to see that you didn't need him, Maggie. That even if he takes you to the zoo or carries a plate of sandwiches into a village hall for you, that you are amazing as you are. It doesn't matter if he is here or not, Maggie. It doesn't matter that she never came back. We can do all of it without them. We always have.'

Maggie looked at Liz, her eyes wide and fierce, her nostrils slightly flared, and she wondered if anyone would ever drag her along with them into life as forcefully as her sister did. She campaigned for Maggie. She always had.

'So what do we do now, then?' Maggie asked, and Liz looked startled for a second, as if she had been asked a tricky maths question.

'Now?'

'Yes. What are we going to do?'

'We carry on,' she said. 'We're just going to carry on.'

Maggie nodded at her, neither of them knowing what it really meant, but both determined to hold each other up.

PART THREE
Autumn/Winter

Chapter 25

There was a time when being George Addison was the best thing you could ever imagine. When the business was doing well and your children were sweet and adoring and could see no wrong in the things that you did, when your wife was still wide-eyed and unquestioning, and your mother thought that the good still outweighed the bad. When you could walk down the street and people would be happy to see you and want to shake your hand or buy you a drink, and the stories you told over pints of beer still wanted to be heard. When you could do anything or go anywhere but all you actually wanted to do was to be just where you were, where everything came so easily, at the Manor House in Little Martin, in the Cotswolds, in England.

Maggie wondered, as she so often had, when it was that George's life had gone off course. Is there an exact moment where the balance irreversibly shifts, the switch operator finally pulling a lever after years of dreadful behaviour and rerouting you onto a completely different track? Did you feel something happen, a change in the wind, a lurch in your stomach? Did you wake the following morning and know that things were going to change, that life was going to unfold in an altogether different way? Perhaps there was just a sense of relief, a lightness in your bones, an understanding that you didn't need to bother making an effort anymore, and even though the path you were now on was darker, perhaps it would be easier to navigate because it was just so familiar.

Maggie wanted to know when it had happened to George. Had it been there all along, bred into his bones, or was it just in adulthood that the first infidelities, the selfishness and arrogance had started to creep in? Was his course already set then, or was it later, becoming a father; the children he couldn't quite love enough, the wife who left, the mother who he didn't care for? Perhaps it was much, much later. Perhaps it was only now? Perhaps she could have done something about it, done more with the list? Perhaps she could have tried just a little bit harder?

Autumn was not pretty that year, and Maggie felt relieved. She didn't think she deserved the wonder and the beauty of the leaves changing colour, the low mists on the fields, the warmth of the ironstone walls from months of baking in the summer sun. The seasons changed sharply with a two-day storm that blasted all the leaves from their trees leaving everything suddenly bare, exposed and vulnerable. Maggie hid inside the Manor House, thinking about forgiveness. She wondered, if she was to be forgiven, must she in turn forgive someone else? The checks and balances of life bothered her, the list of good things over bad, the passing of batons from one person to the next. Even the house itself, back on the market with Susie after the second buyer pulled out. The market was shifting, but it would come back again, and on and on it went, round and round and round.

Pamela had no trouble selling the house at Martin's Rest. She had wondered whether keeping a foot in the UK might be a good idea, what with US presidents being so unpredictable and the aged aunt in Devon. But the house had gone up so much since she had bought it, and she'd never quite made it down to the south-west, so it made financial sense to cut her all her British ties and just say goodbye.

She had grasped the Georgeness of George almost as soon as she had met him, but she'd liked him, even grown to love him in her own Pamela Hamilton III way. Rhonda's brief cameo hadn't troubled her in the slightest. She claimed that she couldn't possibly take a woman with hair as short as hers seriously, and why on earth should she be bothered about what George had got up to on some holiday in Spain? But then the play had ended, and life returned to normal, and she realised that being in England wasn't quite what she wanted, after all. The troubling emptiness in her stomach wasn't for the end of summer, the end of the cast parties and the glasses of rosé on the grass, it was homesickness. Despite the Jeffness of Jeff and the BBQs and the Christians, she rather missed Florida and wanted to go home.

Liz hadn't been at all surprised by the news, claiming that she'd known all along that Pamela wouldn't be able to hack village life, but Maggie was surprised. It wasn't that she thought Pamela and George would settle down together, more that she had come to imagine Pamela rising up the ranks of the Martins, opening more village halls, charming the vicar, or starting a dating service for dogs while also throwing wild 80s discos at Martin's Rest. She would become the new Queen of the village, completely different from the outgoing one, of course, but regal all the same; with a silk turban on her head and a cocktail in her hand, she would take Maggie under her wing and together they would make it all work somehow.

'So, when do you fly?' Maggie asked. They had met at a bar in Chipping Norton. It was early afternoon and very quiet, but Pamela ordered cocktails, margaritas with little umbrellas on the side, and the barman had looked confused and pained while making them.

'A day or two. We're all packed up, pretty much. Hermione is being picked up by the pet courier first thing tomorrow so I'm going so slip a little Valium into her porridge.' She fed Hermione a crisp from a bowl on the bar and Maggie watched as the little dog ate it as carefully and as solemnly as if it was a communion wafer.

'And you're going back to your ex-husband?'

'We'll see,' she said, taking a sip of her drink and then grimacing at its taste. 'Jeff is keen. He's been sending me fruit! The whole house is filled with goddam fruit. We never got fully divorced, you know, so I could just slot back into the other wing of the house and just pretend none of this ever happened.'

She flicked her hand dismissively through the air as if she might have been talking about a bad evening out or a stomach bug rather than a romantic relationship.

'What about all the salads? And the Republicans?' Maggie asked. 'What about Jesus?'

'The Jesus stuff is all right, really. I can handle Jesus. I mean it's a bit wacky in places, sure, but we can all get on board with absolution, right? I mean what's not to like about waving all those sins goodbye?'

Maggie smiled and raised her glass to meet Pamela's, although she felt a heaviness sitting on her shoulders like a thick wool cloak that she could not shake off.

'How is George?' Pamela asked. 'Hermione misses him dreadfully, you know.'

On cue, Hermione sighed heavily on Pamela's lap. She was wearing a fur-lined tweed jacket and Maggie wondered if she'd perhaps lost weight.

'George is OK. He's fine. He's renting a little terraced house not far from the Manor. The sale isn't actually going through anymore. The buyer pulled out, but there's new people interested so I am sure it will sell soon.'

'I know I have said it before, but you know I don't think you should sell that house, Maggie. That buyer pulling out, that's a sign that you're meant to keep hold of it.'

'The buyer pulled out because their sale fell through.'

Pamela shrugged and sipped her cocktail.

'We have to sell it, Pamela. There are debts to pay off.'

'Your dear old dead grandma wanted *you* to have that house, not sell it to some developer. I mean how many houses are there like that in England, huh? Big old Manor Houses? Not many, I can tell you.'

'I think there's probably quite a few, actually.'

'That's why she left it to you guys, to you and Liz and not to George. She wanted you two to look after it, to *do* something with it.'

'She just didn't trust *him* with it, that's all. She knew what he was like.'

'She was a smart lady, your grandma. Very smart,' Pamela said, narrowing her eyes.

'With all due respect,' Maggie said, feeling the first prickles of irritation. 'I think it's probably easier to think about not selling when your *not*-ex-husband owns the biggest house in Florida.'

Pamela smiled coyly and patted her hair before taking the cocktail umbrella from her drink and placing it among her curls. 'Think about it,' she said. 'You'll figure out what to do.'

Maggie felt a sudden swell of exasperation and she desperately wanted to leave.

'Look, I'm sorry that this whole thing with George hasn't worked out, Pamela,' Maggie said, finishing her drink. 'It hasn't worked out for any of us if that makes it any easier.'

'You do know that the whole thing with Rhonda wasn't his idea?' she said quietly, leaning in on her chair so that her face was very close to Maggie's. 'He wasn't going to tell you.'

'What? What do you mean?' Maggie said.

'It wasn't his idea to contest the will. She was the one who thought she could get all the money. I know he went along with it at the start, but his heart was never in it. He phoned her to call it off. He emailed, he said he didn't want anything to do with it, he didn't want anything to do with her, but she came to find him anyway.'

'But . . . he was involved, wasn't he? It's why he came back.'

'Who knows, Maggie? He's a fool, we all know that. I think he thought he might get a little a bit of money when the sale went through, but that wasn't why he came back. He missed it here. He missed all of you. I mean, he certainly didn't plan any of it. He's not a *con artist*. He might actually have some cash if he was!'

Pamela found this hilarious, and the stream of Ss that left her mouth reached all the way to the back of the room where the barman turned to see what the noise was. Maggie thought back to the zoo, to the penguins and the meerkats, and how sure George must have been that Rhonda was never coming back.

'Listen, Maggie, I know your dad is a bit all over the place at the moment, and he's silly and pompous and he makes terrible mistakes, but, you know, he's funny. He's sweet. He's romantic. He laughs and he wants to have a good time and you just don't meet guys like that at my age. They're all bent over and achey and worried about their knees or their prostates and they sit on the toilet for *hours,* or they don't drink, or they just want *a cuddle. God,* the cuddlers! I knew it was probably not going to last, Maggie. I just miss my old life. I miss Florida.'

'So, take George with you. He can be a pool boy or something. A tennis instructor!'

'You're kidding, right?' she laughed again, the Ss as crisp and as sharp as the drinks in front of them. 'Your father will never leave here again! He's baked into this place. He's the old bones of this country, an old English fossil dug deep into the ground. I loved that about him.'

Maggie smiled but thought that she actually might be about to cry. There was something about George's old bones that had suddenly made him seem so painfully mortal and weary, the bluster and the bravado all fallen away, the skeleton underneath.

'Liz and I, we tried to make him into a father after he came back. We thought about what it was that makes a good one, what he could do to show us that he cared. It all seems so, so stupid now, but at the time I really thought we were getting somewhere. I thought he was enjoying it.'

'He did enjoy it, Maggie,' she said, reaching over to hold Maggie's hand. 'He loved it. I know he did. He never stopped talking about you. He was so proud.'

'He lied though. He lied to all of us,' Maggie said, and then she was crying, much to her embarrassment. Pamela did not look like a crier.

'We *all* lie, Maggie!' Pamela said. 'We all fuck things up. Listen, you don't want advice from me, I'm sure, but if you are expecting George to be like some TV dad that you've put together from a list, then you guys are going to be very disappointed.'

'That's not what we wanted, Pamela. It's not like that.'

Maggie felt irritated. She hadn't wanted advice from Pamela, a woman she barely knew, a woman who wore pineapple earrings and pink polka-dot dresses and put plates with garlic bread still on them in the dishwasher. It was easy for her to say all that, cocktail umbrella in her solid yellow hair, pug on her lap, preparing to fly back to Florida and pick up her old life with Jeff and Jesus and all the dolphins. It wasn't *her* father. She hadn't been waiting for years and years, waiting forever, for George to turn and see that she had been there all along.

Pamela must have sensed her annoyance as she said, 'Look, maybe he will change, Maggie. Maybe this whole thing is exactly what he needed. A good kick up the ass once and for all to realise that it's not just some blonde from Florida that he's going to lose, but all of *this*, you and Liz everything you have here. I don't need Jeff, but you know what, I guess I am choosing him. It's *your* choice, Maggie. You can do it all without him, without anyone for that matter.'

Maggie looked up at her and nodded as Pamela downed the rest of her drink.

'Although, you know, I think that guy Joe is probably worth bringing along for the ride.'

'We broke up, actually,' Maggie said, wiping her nose. 'I had a bit of a wobble.'

'What the heck is a *wobble*?'

'It's when you make a huge, awful mistake,' Maggie said.

They went outside to say their goodbyes and neither of them made any fuss. Maggie was half expecting Pamela to make a scene, but she simply hugged her and said she must get in touch if she ever found herself in Florida. They'd drink proper margaritas and see the dolphins and it would all be so wonderful, but they both knew it would never happen and that was absolutely fine.

Chapter 26

The news about Rhonda had taken some time to digest.

Liz had not wanted to believe it at first, despite the evidence. She had, at least for the time being, carefully parcelled George away in her mind, and now that he was finally out of the Manor and living in his own house, she was loathe to unwrap him all over again.

Maggie sat with the facts, breaking them up and turning them over and then back again, as if it was a recipe she couldn't get quite right. Why hadn't George just told them the truth? Why had he not said anything the night they were all sat there in the headmaster's office? The night when Rhonda put on a performance far better than anyone had on the actual stage. Or later, after she had gone, why had he not explained it to them, helped them to understand? George was no stranger to duplicity, but he was also the first to put his hand up if he felt that he had been wronged. She pictured him in The Owl, surrounded by concerned looking women, recounting the dramatic plot of how he came to be ensnared by a petite Welsh honey trap in the wilds of the Costa Blanca. It was a good story after all, and if George loved anything it was a tale of his own misfortune delivered directly into a sympathetic female ear.

But there had been nothing. No protestations. No excuses, no blaming anyone else. No heart attacks or brain tumours or cancers of the belly button. There had been an apology, and then silence, a silence so deafening, so uncharacteristic, that both Maggie and Liz began to wonder if something in George had actually changed.

It had been a particularly awful day in Leeds that had given Liz the idea to go to Brighton. Her clients, Ross Taylor and his very irritating son, Jack, had insisted that Liz stay on into the late afternoon to join in with some trust-building exercises with their colleagues, and as they were placed into teams and asked to complete a scavenger hunt around the office, Liz wanted to scream at them that she may as well be doing that at home. Not that she enjoyed scavenger hunts, or hide-and-seek, or grandmother's footsteps or any nursery games for that matter. She hated them all, which was precisely why she kept returning to work in the first place.

Searching the third floor of the City West Business Park for 'the blue stapler' or 'Oli's special red water bottle' with Dani from reception and Trevor from sales on a wet Wednesday afternoon felt very much like an all-time low, even for Liz. Then she had missed her usual train home, which meant that Doug had to collect Lily from nursery and Tom and Sophie from after-school club, and when she got home everyone was fractious and grumpy and out of their usual routine and, quite frankly, what on earth was the point of it all?

Not that the days spent in the Oxford office had been much better. Teenage line manager, Rachel, was a fan of performance reviews and morning check-in meetings and signing off on *all* of Liz's work. She was not a fan of home working or letting Liz just get on with it or, in fact, just ever leaving her alone.

Doug reassured her that everything would settle. She would get back into the rhythm of it all. She would find her feet again, those forward moving, work loving, sensible-shoe wearing feet. After all, it had only been a short amount of time since she had been back in the office and work had always, always been where she felt most at home.

But as the weeks went on, she found to her great surprise that it was actually *home* that felt like home. Home was where she wanted to be.

'What is the matter with me, Maggie?' she moaned down the phone as she walked to the train station one dark evening in November.

'Nothing is the matter with you, Liz. It's grey and miserable and it's freezing cold. It's probably raining too. Is it?'

'Yes.'

'It's raining, it's cold. *Everyone* wants to be at home. Being in an office all the time is rubbish. Everyone knows that.'

'*I* was different though, Maggie. I used to like it. I think I might be having a midlife crisis.'

'You are *not* having a midlife crisis, Liz. It's just November!'

Liz had cried as she pushed her way through the turnstiles at Oxford station, and sobbing her way up the stairs to cross over to the northbound platform, Maggie had found herself in the unusual position of telling her older sister, the sister who had only ever looked after her, that everything was going to be all right. She thought back to the nights at the Manor after Pat had left, when she would climb into her sister's bed and they would curl into each other and Maggie hoped that if she lay as close and as still as she could, that she might become a little bit more like Liz, that just being near her would be enough.

'There's so much love for you in that Executive Family Dwelling, Liz. If it was me, I would never want to leave either.'

Liz had been in Leeds the day after that, and the following morning, quite out of the blue, she decided that she was going to take the day off. She was going to take the whole day off and she was going to spend some time with Tom. They would go to the beach. They would go to Brighton! Of course they would, and as soon as the plan had formed in her mind, it seemed like the most obvious thing in the world.

Tom, however, had needed some persuading.

'But it's cold, Mum,' he moaned as he tried to tie the laces on his trainers. He had moved out of Velcro shoes a couple of months earlier but couldn't quite get to grips with the new ones, despite the hours and hours that Doug had spent trying to help him.

'There's no cold, darling, only bad coats,' she said, in the same sing-song tone that Queen Vic had used with her. She said more and more things like her grandmother these days.

Liz couldn't face the train again and so they drove, stopping on the M40 to get hot chocolates and to call the office, and then school, to tell them that neither of them would be in, the thrill of it making her feel quite giddy. They then drove all the way down to the coast as Tom played on his Switch in the passenger seat beside her, and as the signs for Brighton started to appear on the M23, she realised that she did not have a plan. She always had a plan, and there she was, without a single clue as to what they were going to do.

She had always known that she would go there one day. Brighton would be warm and bright and full of colour, with buckets and spades and fish and chips and the sun shining as people ran in and out of the sea. The pier was there, stretching out into the deep navy sea, and the air would smell of sun cream and salt and homemade sandwiches. She imagined seeing Pat on the corner of a street somewhere; wearing a long summer dress. She would be laughing with friends, the sea breeze in her hair and her cheeks all rosy and freckled, and when they finally caught sight of each other, as Liz knew that they must, she would understand then what had gone wrong. She would understand why she left.

They had pulled over on a street not far from the sea, the day still stubbornly wet and grey. The arcades blinked neon pinks, yellows and blues into the puddles on the pavement, and as the rain thundered down onto the windscreen, Liz suddenly felt overwhelmingly foolish that she had thought, even for one moment, that this would be anything other than an enormous mistake.

'Mum. Mum, I'm hungry,' Tom said. He was tapping the dashboard with his foot, and Liz realised she had been staring out of the window for quite some time.

'Yeah, me too, Tom.'

'Can we get an ice cream?'

'Ice cream? Yeah, why not. What about chips?'

'Chips *and* ice cream?'

'Do you think they'll taste good together?'

Tom thought about this for a moment. 'Josh Clear says that he dips his chips into his dad's beer.'

'Who's *Josh Clear*?'

'He's in Class 3. He's a knob.'

'A *knob*? Are you allowed to say knob?'

'Everyone else does,' Tom replied in a voice implying that his mother knew nothing.

'Right.'

They got a Mr Whippy from a van in front of the beach and then some chips from a fish and chip place on the corner of the seafront before going down to sit on the pebbles. They pulled their coats in tightly as the sea frothed and foamed in front of them, and Liz realised that she wasn't feeling sad. She felt empty more than anything else, as if everything had been poured out of her, and the feeling wasn't alarming or unpleasant, but more like she had made room for something else.

'I'm really sorry, Tom, about today,' she said after they had settled down. The rain had stopped, and Liz had laid out her foldable raincoat so their bottoms didn't get too wet. 'This was all a bit silly, wasn't it? Coming all the way down here, in the rain.'

Tom shrugged. 'It's OK, Mum.'

'I just thought we could bunk off school and have a bit of an adventure together.' How she longed for him to think of her as cool.

'We can have an adventure at home.'

'You're right,' she said. 'You're absolutely right, Tom. Thank you.'

'That's OK.'

'And I'm sorry we haven't hung out much recently. It's been a busy year, one way or another and I've really missed spending time with you.'

He smiled up at her, his face so bright and beautiful, his eyelashes so ridiculously long, his pale floppy hair just skimming the edges of his eyebrows. 'Me too,' he said.

'Lily coming along was a bit of a surprise for all of us, wasn't it?'

'It's OK,' he shrugged again. 'It's not her fault.'

'No, no of course not. Anyway, she's at nursery now, isn't she? Terrorising those poor ladies at Puddle Ducks.'

Tom smiled to himself. 'I liked it when she was around.'

'Did you?'

'Maybe not at first. She was always crying and you had to pick her up all the time and then we didn't really get to hug you anymore. And you were always really grumpy.'

'Was I?'

'*Really* grumpy. Especially with Daddy.'

'All mums are grumpy at daddies, Tom.'

'You were probably *more grumpy* before Lily though.'

'Really? So, I'm just grumpy all the time, then?'

Tom exhaled sharply, puffing out his lips with air. 'I think so, yeah.'

'Oh,' she said, feeling as though she had just been told off.

'It's nice when we're all together though.'

'Yeah, it is nice.'

'And Grandpa George, when he came over. And Aunty Maggie. I like it when *everyone* is there.'

'Me too, Tom. And that doesn't have to change. We can get them all over whenever you want.'

Tom looked up at her and then back out to sea. There was a ship in the distance, way out in the Channel, and Tom watched it for a while, his eyes blinking into the salty air.

'Do you know why we're really here?' she eventually said.

'You wanted to bunk off work for the day?'

'No. Well, yes, and I wanted to see you, and to have an adventure together, but we came here, to this town, because this is where my mother used to live.'

'*Your* mother?'

'Yes. My mother, and Aunty Maggie's mother. Her name was Pat. You never met her, and we don't talk about her very much because she came to live here when Aunty Maggie and I were much younger and then she died. Maggie was the age that Sophie is now, but I was a bit older and, well, Queen Vic looked after us after that.'

'How did she die?

'She was in a car accident.'

'That's sad.'

'It is sad. It's very sad. We would have liked to know her for a bit longer, and for a while I thought she might come back . . . but that's not the way it worked out and life is like that sometimes. You have to move past the sad bits.'

'Did she look like you?'

'A little bit. We had the same colour hair. But we were very different. I don't think she wanted to be a mother really. She much preferred working and seeing her friends and so she left.'

'Do you not want to be a mother?' Tom asked, his voice now full of worry.

'No, no, Tom, I want to be a mother more than anything,' she said, squeezing up next to him and putting her arm around his shoulders. 'Being a mum to you and Sophie and Lily is the best job in the whole wide world and I would never, ever leave you. I think my mother just felt that she didn't really fit in with us. It wasn't anyone's fault and nobody is to blame. It was just one of those things. She just wanted something different, and so she came to live here, by the sea.'

'She was a knob, then?'

Liz laughed. 'She was a bit of a knob.'

'She sounds like a massive knob!'

'I'm pretty sure knob is *not* an OK word for an eight-year-old!'

Tom shrugged. 'I think it's OK this time, Mum.'

They sat for a little while longer, throwing pebbles on the beach until the rain started again, then they walked hand in hand up the shingle and back towards the car. Tom slept most of the way home and Liz could only think about Doug and how much she loved him. Was there anyone kinder, gentler, or more caring than her husband? Was there anyone sweeter or funnier or more joyful than her children? How lucky she was to have him. How lucky she was to have all of them. How extraordinary lucky.

Chapter 27

Of all the villages to will a restaurant into life, it would, of course, be Little Martin. The other villages might have had their new halls or their exclusive modern developments, but it could have only been Little Martin who had the creativity, the foresight and the sheer determination to make it happen. Small, yes, but underestimated.

It seemed obvious really, the pieces of the puzzle all laid out in front of them just asking for someone to put them together, urging them to just put one more foot in front of the other until they realised they had reached the same place. Maggie, more in demand than ever, people queuing up for cooking and everyone asking when a new venture might be appearing, and then Liz, handing her notice in the week after she got back from Brighton. She didn't want to get up and go to Leeds anymore. She didn't want to go Oxford. She wanted to do something different, *be* someone different, and there the two sisters were, waiting for someone to just nudge them together.

Maggie had not intended to see Callum. She had not intended to see Callum ever again, despite his best efforts, but she had been on her way to drop food off to a family party on Horn Hill and happened to pass his house. The van with the rat on top was parked outside and the sight of his front doorstep, the memory of when she had last been on it, filled Maggie such an enormous surge of rage and frustration, an actual physical energy at her own stupidity, that before she knew it she was right there, banging on his door.

'Why are you in your pants?' she said as Callum appeared in his boxers. He looked particularly dishevelled and bewildered, as if he might have just been thawed out from another century.

'I dunno,' he shrugged. 'It's a Wednesday. I don't work on a Wednesday.'

'Right. Well, I have come to tell you something,' she said, the words coming out quickly before her resolve had a chance to run away.

'Yeah?'

'I have come to tell you . . . I have come to tell you, Callum, that I am going to do something.'

'What does that mean?'

'I am going to open a restaurant.'

'You *what*?'

'Yes! I am going to open a restaurant, at the house, and it's going to be amazing and I needed to tell you that.'

'What do you want me to do about it?' he said, leaning against the door frame.

'Nothing. You don't have to do anything. But I wanted you to know that *I* am doing something. I am going to do something great.'

He looked confused then, his mouth hanging open slightly, and she wondered if she had thrown too much information at him in too short a space of time.

'Aren't you cold, Callum?' she said. 'It's freezing.'

'I didn't expect to be standing out here, did I? I thought you were Amazon.'

'Right. Well, you can go in now. That's it.'

'*That's it?*' he smirked.

'Oh, no, wait. Hang on. I'm also *not* going to sleep with you again. Ever. Sorry.'

'What do I care?' Callum said, his top lip all curled up like a grumpy dog.

'I love someone else. He doesn't know that I love him, not anymore anyway, but he's brilliant. He's really brilliant. His name is Joe, and he's an estate agent.'

Maggie thought Callum's face might have softened ever so slightly before he closed the door, but she was already turning away, and then she was walking back down Ivy Lane towards the holiday house, towards better things, two large shepherd's pies in her bag and an enormous smile on her face. The words were out there then, floating somewhere above the village, and she couldn't now put them back.

And across the village, another doorstep conversation was taking place.

'This is a lovely surprise,' George said as he opened the door. The little house on Rosebank was looking bright, clean and spruce in the winter sunshine and despite the significant shrinkage of George's living quarters, he was looking remarkably content with life.

'I can't stay long,' Liz said. 'How are you?'

'Very well,' he said, and he looked it, smart as ever in a navy V-neck and corduroys, Albert waddling out by his side. 'Very well indeed.'

'I can't stay long, I have to pick up Lily. I just wanted to tell you that I've been having a think about things and I realise that I might have been wrong, very wrong, about lots of it.'

'Golly,' George said, startled. 'It's usually me in the wrong.'

'You're a terrible man, and a terrible father, but you're not to blame for everything.'

'Right,' he said, nodding his head for a few seconds, and then with a smile, 'Do you think I could have that on my gravestone?'

Liz laughed. 'I am sure that can be arranged, Dad.'

'Jolly good,' he said. 'I couldn't for the life of me think what to put on there.'

'Well, you've got plenty of time to think about it, haven't you?'

'You're right,' he said, smiling. They looked at each other for a moment, those bright blue eyes just the same.

'I can't stay,' Liz said. Not this time anyway, but I wondered if you, and Albert, might like to come with me on an outing one day soon, you know, if you have time.'

'Ah, for 'the list'?'

'No,' she sniffed. 'Not the list. I wanted to go and choose a rescue dog, for the kids, and I thought you might like to come with me. You could help me choose, see which one Albert likes best. I am sure he must be missing Hermione?'

George was very still for a moment and Liz wondered if he had taken in what she had said.

'Dad?' she said. 'What do you think?'

'I think we'd like that very much,' he said, smiling down at Albert.

'Well, Tom's been asking for years and years now and as I'm not going to be in the office anymore—'

'—Oh?'

'Yes, I thought I might try something different.'

'That's excellent news,' he said. 'Really excellent.'

'Is it?'

'I never thought you should be an accountant.'

'*Really*? Why didn't you say anything?'

'I wasn't around, darling.'

'Right,' Liz said, the matter of factness of it all taking a second to sink in. She looked down at her feet, the sensible shoes, the uniform she had been wearing all of her life. It suddenly seemed so simple to just put them to one side.

'You're very good with people, Liz,' George said softly. 'I always thought that.'

'Am I? Yes, well I might set up my own thing,' she said, feeling a sudden of jog of confidence. 'We'll see.'

'Maggie will need someone, won't she?'

'Maggie?'

'She'll get round to opening that restaurant one day.'

There were the smaller puzzle pieces that fitted in alongside, the kind bank manager who loved their idea, the debts they could pay back slowly over time, the second buyer of the Manor House pulling out, a house full of antiques, a freezer full of meat. There was George too, full of enthusiasm and energy, full of pride for his daughters and telling anyone he could about their exciting new project. George would be involved too, helping them with publicity, selling some of the better antiques and curating the ones they had left. But the final piece of the puzzle, that little piece that could have been missed, the piece they realised holds the whole thing together, had been put there by Queen Vic.

'Any other business, ladies?' Carolyn Sewell, the parish council chair, said towards the end of their December meeting. Liz was hosting again, but this time at the Manor House. She couldn't quite face another evening of the moaning about Fair Meadows, not when she had something so important to say. What's more, there wasn't anywhere as festive as the Manor House, all decked out in fairy lights, tinsel and holly, with the enormous tree in the hallway. There wasn't anywhere prettier in the whole of the Cotswolds.

'Are we any further forward with the dog-poo bins, Miranda?' Carolyn added.

'Ah, no, I don't think so. There's a hold up, apparently.'

'Right, right,' Carolyn sighed. 'Anything else at all? Anyone?'

'I have something, actually,' Liz said, standing up. 'It's not in the notes, I am afraid.'

'Oh, I see. Well, that is rather irregular, Elizabeth,' Carolyn said, looking around the group for support.

'I don't think it needs putting on the minutes actually,' Liz continued. 'It's more of an announcement really. A courtesy message. And an invitation, I suppose.'

Carolyn cleared her throat sharply, while Mrs Wilson, newly appointed to parish council secretary, hovered her pen above her notepad. 'Shall I jot it down anyway?' she asked.

'Yes, please, Mrs Wilson,' Carolyn said firmly. 'Carry on, Elizabeth.'

'My sister, Maggie, and I are going to be opening a pop-up restaurant, here at the Manor, and the first date will be in a couple of weeks, just before Christmas.'

'Oh, how wonderful!' exclaimed Mrs Wilson, clapping her hands. 'That is good news, isn't it? We have been wondering, haven't we?'

'We would of course be delighted for you all to come along. I am sure you all know that my sister is an excellent chef, and we both feel that the space here, this wonderful, beautiful, magical house that my grandmother wanted us to keep, that she wanted us to do something with, will make the most perfect restaurant setting. We will be serving traditional English dishes, comfort food, things you might have eaten and loved when you were younger. Food that will make you happy.'

'What's a *pop-up*?' one of the older women asked, her hand raised.

'It means it's temporary. Like a supper club.'

'Nothing jumps out at you, then?'

'No.'

'I don't like loud, jumpy things,' she said, putting her hand back down again.

'Is there live music?' someone else asked.

'We are looking into that, providing it doesn't go on too late. We don't want to upset any of the neighbours,' Liz said, looking directly at Carolyn.

'Oh, how exciting,' Mrs Wilson said, sitting forward in her seat. 'There might be dancing then!'

'Well, we'll see. It's early days but we are looking at lots of different options, possibly also opening up some the bedrooms so people from further afield can stay the night.'

There was then some general whispering and chatting among the group before Carolyn abruptly called the meeting to order. 'Excuse me, excuse me everyone, can I have everyone's attention please! Quieten down everyone.'

Liz sat down as Carolyn stood up, the two women eyeing each other across the room.

'I do believe, Elizabeth, that there are all sorts of licences involved with any sort of endeavour such as this, health and safety, to name but one. Those take time to gather, longer I suspect than a couple of weeks. We would expect to see them all in advance, of course, and they will need checking over.'

'Yes, *of course*, Carolyn. We have all of those already,' Liz said, lifting up a file that had been on the footrest in front of her. 'Would you like to have a look now or shall I drop them over to you tomorrow?'

'Do you think she'll have the chicken pie on the menu, Liz?' Mrs Wilson said, leaning forward towards Liz. 'I haven't stopped thinking about that pie.'

'I'm not sure, Penny. I think she is keeping the final menu a surprise until the actual day, although I think there will be something for everyone.'

'People can't just open restaurants *willy nilly*,' Carolyn said. 'The council themselves will need to be notified and permission will have to be granted. There are systems in place, thank the lord!'

'I can assure you that I have looked into it all, Carolyn. I looked into it extensively. It will only count as a temporary restaurant for the time being, so most council regulations don't actually apply.'

'Well, I can assure *you* that I will be contacting them first thing in the morning.'

Liz smiled sweetly at her. 'Do ask for Jim McFarlane when you call. Lovely man, very knowledgeable, he knows all about it. He's expecting to hear from you.'

'Right, well I will,' Carolyn huffed.

'The funny thing is,' Liz continued, very much on a roll. 'The funny thing is, that it was actually my grandmother, Victoria, when she was on this parish council, who helped to ensure that small businesses like this are allowed to operate without any opposition from parish councillors.'

'What are you talking about?' Carolyn snapped.

'I think it must have been the reason she stepped down all those years ago. She couldn't understand why anyone would oppose resourcefulness or creativity.'

'There are rules, Elizabeth. We all have to follow them.'

'I wouldn't dream of breaking any rules, Carolyn. I happen to be rather keen on rules. But this very small exception to the rule was actually set by *this* parish council. Mrs Wilson kindly reminded me of that. It was a long time ago now, but some of you might remember a lady called Hilary Davies? She sold some homemade jumpers and scarves from her house on Ells Lane, a sort of pop-up shop I suppose, and some people on the council got a bit agitated about it.'

'That was very different,' Carolyn said. '*That* was knitwear.'

'It wasn't so different,' Mrs Wilson added. 'The principle is the same.'

'Knitwear or chicken pie, Victoria thought that it should be added to the Little Martin parish council's own list of regulations, just in case the issue ever came up again. And, well, here we are!'

Carolyn glared at Liz. 'Surely this all needs looking at again?' she said. 'How many years ago was it, exactly? Things have moved on since then.'

'I suppose there is no harm in putting it to the vote again,' Mrs Wilson said. 'Just so we can keep everyone happy?'

'Yes. Exactly,' Carolyn said, jumping up from her seat again. 'Thank you, Mrs Wilson. A show of hands please as to who would like to return to this subject and do another vote?'

The room was silent for a moment or two before one woman gingerly raised her hand, before quickly pulling it back down again.

'Right!' muttered Carolyn, her face rigid and furious. 'And who here is happy for a restaurant to just spring up out of the blue and cause all kinds of reckless, dangerous chaos?'

The women all looked around at each other, wondering who, if anyone, would be the first to break cover. Mrs Wilson then raised her hand in such a firm and decisive manner that the woman next to her shot hers up too, and then there was a rush of hands all rising upwards in the air until the only ones without them lifted were Carolyn and Liz.

Liz then raised hers very slowly and smiled at the group.

'We would so love to see you all on the opening night,' she said, and even though Carolyn had simply lifted her nose in reply, Liz knew she wouldn't miss it for the world.

Chapter 28

One of Maggie's favourite recipes was one that Queen Vic had taught her just before she left for Paris. It had become one of her most popular dishes, the one she kept coming back to, the one she made when she needed to feel warm and comforted and safe. She wasn't sure if this was because it reminded her of her grandmother, or because it just tasted so good, but the two things were so intertwined that it didn't really matter anymore. All of her cooking was down to Queen Vic, in one way or another, and as soon as she and Liz decided to open the restaurant, this was one of the recipes she knew she would serve on the first night.

'You'll be served something like this over there, but it won't be as good,' she had told Maggie as she chopped the onions and celery on her large wooden chopping board in the kitchen. She'd had a rough chopping style, the knife working quickly in spite of arthritic joints, and she didn't care much for precision.

'Is it from a recipe book?' Maggie had asked, although she should have known better. Queen Vic had never taught her from a book.

'Of course not,' she had replied. She could be brusque when the subject was deemed important. 'The recipes are part of you, and you part of them. You have to adapt and adjust and decide how to make it yours. Maybe a few different herbs, different vegetables, more wine.'

The recipe, a traditional cassoulet, couldn't have been more French in origin but that didn't matter to Queen Vic. If you had made it, then it was the best. That was the way she had always taught Maggie to cook, right back from when she was six and standing on a stool at the side of the Aga. She taught her to cook with confidence and irreverence and a love of flavour above everything else, because the joy of eating good food with the people you loved was all that you really needed in life.

Queen Vic had been ailing by then. She was frail and often weak, but she was still restless, still eager to impart wisdom. Despite the joints, the blood-pressure issues, the heart disease and the failing eyesight, Victoria had suited this late stage in her life, and to Maggie, she had never looked more beautiful or more elegant. When not in the kitchen or in the garden tending to her roses, she liked to spend large parts of the day in her cream cano-pied four-poster bed, the corgis snoring gently in their baskets, surrounded by her books, her newspapers and magazines, her custard coloured rotary telephone and a selection of her green-inked correspondence.

Victoria's bedroom had always been Maggie's favour-ite room in the house. The smell of her French musk perfume, the dusky apricot damask wallpaper and heavy silk embroidered curtains, the framed watercolours on the walls, the still lifes of peonies and lemons and the English country landscapes. In the corner of the room stood her kidney-shaped, rose-skirted dressing table with the tri-fold mirror and the boxes full of necklaces and brooches, lipsticks and powder puffs. Maggie had sat there as a child over and over again and dreamt she was a princess. You couldn't be in that room and not want to be a little more poised, a little more elegant and feminine and majestic, imagining yourself getting ready for a party and the world all yours for the taking.

Maggie had spent a lot of time in that room over the autumn, remembering their last conversations, looking for clues in what she had said. The bed had gone but the furnishings were still the same, the dressing table still there in the corner, a box of her jewellery still sitting open. There was the smell of her too, the delicate perfume, the slightly musty smell of old precious things, and Maggie had sat on the stool and looked in the dressing-table mirror and with her grandmother's necklaces around her neck and her rings on her fingers, she knew that if she just sat there long enough, she would know what to do to make everything right.

'You'll have a wonderful, wonderful time,' Queen Vic had said to her, not long before Maggie left. 'It will all be wonderful.'

'I hope so,' Maggie had replied, not meaning to sound quite so nervous. She had been sat on Queen Vic's bed, a younger Albert asleep at her feet and it was early evening, summer.

'Nonsense! What on earth is there to be worried about?'

'I don't know really. Change makes you feel a bit anxious, doesn't it?'

'Change is good. Change is what keeps us alive. We have to keep pushing forward, Maggie, keep improving.

You'll find your way back here before long. Home has a funny way of pulling you back in.'

'I thought you were meant to want to get away from home when you're my age?'

'Not this one,' she said, her eyes narrowing, and Maggie realised she wasn't talking about the country or even the village, but the Manor House itself.

'What if I meet some gorgeous, handsome sailor, Granny? What if I want to get married and sail across the seas forever?' Maggie asked with a cheeky smile.

Queen Vic laughed heartily, the laugh of an older, wiser person who knows how foolish the young can be. 'Nonsense,' she said. 'That's not you at all.'

'Isn't it? OK, what about a nice doctor, then? Or an architect! Someone tall and well-mannered and sensible and educated. Someone who loves dogs and food and the countryside. That would be OK, wouldn't it?'

She shook her head from side to side and gently patted Maggie's hand. 'You'll find someone from *here*,' she had said.

They all had Queen Vic on their mind as they planned and organised and arranged. George and Albert came over to the Manor House every Wednesday and Friday morning for scrambled eggs and coffee and to help Maggie clear out the attic. Liz sometimes came over too, often with Fergie, her small russet-coloured rescue terrier. Fergie hadn't quite got over the excitement of her new life and often ran in circles around Albert, darting at him with small but persistent barks, which Albert felt only required a few thumps of his tail in response.

One afternoon, George had found them asleep together, curled around each other's bodies by the fire in Tea, and he had managed to operate the camera on his phone for the very first time to take a photograph. The picture, slightly off-centre but still recognisably canine, would be at the top of the restaurant menu, a representation of the old, the new and everything in between. They will call it Victoria's, which Liz likes because she thinks it sounds like victorious, and Maggie likes because she hopes that this is exactly what their grandmother had in mind.

They cleared the Blue, Dark and Light Green rooms, the basement and the kitchen and then laid all the furniture and paintings out in the hallway. Doug came over after work and helped to bring down spare tables and chairs from the bedrooms and the corridors, and then the girls began to reassemble and arrange it all in the downstairs rooms. From the attic they brought down pictures, rugs, lamps and vases, mismatched bone-handled cutlery and plates, bowls and cups. There was a jumble of French wine glasses and crystal tumblers, dusty linen tablecloths and delicately embroidered napkins and a box of grubby silver candlesticks that Liz polished late into the night.

Then there was the taxidermy. Maggie, Liz and the children lined up the animals that weren't too moth-eaten or terrifying and gave them all names. The bear was Jeremy, the fox, Daisy, the antelope, Ronaldo, and the badger was Toodle Pip. Liz wanted to call the wild boar Carolyn, but they settled on Persephone, with her middle name being Dawn. There was a goat they called Artemis and a squirrel called Keith, a weasel called Captain Weasel as nothing else seemed to fit, and a huge barn owl that Sophie wanted to call Wol, after the owl in Winnie the Pooh, and Tom wanted to call Sonic, so they compromised on Hedwig which made Maggie happy. She liked to think of Pamela being there somehow.

Above the front door, watching over them all, Doug climbed up a rickety ladder to hang a large mounted, deer's head, a female, with bright sparkling eyes. They called that one The Queen. Maggie stood in the hallway and looked up at it when everyone else had gone home and she thought about the last time she had seen her grandmother. It was the night before she left for Paris, and after all the French cooking they had done, Maggie had made roast chicken. Just roast chicken, in an English a way as possible, with bread sauce and Yorkshire puddings and gravy, and Queen Vic had laughed and said 'touché' in that elegant way of hers. It was the first recipe that she had ever taught Maggie, and Maggie knew it was also her favourite.

'You must always make this for someone you love,' she had said to her as they ate, and Maggie had smiled at her and thought she had meant family, for her, for Liz, for all of them when they were together.

'We have to say goodbye now,' Queen Vic said, as Maggie had washed the last of the plates and dishes and put the leftovers into the fridge.

'I'll see you in the morning, won't I?' Maggie had said. 'I'm not leaving till eight.'

'No, no, it's far too early for me. Let's say goodbye now.'

And so they had.

Chapter 29

It wasn't until she heard the bell that Maggie believed he might actually come. Even then, as she was walking towards the front door, wiping her hands on her apron and hoping that she didn't completely smell of gravy, she thought it might be Liz dropping off something last minute, or Mrs Wilson trying to get a sneak preview, or the postman, or anyone but him. As she'd worked in the kitchen in the fading light of the late afternoon, it had seemed like the whole thing might be the most ridiculous, stupid idea, the sort of thing that people did in films and books, in Hollywood, or even just London, but not in Little Martin.

'You have to do something big,' Liz had told her. 'That's what people do in films when a character wants to win someone back. You have to make a grand gesture.'

'I'm not a grand-gesture type of person,' Maggie had said, because really, who was?

'Then do something that only you could do,' Liz said, and then it had all made sense to Maggie. Then she had known what she needed to do.

It was dark now. It was six o'clock, and the bell was tinkling, and there behind the large Manor House door was Joe, standing at the top of the stairs with his hands

296

in his pockets and that smile that leant just a little to the right. The night was cold, well below zero they had said, and against the deep blackness of the freezing December air Joe was everything warm and good, and it wasn't until she saw him right there that she realised that she wanted to spend every possible minute of her life with him. How on earth could she have ever thought anything different?

'Hi,' he said, a small wisp of warm air rising up from his mouth and into the air.

'Hi. Joe. Hi.'

'How are you?'

'I'm well. I'm good. You look well too. Really well.'

He looked smart and groomed and far more handsome than seemed reasonable, considering the circumstances. He had made an effort.

'It's a new suit,' he said, looking down at his jacket and trousers. 'Special occasion. I thought I would I try and wear something that actually sat on my body in some sort of normal, human way.'

'You look very handsome,' she said, and then laughed nervously, the awkwardness feeling thick between them.

'You look very . . . lovely,' he said, the smile there again.

'Work attire,' she said, pulling up the edge of her apron.

'The restaurant. You did it.'

'We gave it a go.'

'I told you that you knew what you were doing, Maggie Addison,' he said, smiling broadly now.

'We're just making it up as we go along really,' Maggie shrugged.

'It's the only way,' he said, and there was a pause then as Maggie recomposed herself.

'Do you . . . have a reservation, Sir?' she said.

'I have an invitation,' he said, holding up the hand-drawn card that Maggie had made with Sophie, a picture of the Manor covered in ivy and wisteria and surrounded by roses.

'Well then, you'd better come in,' Maggie said, and she stood back, opening the door wide to let him pass. Joe took a few steps into the hallway and then stopped, just as she hoped he would do, just as she had pictured him doing so many times, as he took in what was in front of him. She had wanted him to be the first to see it, the house now completely transformed.

The hallway, the Blue Room, the Dark and Light Green, the Pink Room and Tea were all opened out in front of them, each one somehow its own little restaurant with its own colour scheme, and yet still all connected. The tables were laid out among the rooms and beautifully set with the tablecloths and the wine glasses and the mismatched plates and chairs, coloured lamps and little candles flickering on every surface and vases and bowls filled with sprigs of holly, oranges and pinecones. The walls had become a gallery, every surface hung with portraits and landscapes and still lifes, a glorious mishmash of old master oils, watercolours of flowers and trees and birds, and large acrylic canvases in gilt frames of the rolling Cotswold hills and scenes of endless green fields in the sunshine. Charcoal sketches of unknown faces sat among a collection of old family photographs and the corgi portraits had all been hung in a row in the hallway, from Caroline and Diana to Ham and Albert and all the others in between.

In a corner of the hallway stood a huge Christmas tree decorated with fairy lights and ribbons and the glass baubles that Maggie and Liz had had since childhood, and in the grates the fires had been lit, shading the rooms with a warm orange glow and inky dancing shadows. The animals, the strange little taxidermy zoo that had been collected by her grandmother over the years, stood proudly next to their assigned tables as if they knew somehow how very important this moment was, as if they were holding their breath right then for Maggie and Joe.

'Wow, Maggie,' Joe said, turning back to look at her, his eyes so wide and bright.

'She scrubs up well,' Maggie said, coming to stand next to him.

'I've never seen anything quite like it before. It's completely . . . *bonkers*!'

Maggie laughed. 'I was hoping you would say that.'

'All this *stuff*.'

'We didn't even use all of it. There was a mouldy muntjac that didn't quite make the cut, and a whole tonne of other things. A lot of these bits and bobs have little stickers on them in case anyone wants to buy them. George is going to be in charge of all of that.'

'This is what she wanted you to do with it,' he said, turning to look at her. 'This is why she wanted you to have the house.'

'I hope so,' Maggie said, and saying it out loud then, saying it to Joe, seemed to help it all make sense. They stood facing each other for a moment, a second or two at most, but Maggie felt a rush of sorrow and love and so much hope crash over her that she felt her legs begin to tremble.

'So, um,' she said, swallowing hard and looking away. 'The tables are all named after the animals. You could sit on Persephone or Captain Weasel, although those are for four people, so perhaps you could go on Keith? That's a table for two.'

'*Keith*?'

'He's the squirrel, over there.' She pointed to a small table with two chairs in Tea. Keith had been affixed above it onto the panelled wall, as though he might be scaling down an oak tree to take a nut from the glass bowl below.

'Keith,' he said as he began to move towards Tea, but then he paused and slowly turned around to face her again. 'There's nobody here, Maggie.'

'No,' she said. 'Not yet anyway. There will be later,' and then, as his face began to register what he had been led in to, 'hopefully.'

'That's why you said six?' he said, and she thought for one awful moment that he sounded disappointed, even cross.

'I wanted you to be my first customer.'

'Right,' he said, smiling at her. 'Right. Well, I'd better sit down, then.'

She sat him down at Keith, placing the napkin on his lap and pouring him a glass of water, her hand slightly shaky, the ebb and flow of her nerves racing through her body. She had intended to say everything to him the moment she opened the door, get it all out and over and done with so that she didn't have to prolong the agony of it all, but Joe had a way about him that led her away from herself. It was one of her favourite things about him.

'Perhaps I could have a menu?' he said, helping her out. 'Or, I don't even need a menu, really. Don't bring me one. I'll just have whatever is on offer, a piece of toast, crisps, anything.'

'What about a drink? Would you like a drink?'

'Yes! Yes, actually, a drink would be great,' he said with a big puff of breath. 'Did that sound desperate? I didn't mean to sound quite so desperate.'

'That's OK. I think I'm desperate for one too,' she said, and she hurried into the kitchen to get a bottle of wine, her heart beating so fast that she thought she might need to sit down and put her head between her legs.

'Your wine, Sir,' she said, placing a bottle of red on the table and perching awkwardly on the opposite chair, and then, because she could not bear it any longer, 'Why did you come, Joe?'

'Did you not want me to?'

'I wanted you to. I just wasn't sure that you would.'

'Well there's a brand new *Midsomer Murders* on tonight and Mum really likes to stay quiet and focused, bang, right there, front and centre on DCI Barnaby. They have a bit of a thing going on and I would only be in the way.'

Maggie smiled. 'How is she?'

'She's good. She says hi. And she says come over, have a sherry, whenever you like. I don't have to be there, or I can be as well. Either way.'

'I'd like that.'

'I missed you, Maggie,' he then said, and it caught her so off guard that she said, 'Oh.'

They looked at each other across the table. His face had hardened a little, the charade of it all suddenly dropped. He means that she hurt him.

'I've missed you too, Joe,' she said, and she means that she's sorry, more sorry than she can possibly say.

'Liz came to see me.'

'Liz?'

'She came over a few times actually.'

'Why?'

'Well, she's made friends with Mum. She's on the parish council now and involved in all sorts of village clubs.'

'Oh, God,' Maggie said, putting her head in her hands.

'No, no it's great. She's out and about and doing all sorts of things.'

'That's good.'

'But she wanted to try and explain how you were feeling and to tell me about everything that had happened. She said you were just having a wobble, and that the good thing about something that wobbles is that it always comes back to stillness.'

'She said that?'

'I think she was picturing a sort of trifle or jelly. Maybe a blancmange. What is a blancmange by the way?'

Maggie laughed then. 'I am not sure I really know.'

'I don't think there's anyone who could possibly love you or believe in you more, Maggie. Except possibly for me.'

He pushed his hand across the table towards her and she took it in hers, the warmth and familiarity of it bringing tears to her eyes.

'We've been here before,' she whispered.

'I like it here,' he said. 'I like it here more than I like it anywhere else, Maggie.'

'But I've been such a terrible, stupid idiot. Can you ever forgive me?'

'There's nobody else for me, Maggie Addison. I'm yours, if you want me to be,' and he got up from the table to pull to her feet, kissing her softly on the lips, his hands resting gently on her face. They held each other then, for quite some time, and Maggie felt her whole body come to stillness.

There was just enough time to serve Joe the roast chicken she had made for him with roast potatoes, carrots, beans and gravy, before everyone else started to flood in, Tammy and Kathy first into the kitchen to start getting the food ready to serve, and then Liz and Doug and the children, all dressed in Christmas jumpers and covered in tinsel. George arrived shortly after, looking very handsome in a forest-green smoking jacket he had found in an attic box labelled, 'Festive, George', and not long after that, guests from the village began to file in and take their places at the different tables. George stood at the Manor House front door with Albert by his side to welcome everyone in before pulling up a chair at Hedwig where a large, merry table of women were enjoying their starters.

Mrs Wilson had bought a large party of friends, including a very happy looking Carolyn, who Liz seated on Captain Weasel as it was the warmest table nearest the fire. Most of the cast of the play were also there, having been invited by George, as well as Liz's new friends all dolled up in dresses and pretty shoes. They managed two sittings at each table but could have easily done four, and the old rotary phone of Queen Vic's had not stopped ringing for future reservations.

Towards the end of the evening, when almost everyone had gone home and Tammy and Kathy were helping to clear the last of the tables, Maggie and Liz found themselves lying together on the sofa in Tea, the tail end of a bottle of wine in their glasses and their shoes kicked off.

'Headline, please,' Liz said wearily.

'"Tired woman sits down after making food for half a village".'

'Oh, come on,' Liz said. 'You can spice that up a bit. "Brilliant chef opens pop-up restaurant to huge acclaim" more like.'

'Let's just wait and see,' Maggie said, taking a sip of her wine and curling her legs underneath her. 'They've only just left. They might all be back later asking for a refund.'

'Don't be silly. It was all amazing. More than amazing.'

'How about, "Sisters save house from hot tub fate".'

Liz laughed. 'Oh, I see. It's like that, is it?'

'No, no. I'm just very relieved for you, Liz, that's all,' Maggie said, grinning at her. 'I know what a huge, awful worry it must have been for you to think of the Lay-Z Mega Whirlpool 500 littering your grandmother's beloved garden.'

'Oh, OK,' Liz said playfully, nudging her sister's leg with her foot. 'The challenge is on. Let's have a think . . . "Middle-aged woman—"'

'—*middle-aged*? Jesus! I'm still a baby compared to you!'

'Fine, fine! "Young adult finally realises that a very nice, handsome man who loves her is not a terrible thing."'

'"Older woman finally realises she has the world's greatest husband."'

Liz started to laugh. 'Oh, my God! OK, fine, you win, you win.'

'*You* win, Liz.' Maggie said, and she rested her head on her sister's leg, the tiredness of the day slowly taking over. 'You win.'

'By the way,' Liz said a few moments later as she took a sip of her wine. 'Did I ever tell you what George said to some of the school mums at that fête thing in the summer?'

'No?'

'That before I married Doug, I had a fling with Mick Jagger.'

'*What*?' Maggie sat up again, a look of absolute astonishment on her face. '*Mick Jagger*?'

'I know! They were asking me all about it when we went out the other week. And then there was something about working for the government and doing something top secret that he wasn't allowed to talk about. He did a whole back story on me.'

'What did you say?'

'I sort of went along with it.'

'I guess you would have to.'

'It's fine though because they've got to know me a bit now and I have got to know them, and I quite like them all, actually. We're friends now, I suppose.'

'That's great, Liz. I'm really happy for you.'

'Doug said it makes him look like a dark horse.'

Maggie chuckled. 'Of course it does. Doug the dark horse. That's brilliant. I might get him a T-shirt with that on.'

There was a knock, then and standing in the doorway of Tea was George with a large bag in his hand.

'Knock, knock, girls,' he said.

'I thought you'd gone, Dad,' Liz said, looking up.

'No, no. I've just been sorting through a few bits. Left-overs,' he said, lifting the bag up. 'Any takers? Tammy and Kathy have taken quite a bit home with them.'

'You take them, Dad,' Maggie said. 'We've got more than enough here.'

'Righty-ho,' he said. 'I'm off then, girls.'

'Are you?' Liz said, sitting up. 'Why don't you come and sit down for a minute?'

'Well, it's just you girls, isn't it?' he said. 'You don't want me cramping your style.'

'Don't be ridiculous, Dad,' Maggie said as she squidged up alongside her sister. 'Come and sit down. We're just chatting.'

She patted the space next to her on the sofa and he came to sit down, tentatively at first, but then relaxing back onto the large cream cushions.

'This was always my favourite room,' he said after a moment or two, looking around at the bookshelves and the paintings on the wall.

'Really?' Liz said. 'I didn't think you liked it in here. I thought Dark Green was more your style.'

'This was where I always came as a child. I'd bring all my toys in, my cars and little soldiers, and pile up the cushions to make forts and castles. There used to be an old record player in the corner, and I would listen to Johnnie Ray and Buddy Holly while waiting for someone to come and play with me. One of the corgis, usually. I think it was Beatrice back then, or possibly Mary.'

'Mary came first,' Liz said. 'She was the one with the two black ears who had the litter with the local farm dog. I remember Granny telling me about it.'

'Where was Granny?' Maggie asked. 'While you were in here?'

'She was working mainly. She was always very busy, your grandma.'

'So you were on your own a lot?' Liz said, more as a statement than a question.

'She would always come and find me at the end of the day, and we would play Snakes and Ladders or Dominoes or Clue together.'

'What's *Clue*?' Maggie asked.

'You know, vicar in the library with a gun, professor in the hallway with the candlestick.'

'You mean *Cluedo*?' Liz said.

'Do I?'

'Yes! It's called Cluedo,' Maggie said.

'Doug always insists that Snakes and Ladders is really called Ups and Downs and has something to do with the Bible.'

'*What?*' Maggie chuckled.

'His family are nuts,' Liz said.

'Right, well, anyway,' George continued. 'Granny used to say that Clue was based on this house: the study, the library, the kitchen, and all the people who used to come over were all the different characters. I used to get upset if it was Mrs Peacock who did it as we knew a lady with that name and I took rather a shine to her.'

'Oh, well there's a surprise,' giggled Liz.

'Yes, what a shocker, Dad!' Maggie said, nudging George in the ribs.

'I think it's still here, somewhere,' George said, his eyes then searching the bookshelves.

'Is it?' Maggie said.

'Ah, there we go.' George was up on his feet then, tiptoeing to a top shelf and pulling down an old box that rattled slightly as he moved. He laid it out on the ottoman in front of the sofa and took the lid off. The board was frayed and dusty, its colours slightly muted, but when it was fully opened up it looked in very good condition, and all the pieces were there, perfectly intact.

'Not much changes really, does it?' he said, giving the dust a quick blow. 'Who's up for a quick game, then?' he said.

And so they settled down to play.

Acknowledgements

I can honestly say that writing this book has been one of the most amazing experiences, and for that I am forever grateful to my wise and wonderful agent, Laura. Thank you also to the lovely Olivia and all the gang at United Agents books for their continuing support. A huge thank you to Susannah for giving me the privilege and to Melissa for holding my hand through the many wobbles I had along the way. I have loved working with you so much. Thank you to everyone at Bonnier, particularly Salma, Misha, Margaret, Claire, Emily and to Alice for her copy edit. I feel so immensely proud to have been on your team.

One day I might write a book set somewhere very exotic and mention a lot of glamourous sounding people, but this time my heartfelt thanks go to the staff at the M&S café in Banbury where I often sat to write; the doctors and nurses at Horton General Hospital's critical care unit; the brilliant primary school teachers who look after my children; the North Newington parish council; my very kind early readers Clem, Karra and Katy, and the many antique shops, auction houses, tea rooms, pubs, hills and dales in the Cotswolds that helped to inspire the setting.

I couldn't have done any of it without my family and my friends. Thank you all so much. I am unbelievably lucky to have you all in my life.

If you enjoyed *Good Things*, you will love
Kate MacDougall's charming novel,
London's No. 1 Dog-Walking Agency.

Kate MacDougall always knew her heart wasn't really in her
job at Sotheby's. All around her, friends were finding their
dream jobs and whooshing up career ladders. After yet another
breakage, this time of two precious, porcelain pigeons, she had
enough, and walked out of her snoozy, back-office existence
into the unknown world of the then-nascent gig economy.

London's No. 1 Dog-Walking Agency is the story of her next
nine years and the dogs (and people) she meets along the way.
There's Winston, the Labrador, who isn't allowed to get muddy,
even after his owners split up and then enlist Kate in their
custody battle. There's the chic trio of Islington couples whose
immaculately arranged dog-walking schedule is thrown off when
one of them gets off with the dog walker Kate has employed.
There's Kate's long-suffering, dog-agnostic boyfriend, Finlay,
and her mother, who is always on the alert for wedding bells.

Among all this, there's Kate herself, trying to work out what
she wants from life, and when and how to get there.